Surviving Him

Jo Johnson

MYH - Mind Your Head

This edition first published in 2023

ISBN (Paperback): 978-1-3999-7007-5

Cover design by Lauren Densham

Ecclesiastes 12:12-13 (MSG)

'But regarding anything beyond this, dear friend, go easy. There's no end to the publishing of books, and constant study wears you out so you're no good for anything else. The last and final word is this:

Fear God.

Do what he tells you.'

This novel is dedicated to all the people who are living with dementia and their families but especially Brian Frost, Enid Wroe and Peter Chadwick. True heroes who show that the best way to live life is with courage and a cheeky smile.

And finally, to dearest, delightful, diligent Dr Camilla who so loves an endearing dedication.

Family Tree

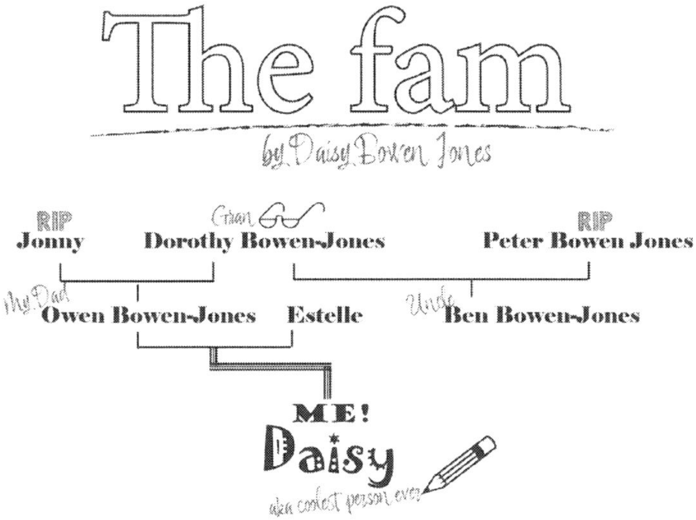

The fam
by Daisy Bowen Jones
RIP
Jonny
Gran
Dorothy Bowen-Jones
RIP
Peter Bowen Jones
My Dad
Owen Bowen-Jones
Estelle
Uncle
Ben Bowen-Jones
ME!
Daisy
aka coolest person ever

Darling Daisy,

By the time you read this, I'll most probably be gone.

But, right now, we're together in our favourite spot, the kitchen table. The one you chose, with the pink glossy top. Your rainbow swimsuit is drying on your mum's fancy Aga. When she gets home we'll go with Gran and Ben to your favourite pizza place in town. We'll eat, laugh and blow out your candles.

You're scribbling a homework story about Arundel Castle whilst rabbiting about your day. James fell over Lily's skipping rope. Mrs Sale was angry at Toby for ripping Reuben's book. The dinner lady bit your head off when you asked for a tissue. We laughed at that phrase, the idea someone might bite your head off. You used the word metaphorically – Daisy dramas, your mum calls these verbose explanations. The small things that make your world colourful. I love it; I hang on your every word.

Between writing each sentence, you look up, rightly demanding your daddy's affirmation. You have my eyes and unruly raven hair but thankfully you've inherited Mum's nose and perfectly shaped lips. You're not a fan of your front teeth but, believe me, nothing can detract from your glory. My pint-sized genius. My strong, beautiful, Daisy girl.

I'll never forget the first time we met. You, a pounding blip on a colourless screen. Me, awkwardly perched on a wonky stool. From that moment, I knew you would be my forever girl. Today, as always, you're beaming your megawatt smile because you don't know. You don't know life has come to a shocking end. You don't know I can't keep my promises. You don't know that today, a devastating, life-erasing bomb has exploded in our living room.

My heart is broken. It's not for me, soon I won't know. Not even for Mum, she'll find another prince. My heart has shattered into a million pieces because of you, for you.

Daisy, I'm so, so sorry. This was not how it was meant to be.

Please forgive me.

Love,

Daddy

1

Ben

Right now, the last thing Ben needs is to be arrested for ogling a teenage girl, so he slopes into an abandoned doorway and hides. He's incredibly thankful Daisy has pitched up but before she spots him, he's got to ramp up strength, get his words in order and repeat a silent prayer.

He leans against the filthy door, trying to ignore the stench of pee and cannabis, and watches. Ben has never felt this way before. He adores this kid: Daisy is his raison d'etre. Not in law, or biology, but she's his. He yearns to give her a hug, make her giggle and stop her pain. Inside the oversized hood and heavy boots, she's tiny, thinner than ever. It's hard to believe she's almost an adult.

Is it already too late?

She lights a cigarette; her nails are painted to match her hair. She's gorgeous, there's no denying that. Despite her attempts to self-disguise with bleached hair that drains her complexion and fake eyelashes that are asymmetrical, the family likeness is unmistakable.

She looks around, agitated. He needs to go before she loses her bottle. He grips the front straps of his rucky and sucks in a lungful of air. He's ready to sprint across in the next gap and drag her to get saved. If he gets there before she spots him, he'll have a shot at success.

he'll fulfil the promises he made to his brother, even if it means sacrificing everything.

When Ben had last seen Dr Staples, she had been working out of a log cabin in her garden. This glassy-cool building is different, intimidating.

'Look, we're here now. Maybe you can give it a go for Uncle Ben.'

She turns toward him. The top of her head is in line with his mouth, but she won't look up. He gives her hair a light kiss. It smells of vanilla and apple and nicotine.

She looks away.

'*Give it a go for Uncle.*' Her voice is mocking. He can hear the tears, but she won't let him see her cry. But as they scan the businesses listed on a panel, Daisy grabs his hand. He can't steady his finger as he jabs at the buzzer for Clinical Psychology. The automatic doors swish open, inviting them onto a freshly hoovered carpet.

She tightens her grip for a moment as they walk towards the reception desk, he can feel her sharp nails against his palm. Then she lets go, pulls up her hood and shoves both hands into her pockets.

'Hello. This is Daisy Bowen-Jones to see Dr Staples,' Ben tells the receptionist.

Ben barely has a moment to get comfy in the waiting area when a door flies open and a familiar woman strides in, clutching a flimsy file to her chest. The receptionist looks up from her computer and nods towards them. He knows what she's thinking about the hunched teenager next to the scruffy bloke with too much stubble and unruly hair.

For a few seconds, although he's had years to recover, to prepare for the assault of memories, anticipate those old feelings of shame, he can hardly meet her eyes, let alone speak.

'Hello, Ben. It's great to see you.' She leans close, touching the top of his arm. She waits for him to meet her gaze; Dr Staples's smile is warm and open. 'And you must be Daisy. Would you like to come through?'

Daisy stays put. Head down, eyes to the floor, staring at cuffs pulled over balled fists.

Ben daren't move. She's so unpredictable at the moment, so different to the fun bundle who had jumped on his back and teased him mercilessly about his choice of clothes. Will she stay huddled there until the building closes, in defiant silence, refusing to speak? Will she do a runner as soon as he leaves?

There is a deep sigh, and then she looks up.

Dr Staples smiles down at Daisy.

Daisy repays her with a defiant stare. The teenager's focus rests at the top of the psychologist's head, then drifts downwards, past the long blonde hair, across to a bold necklace, and over a more curvaceous body than Ben remembers. Still silent, still slow, Daisy's eyes stop on shiny black brogues.

Ben can feel a warm flush creeping up his neckline. The doctor waits, unflustered, clutching the beige file with her patient's name in capital letters.

Finally, with a loud smirk, Daisy pronounces her long-awaited judgement.

'So, you're the magic fix-it fairy. I thought you'd be thinner.'

2

Daisy

Daisy is pretty impressed. Four days without a lunch detention. She won't admit it, but life is easier since Kiera got kicked out.

Mrs Smith is waiting by the main entrance, arms folded. Her specs resting on the end of her pointy nose. Her head teacher is one of many irritants Daisy despises. Today, Mrs Try Hard is wearing a mustard cardie over a mismatched dress that's too short for her age. Mrs Smith owns many cardies but obviously not a bobble remover. Rooky error, Miss!

'Good morning, come to my office.'

Before Daisy can reply, Mrs Smith turns around and marches off. Following that lardy backside swishing from side to side, Daisy wants to spin her teacher around and slap her smug face. Unfortunately, too often her daddy's chants echo in her head.

Daisy, you are being spoken to.

Daisy, what do you say?

Daisy, where are your manners?

Daisy's manners went with him. When he went, he didn't say goodbye. They'd been to Pizza Express for what turned out to be their last day. He was wearing his grey woollen coat with the silky red inside. It had ketchup on the sleeve. After he went, every day, Daisy hid in the downstairs cloakroom and pushed her nose into the lining until she could smell him. Whilst she was there, she ate a sucky sweet from his pocket. Each day she had to push harder until a small red patch developed on the side of her cheek. She couldn't keep his smell from fading and the sherbet lemons ran out. In their grubby little semi, there's no trace of his heavy coat, no trace of his vinyl, and his crazy shirts. There's no trace of him.

Daddy got stolen from the inside out. His smile went first, he stopped smiling with his eyes, then with his face, and then he just stopped smiling.

Daisy takes a sharp intake of breath when Mrs Smith opens the office door and there, perched on the edge of the sofa, is her mother. Daisy knows something awful has happened. *Please don't let it be Ben or Gran.* Her mother looks up but doesn't speak. She hasn't been crying and her hair is in place. For a change, she's dressed up like lady muck, her lips are tight like she's supressing a fart.

'Have a seat.' Mrs Smith gestures as if Daisy's too stupid to recognise a chair, before retreating behind her grotesque desk and laying her glasses in front of her. She squeezes her hands together like she's leading morning prayers. Daisy drags the chair as far away from her mother and teacher as possible before plonking herself down. She slides forward, legs stretched out, arms folded. Her skirt is hitched high so Mrs Smith can see her floral pants. At least in sixth-form college, you can wear what you want.

Mrs Smith expresses an exaggerated sigh before speaking. *Drama llama*, Daisy thinks.

'Oh, Daisy, you've had so many opportunities. I had hoped sixth form would be a new start, especially now Kiera isn't here, but you've blown it now, haven't you?' she says, putting her glasses back on to squint at Daisy.

Daisy's been here stacks of times. For smoking. For bunking off. And for one assault that wasn't her fault. Usually, Mrs Smith dishes out a lunchtime detention. When she got done three days in a row, she got excluded for a week, Today, Miss looks proper stressy.

'Mrs Bowen-Jones, I'm sorry to call this meeting in the working day, I know you are exceptionally busy, but there's been a very serious incident. It changes everything. Yesterday, Daisy was part of a group' – she pauses for dramatic effect – 'who intentionally started a fire!' Another too-long pause. Daisy knows Mrs Smith wants to be an actress. Pathetic.

'The police are involved as the incident is considered to be arson. As you know, Daisy has been given many chances already. I know this isn't who Daisy is, or wants to be, but I've tried everything.'

Daisy can't believe they're making such a fuss over this, after everything she's got away with. Now, when she's trying to retrieve Dad's pride by studying and accepting Ben's help, this stupid, stupid cow is getting hysterical over an air freshener.

'It was just the stick. I didn't mean for it to make flames,' Daisy explains.

Surely, they don't think she set out to destroy the school? She's messed up but not that much. She was showing Dan what a dick he is, that he was wrong, and that the liquid in an air freshener isn't flammable.

Mrs Smith continues as if there hasn't been an interruption.

'Daisy, you need help. We'll support a referral for psychological help.'

Daisy releases a sigh of relief. For a horrible minute she thought this was it, that she was following Kiera and Ryan.

She doesn't want to be chucked out. She's blown Cambridge and won't fulfil her father's expectations and she's disappointed Ben and Gran. But she's not a total loser, she doesn't want to end up working in a factory or at Maccies. If she passes this year, she'll be allowed to start A levels. She'll be dead by fifty but she's gotta fill the between years with something.

Mrs Smith passes Mum a piece of paper with a telephone number. 'You'll need a GP referral to the child and adolescent mental health service, the CAMHS team. Fortunately, she's eligible until she's eighteen. The good thing is what she's done will move her up an ever-growing list.'

'Whoopee, top of the list, eh Mum? That's been a while.'

'Shut up,' her mother snaps.

Daisy supresses a smirk. Her mother hates showing her home self in public. Daisy knows her mother has no clue what to do. Dad sorted everything.

'My husband's family have already found therapy for Daisy so it's with the academic situation I'd appreciate the school's guidance.'

Mrs Smith looks at Daisy and then her mother. She flattens her hands on her desk and pushes up to stand.

'I'm afraid that's all we can do. I'll call the council to let them know. Daisy, it gives me no pleasure to do this, but I'm terminating your place.'

Mrs Smith shuffles behind Daisy's chair and opens the office door. The credits are rolling. There's nothing left to say.

Daisy's heart plummets. She can't believe it. She was expecting litter duty in junior playground. She got less punishment when she slapped Katie and smashed her glasses. But this is really it. She's being expelled. Just like Kiera.

By the time she reaches the car park, her mother's second-hand Peugeot is screeching through the school gates.

At first, her wild friendship with Kiera was exhilarating. At St Cuthman's for girls, everyone was wealthy and proper like her. When they had moved house and she got dumped at the Steyning Academy she managed to find nice girls. Girls with ironed skirts from homes with well-stocked fridges and fathers in suits, who drove clean cars.

But when she couldn't focus on her GCSEs, those friends moved on. They avoided her to geek in the library, puzzling over algorithms and chemical symbols. There was no place for her. Her, with her absent father. Her, in her two-bed semi. Her, studying for a BTEC in health and social.

After Christmas in Year 10, she was alone. She moped around school looking for corners to be invisible in. Then, she stumbled across Ryan at the bus stop. She remembered him from her first form class. He'd been excluded soon after she arrived. At the park, Ryan introduced her to Kiera and a whole new world opened up. A world she hadn't known. Housing estates and high-rise blocks. Flats with front doors that never closed and lifts that didn't function. At first, it was truly awesome. What's not to like about hanging about, smoking and drinking in a messy kitchen with no rules or tutting adults? But, then it became obvious what Kiera wanted from her wasn't friendship, it was ownership. She wanted slaves to do her dirty work, pick up her mess and do as they were told. These days, Daisy hates Kiera and feels a total misfit wherever she hangs out.

Still, Daisy tries to feel happy about her badge of honour. She was now a fully-fledged member of the dropout club! One of them. She calls Ryan and Kiera to boast, they're ecstatic, laughing and clapping. But it feels hollow, and she can't be bothered to hang in the park so instead she wanders for hours, trying not to imagine Dad's disappointed face.

When she gets home, the house is in darkness and the door is locked. Good. She can sneak upstairs unnoticed; her mum will be sozzled anyway.

She slips off her trainers and pushes the door to their front room, smelling chicken stew. At least the hag cooked tea before she cracked open her second bottle.

As she reaches for the light switch, she hears a noise. There's someone in the darkness and it's not her mother. Daisy's heart is pumping so hard, she can hear it. Her courage has stomped off.

In the furthest corner of the room, the lamp is on. She can see a vague outline. There's a body in the chair. An unmoving shape sitting in silence.

She can't see exactly but there's definitely someone there. For a second, she thinks it's him, her dad. Daddy.

Her breathing speeds up, she can hear her own panting as she turns to leg it in her socks.

Before she can spin around, a rasping voice speaks from the shadows.

'Hello Daisy, I've been waiting.'

'You could've given me a heart attack,' Daisy snaps, stubbing her foot on the door.

'The feeling is mutual. Put the light on and sit. Your mother is with a friend, she needs a break.'

Daisy flops onto the leather settee. She knows she's in big bother when Gran's left in charge.

'Right, young lady. Your mother told me you've been thrown out of sixth form after less than a term—'

'Asked to leave, it's different—'

'I'm talking. You'll be quiet until I give permission, do you understand?'

Daisy understands.

'I know how you feel, Daisy. I understand you're scared and hurt. We all are. I loved your father from the day he was born. I do not, however, go around punishing everyone else. It's not your mother's fault, it's not Ben's fault, and it's not mine. So, stop being an obnoxious selfish brat.'

Gran's face is very wrinkly. *When did she get so ancient?*

'We've tried to ignore your behaviour as is your mother's way. I've allowed Ben to indulge you with spoils, but from now on, I call the shots. First, you'll continue with Ben's therapist until I say otherwise. Second, my friend Penny needs extra staff at The Orchards residential facility. She's agreed to give you an interview. If you want to be a grown-up, you can earn some money and do something useful. Take the pressure off your poor mother. Do you understand me?'

'I heard what you said, but I'm not—'

Gran stands so quickly, Daisy panics she's going to topple forward and kill them both. Gran steadies herself and takes two deliberate steps to look down at her granddaughter. 'Daisy Bowen-Jones, do you understand?'

'Yes.'

Gran's angry eyes are deeply unsettling.

Just as Daisy thinks she's off the hook, the lecture reignites.

'Shift your backside upstairs and get your things out of the master bedroom. From now, that's your mother's room. You will not be in charge of this house. I will not allow it.'

For a minute Daisy worries she's going to be homeless as well as excluded.

'You can choose a reasonable amount to take into the box room. The rest can go in my garage. If you're not in the other room by midnight, I'll kick you out with my own varicose leg.'

Gran continues to stare, breathing as if she's done exactly that.

When Daisy opens her mouth to argue, nothing comes out.

Getting upstairs takes four strides, the house feels like a rabbit hutch.

If she thinks I'm gonna smell of old people's pee, she's more demented than I thought. I hate her. I hate her.

Daisy flings herself on the narrow bed and rips off her skirt. She launches it across the room, knickers still inside. Her mother's desk light falls down like a drunken tramp. She secretly hopes the thud will send Gran running to check she's okay. It doesn't.

Under Mum's duvet, there's a warm safe haven, a comforting dark cave infused with the odour of childhood. She crawls into it; with her right arm wrapped tight around her blue bear, her thumb finds the roof of her mouth. The covers hide the sound of heart-wrenching sobs.

3

Dorothy

Dorothy is desperate for respite from her frazzled mind. Bowen-Jones offspring do not get excluded from school. Neither do they have social workers and shrinks. At the best of times, she's not someone who can relax, sit in a chair, and drink tea. This is not the best of times.

Dorothy has been tossing and turning all night. Daisy had done as she was told and moved into the single, so Dorothy had slept on top of the duvet in the double. The stench of Daisy's stale clothes and used cans was strong enough to wake a tramp. Having read Daisy the riot act last night, she realises her ultimatum is Penny dependent. It's five a.m. but Penny isn't an early riser. Dorothy is not stupid. She knows The Orchards is not an ideal solution. There's so much that could go wrong but she has exhausted all other avenues. But while Penny is wonderfully generous, that Derrick always gets the last word. He'll says it's too complex to manage, that it's not fair on anyone.

Hence, Dorothy needs to catch Penny early, alone, with her cup of tea and the *Guardian* before Derrick slouches downstairs to interfere.

When Estelle called in floods to say Daisy had been kicked out of sixth-form college, Dorothy wasn't at all surprised. Daisy has been raising merry hell for over a year. She was shocked when Mrs Smith let her back given her behaviour and predicted grades. A small part of Dorothy hoped promotion to the sixth-form college might help. She blames that girl from the estate, the one with holes all over her face, and that boy with the crooked cap.

Dorothy had hushed Estelle with the soothing she had used with labouring mothers. She insisted she took a break, a rest from her only daughter. Dorothy reassured Estelle she'd sort it all out, like she always has, that she'd stay over with Daisy and call when things were calmer. Since then, she's busied herself here at Daisy's house, the house where her beloved son should be. If he was here, his wife would be happy, not despairing; and his wayward daughter would be studying for university. Before Owen left, before they moved here, his home was spotless, much like her own.

Scrubbing the sink whilst avoiding the mirror's grubby opinion is not an easy task. How did she get this old? When did her breasts become so droopy and her waist so thick? When did her skin get transparent and her hair so lacklustre? Even as a teenager she got immense pleasure from loosening her locks and swishing them about, especially if she had a male audience. Knowing that season of life is well and truly over pains her.

She races around the double bedroom, frantically dusting anything that doesn't move. What a slut her granddaughter has become. She's determined to make it bright and cheery for Estelle's return. She wonders how her daughter-in-law has coped with so much loss. In their previous home, she and Owen had an en-suite and a dressing room attached to their king-sized expanse. In this room, you couldn't swing a cat. A dirty ashtray and a pair of inside-out knickers are discarded on the rug. Estelle has gotten so soft. More than ever, Daisy needs tight boundaries, clarity, and the occasional smacked bottom.

They can't give up. The Bowen-Jones name means something; they have Owen's reputation to uphold.

'How ruddy dare she?' is the thought that kept Dorothy awake and has sustained the pace of her cleaning. Dorothy hasn't been this furious since Ben's teen dramas. After all they've been through. After the umpteen chances Daisy's had. After the legacy her father left.

That girl is without excuse and when I see her, I'll wring her ruddy neck.

With renewed vigour, Dorothy shoves everything of Daisy's into bin liners. She simply doesn't care if she disturbs that lazy so and so. How can Daisy sleep so soundly after all that's happened, with all her banging and crashing? Dorothy stomps downstairs and piles the overflowing bags into the garage. On her return, she pauses on the landing to catch her breath. The door of Daisy's room remains shut. Long-supressed emotion seizes her as she spots her beloved son, shrunken inside a tiny silver frame. She gives herself a stern talking-to. *Pull yourself together.* Grabbing the frame and some washed bedding from the airing cupboard, Dorothy stomps into the double and slams the door behind her. She sweeps off the ash and sweet papers from the bedside table and replaces them with the photo frame. Exhausted, she collapses into Owen's bedside armchair. In his beloved velvet chair, hugging his favourite cushion, for a fleeting moment, Dorothy reflects on her son. But it's impossible to savour the warmth of her best memories without confronting painful ones of Owen in his last months.

Owen's tender eyes look from the wedding photo tilted towards her. It's as if he's back. Standing in front of a raging fire, a glass of red in hand, badly retelling a senseless joke. Apart from this one photograph, Estelle has removed all traces of her lost husband.

In the picture, Ben is best man in a suit too large for his teenage frame. She and Peter hold hands at Owen's side. Thank goodness nobody knew what their future held.

Sometimes when Dorothy cleans, the photo is face down. She doesn't blame Estelle. She's done much the same. She has his letter and the one small picture in the spare room, her only external reminders. Only Ben is brave enough to display huge collages of his big brother.

'Take a breath, mother. It's not her fault, she's only young. She's finding her feet,'

Owen would reprimand if he was here.

From the moment Dorothy delivered that scrunched-up bundle to her beaming father, Daisy could do no wrong. She had slept, she had fed and then she had grown into a good child, who was replaced by a good teenager. When Owen was disintegrating, it was Daisy who kept everyone going. When they were in despair, Daisy would burst into a peculiar dance or mimic a silly phrase and they'd be in fits. Even Ben could smile when his niece flung herself on his lap. So how did they get here? It's as if when he went, the Daisy they all loved went as well. It would destroy Owen to see Daisy now.

The clock chimes seven a.m. Surely, she can call Penny now.

Penny answers with a hint of impatience unusual for her. 'Oh, hello Dorothy. I'm on my way out to the business network, is it urgent?'

Dorothy hardly knows where to start. It certainly is urgent. Dorothy has been far too candid with her friend. Will she be able to persuade her this could work, be a good idea even? She's desperate, they're all desperate, and she can't think of a solution despite pacing all night.

'Yes,' is all Dorothy can manage before uncharacteristic sobs steal her dignity.

'Oh dear, what on earth's the matter?' Penny asks. 'Take your time, dear,' she adds, as if talking to one of her residents.

Dorothy imagines her standing by the door, car keys in hand, coat on. *Pull yourself together, you stupid old fool.*

'I don't know what came over me, it's nothing really. Daisy has got herself in another spot of bother and Estelle is at the end of her tether.'

'Oh, I'm so sorry to hear that . . . the poor girl . . .'

'I'm not sure about poor girl, my patience is wearing thin, but I was wondering . . . if you might consider giving . . . her some temporary work.'

Dorothy holds her breath. She can hear the surprise in her friend's silence. *Please, please say yes*. Waiting for Daisy to come home last night, an idea had positioned itself: if Dorothy could crowbar Daisy into The Orchards, it could restore her sense of self and perhaps give her granddaughter the space she needs to grieve.

'Well, it's certainly an idea, I'll have to give it some thought . . . I'm sure you can understand that . . . it wouldn't be easy . . . We'd all have to agree some ground rules . . . and how we could handle all the – details . . .'

Dorothy can sense the understandable hesitancy in Penny's voice. In the background, she hears Derrick cough.

'I know. Obviously, she can't work in the palliative care service, but could she be an extra pair of hands on the independent side?'

There's a pause, a longer pause than is natural. Dorothy imagines her friend edging closer to the door, hopping from one foot to the other, trying to think of a valid excuse. No doubt Derrick is shaking his head, mouthing, 'Don't you dare.'

'. . . and only until the autumn when she'll be back in education.'

Another pause. Dorothy's thoughts are coming too fast. This has to work.

'I wonder if the thing would be for her to have a kind of trial period,' Dorothy suggests, detesting the slight whine in her voice.

'Maybe a week?' Penny says, her tone quiet. 'Can I call you later?'

By the time Dorothy takes the phone from her ear, Penny has long gone.

Dorothy retrieves the wire sponge and makes a half-hearted attempt to clean the brass plates that are long overdue, trying hard to centre her mind. She has no idea what she'll do if Penny says no. With a hefty sigh, she gives up, which is so unlike her. She's exasperated with Daisy, with Ben and the rest of the world. Without conscious thought, she struggles a saucepan from the overcrowded drawer and heaps hot chocolate into full-fat milk and a splash of double cream.

Moving to be closer to the family required little thought. She had sold her flat long before Owen left them. He was all over the place and she knew it wasn't going to end well despite her protests. Estelle needed more support so she could work and care for Daisy. But, after a week of unpacking and hoovering her downsized cottage, Dorothy had absolutely nothing to do. Estelle was grateful she was closer, just in case, but there was an unspoken tension between them, and Daisy was no longer a dependent child in need of care.

Work had left no time for pleasure, her job as a midwife was her pleasure. Ben offered to find her some voluntary work, but she knew it was out of pity, so she said, 'No, thank you.'

Desperately lonely, she had taken herself in hand. A gardening club had been the first advert to catch her eye.

Dorothy had met Penny a few times, but they didn't connect until they had stumbled into 'Better Bulbs' at exactly the same moment. As latecomers, they had sat at the back and sniggered like schoolgirls as a characterless chap with a squint mumbled about shades of soil. Instantly, Dorothy warmed to Penny. After that first club, Penny had hauled her from the tepid coffee and introduced her to the wonderful Vintage Rose, a traditional tearoom with proper china. Relaxing in floral armchairs they had put the world to rights. Neither went back to the gardening club but they had become the best of friends.

With a sigh, Dorothy gives the chocolate a final stir before pouring the steaming liquid from the saucepan into her china cup. She'll calm herself with a hot drink and then she'll storm into her granddaughter's room and demand she gets dressed. If Daisy thinks she is going to sleep until lunch time, she can think again. She adds a custard cream to the matching saucer, then changes her mind and adds two more.

An early-morning conflab with Daisy requires more sugar than the diabetic nurse would allow.

4

Ben

It's gone nine and Ben is still in bed; The heavy curtains his mother donated allow him to believe it's the middle of the night. Kasia is opening the gallery this morning and he can't be bothered to move. Callie left early as usual.

He pulls the curtains, ignoring the dust on the sills. Callie has positioned his to-do list on top of the TV remote. He knows she's trying to help, there's heaps to do for the exhibition.

When Callie suggested a fundraiser exhibition, they had both hoped it might inspire him, restore a sense of purpose. Stupidly, they had hoped it might interest Daisy too, to do something in her father's honour. A joint venture to raise money to help people like her father, like their family, like Daisy and Ben. People who had lost everything to frontal temporal dementia, FTD. How can three capital letters hurt so much?

Of course, Daisy had no interest whatsoever. She even mocked his interest. After that, he'd wanted to put the show off for as long as possible, but Callie protested, 'Go for December. Capture the pre-Christmas spirit. Everyone's happy when the fairy lights shine, and the carols are playing. The festivities make them cheery and . . . generous.' She had laughed. 'And you need sloshed sponsors who don't notice what they're giving.'

He hadn't confessed the festivities make him miserable. Christmas has gone from being his favourite time of year to something he dreads whilst still on his summer holiday. The baubles trigger flashes of despair. The carols create a longing for his father that feels physical. Now, he has less than eight weeks until 18 December when the Owen Bowen-Jones exhibition goes live. He should've stuck with New Year.

The list is endless. Exhibitors. Sponsors. Caterers. Invites. He can probably shift some of that onto Kasia, but he promised to produce some art. After his father died, Owen and his mother created a trust. They said it was Dad's idea, a ring-fenced pot so Ben could have his community gallery. Everyone knows the real truth, though: he can't be trusted with a lump sum; he's a disappointment. He isn't a legal genius like his brother or a top surgeon like his father. He's thrilled with the gallery and can't believe how Kasia has transformed the space, but the trust is a veneer to ensure the remaining Bowen-Jones heir is seen as a success. But he's not. Ever since his father died, his art has been crap. Interesting art requires mental energy, a lightness of spirit, and hope. His portfolio is empty of all three.

Downstairs, Ben drains the dregs of his lukewarm tea and flicks through the channels. Emails and to-dos can wait. He points the zapper at the television and takes pleasure when the ugly celebrity, with lips too big for her face, evaporates from the screen. Instead, he turns to mindless phone scrolling. It's as if he's determined to waste his life checking Insta, stalking his wayward niece. Checking how far she's fallen. Checking how much he's failed.

Sure enough, there she is, with her mates making obscene gestures. A cigarette between her pouting lips, empty cans scattered all around. Owen would be appalled. Shamefully, his eyes fill with tears. All their hopes were on Daisy. She's

Owen's only child, his only niece and his mother's only grandkid. She's it. His only responsibility.

It has been over a week, but he hasn't forgotten the look on Daisy's face when he abandoned her at Dr Staples's office. Ben couldn't believe what Daisy said. Owen would've dragged her outside by her furry hood, given some stern words and pushed her back in to apologise. But if her father was here, she'd be studying for A levels.

Ben did what Ben always does. He gave a lopsided half-grin and looked out the window. Sandra ignored the comment, gestured towards the open door, and led the way to her office. Shockingly, Daisy got up. She kept her eyes firmly down but followed like a newborn chick. As she reached the door, she took a sneaky glance over her shoulder to check he was still there. The desolate look in her eyes broke his heart.

Will Dr Staples, the woman who once rescued him, be able to help Daisy? He can't contemplate the alternative. It took him a few seconds to find the green button and exit the psychology building. As he walked out, he remembered the first time he saw Sandra. It was less than a month after he had tried to kill himself.

He hadn't wanted to die but was desperate for the pain to stop. He knows deep within, Daisy is wailing like a toddler, eyes streaming, nose pouring snot, shouting, 'Please help me, someone, anyone, please help me.'

By the kitchen window, Ben hopes Mrs Edgington can't see he's still in his dressing gown. Callie has left out his favourite mug with a teabag placed inside. *Never Question Your Wife's Choices*, the mug advises. In smaller print: *You Are One of Them*. Is Callie sick of him too?

When they met, before his dad died, before Owen left completely, before the mess his mother created with her meddling, he was full of life. When he bumped into Callie at a beach party in Brighton, she was the perfect match. Ten years younger than him, with no interest in settling down like the girls his age. They planned to climb mountains, cycle slopes and travel across the globe. Callie loved his chilled nature.

Right now, dressed in old man PJs and last night's socks, he looks about sixty whilst Callie is not yet thirty. Would they have married if Owen was still here? Was twenty-four too young for her to say, 'I do' and mean it?

Before everything happened with Owen, Ben and Callie were having so much fun. They worked hard but played harder. On warm evenings they'd climb Chantry Hill to the top of the downs and drink beer in the abandoned cow shed. In the winter they had retreated under blankets to watch Bond films until the early hours. Life was reckless and funny.

Back then, his biggest worry was what next to buy: trainers or an expensive canvas and some paints.

Then everything fell apart.

Everyone knew if Ben got married, Owen would be his best man. When Owen dropped the bombshell, Ben wasn't even engaged. With a twelve-year age gap between them, it was Owen who took him to nursery, Owen who hugged him goodnight. Later, it was Owen who threatened the school bullies and Owen who drove him to prom. Owen was the best man, his best man.

Within a fortnight, he had bought a cheap ring from Argos, and proposed whilst eating chips on the shingle at Littlehampton. Callie agreed marriage was what they both wanted. They got engaged in September and said their vows on 15 December. It was the only date the hotel could do. Callie shivered in a short dress that had been reduced in the summer sale. Daisy was their only bridesmaid.

In the wedding photos they were a normal family. Loving, loud and unbreakable with Daisy as the glue. Beautiful, kind, bright spark little Daisy. For a few months they got their happy ever after.

If Ben had known what the next year held, he'd have stolen a gun and annihilated his entire family. The final straw – that thing that drove him to attempt to take his own life – is something Ben tries not to but can't help but blame his mother for. Before he could even think, he was complicit. She had acted impulsively, taken over, in a hurry to create a cover-up. He shouldn't have even been there. It should've been her opening the door, not him. It should've been her faced with an impossible dilemma. He was forced to nod his consent to a wish that wasn't his to grant. A wish that had dire consequences.

However hard he analyses the day he overdosed, he doesn't recognise himself. His only desire was to escape the guilt and fear that relentlessly stalked him. If he lets his mind go there, he sees another bloke holding pills in his palm. Ben remembers the smell of Callie's cosmetics tin as he stole paracetamol just in case his stash wasn't enough. He recognised the smell of her lip gloss. His fingers were smudged with her eyeshadow. For a moment he saw her face, lit up on their wedding day, full of hope for their bright future. The next time he saw his wife, she was pale with red eyes. Her perfect foundation ruined by rivers of mascara. For that he won't forgive himself, ever.

His mother never mentions what she asked him to do. One of many things stuffed under her bulging carpet with all she chooses not to see. The thin silver lining is because she didn't ask him, he didn't need to lie. At least, Owen will never know what they did to his family.

As he pours himself a second espresso, he looks at his phone again. This morning's profile pic shows Daisy hanging off a wall with her skirt hitched so high, you can see her pants. The idiot she's with has positioned himself below, making no effort to hide where he's looking. His mother would ask, 'Has she no shame?' Ben knows that Daisy is far away because she's full of shame. Shame drives everyone away.

His phone vibrates and, as if connected by telepathy, the screen screams 'niece'. When she got her first phone, he refused to encode her by name, to wind her up.

The clock says nine thirty. He has no idea what she's doing up so early. She'll be after a lift or some money. He daren't tell his mother how much Daisy currently owes him. He knows he's a soft touch, but he wants to show his love and she's not accepting anything else.

He jerks his finger on decline.

She'll have to wait until he's lined his stomach with a banana and marmalade toast. He must step up, take responsibility. He's no longer her trendy uncle, he's the father sub. He promised.

Ben listens to three voicemails whilst the toaster glows. Taking his coffee into the lounge, he tentatively presses call. He pulls the phone away from his ear to avoid the tirade of obscenities.

'Slow down, I can't understand a word you're saying . . .'

'Daisy, stop swearing at me or I'll put the phone down . . .'

'An interview for what . . . ?'

'Well, you need to do something now you're not at college . . .'

'They won't ask you to work with the very ill ones . . .'

'There are plenty of old people who don't smell, including your own grandmother. Stop being so ridiculous . . .'

'Daisy? Daisy?'

Silence.

How long has he been talking to himself?

Dear Daddy's girl,

We're heading into a storm but no need to worry because I'm going to write you a hundred letters – whenever you need me, I'll be here.

Let's start at the beginning. They told me being a dad would be extraordinary. I nodded, but secretly I didn't believe them. But, Daisy, when smudgy shades of grey popped up on that screen, you stole my heart. This Dad thing is unlike anything I've ever tasted apart from maybe a Toblerone, our treat on a Sunday night. I can't explain how momentous it was, standing there, holding you. It was like the world stopped in that suffocating hospital and the only people alive were me, you and Mum.

Your birth was the best show I had ever seen. Talk about plot twists. One minute Mum was screaming for relief and then, you were in my arms. A snuffly pink thing in a yellow blanket. I didn't want to hand you back to be weighed. Why didn't I take industrial-strength glue?

We touched noses and I caressed your soft heels hoping they would never crack like mine. When I looked, you were yawning just like me. We had so much in common. I couldn't wait to escape with my new family.

Those first weeks were a whirlwind. Feeding and burping and sleeping and that was just me. I hadn't the faintest clue what I was doing. Try to look surprised when you read that. This Dad stuff was massive, and I didn't want to mess up. Those first months, I'd run home from work and gather you in my arms. I'd sing songs, maybe out of tune. I loved our weekend trips – to the park, to see the ducks, to grab an espresso – but those strolls were mostly to declare your perfection to the village.

The day you were born transformed my life. You love big words, so it could be described as a metamorphosis. I was never going to be a dad who stood on the edge. Before you, I was Owen Bowen-Jones. But, after you, I was Sir Owen, Daisy's father. You are the love of my life, Crazy Daisy. Don't ever lose sight of that. I was, and am, so proud of you.

But, baby girl, there are bad times ahead. It's going to be tough, but you'll be fine. When Ben was your age, Poppa was hardly around so I was his dad. He's promised to be yours. Talk to him. Don't suppress your feelings like your mother does. Spill it out. Tell anyone who'll listen how you're feeling. Bottling things up never helped anyone. Daisy. Take courage; when I go, it'll hurt but you're a strong soul. Trust me. The bad times won't last.

One last thing, when you find out what I'm about to do, you'll be angry. Don't be. From your first moment, my one desire was to do what's right by you. To protect you. To love you. To give you the very best chance. This is no different. One day, you'll understand and be grateful for how it ended.

Lots of love,

Sir Owen, Daisy's Daddy xx

5

Daisy

Daisy saunters over, deliberately wiggling her hips as she approaches. Gran is standing against her car bonnet squinting at her wristwatch.

'You are ten minutes late,' Gran snaps when Daisy gets close.

She meets Gran's gaze, stubs out her cigarette and pops it into the post box.

Daisy doesn't say hello.

'And over my dead body are you going in dressed like that.'

'What? I've dressed up. My top and skirt meet, so you can't complain about "my midriff", and my shoes are clean.'

'That skirt is a pelmet, and your top is fit for a strip club. I'm surprised you don't get attacked in the streets.'

'Yeah right, like in the 1900s when men had the right to do that.'

Gran ignores Daisy to fling open her car boot and yank out a battered case. Daisy can't help herself rushing to help. Together they lower the case onto the concrete. Gran opens the clasp.

'Oh well, if I'm too casual, your friend will have to give that skanky job to another desperado. Poor old me, missing out,’ Daisy says, plonking herself down in middle of the car park.

Without comment, Gran searches through a pile of neatly folded old women’s clothes.

The sneer on Daisy’s face runs for dear life when she sees the metal hanger Gran is holding high. A diarrhoea-coloured jacket hangs shapelessly over a matching checked skirt the width of an elephant’s butt.

‘It’s your lucky day. Last week I went on a jolly with my choir. When your mother called, I didn’t bother to repack my overnight bag. Isn’t it good that we share the same taste?’ Gran chuckles. ‘With the help of a few safety pins, this two-piece will be perfect for your interview.’

‘You can’t be serious.’

‘Look at my face, little lady. Do I look like I’m joking?’

She shoves the terrifying clothes towards Daisy’s nicotine-stained fingers. ‘Hold these,’ she says, before locking the case and slamming the boot lid.

‘Right, there’s a toilet in that pub, follow me or I’ll hold your hand.’

As they walk across the car park, Daisy sees an open-mouthed rubbish bin, she reckons she could squash in the entire suit and run before Gran turns around.

Before she can action her plan, the part of Daisy that she despises – that she wishes had disappeared with her dad – takes over. The part that struggles to punch as hard as she desires, the part that helps Gran with heavy things, that insists on good manners when she wants to shout and kick. The part Dad nurtured all her life. She so wishes that part had gone with him. It’s the part that ruins her life and destroys her plans. That good girl part couldn’t possibly defy Gran. So, with her head down, kicking up the stones she follows Gran to the entrance of a dodgy-looking pub.

‘Get in there and change.’ Gran pushes Daisy towards the door with a large F on it.

The clock on the wall says two p.m. Daisy remembers her Plan A.

‘Hey, bad news – I’ve missed my interview,’ Daisy says, pointing to the cheap clock positioned above the bar.

‘To be on the safe side, I gave you an earlier time. Your interview is in twenty-five minutes.’

Daisy is about to lock the cubicle when the door is forced back open. A liver-spotted hand waves a baby wipe through the crack.

‘Get that muck off your face and remove three bits of metal. I’ll let you choose.’

Furious, Daisy stomps out of her clothes and checks her face in the cubicle mirror. Her eyelashes look good, she likes the new eye shadow Kiera swiped from the chemist.

With her head held high, Daisy strolls out. Hearing the click-click of Gran’s heels as she speeds to catch up, Daisy mutters under her breath, ‘You can force me into the right clothes, but you can’t force manners into my mouth.’

‘Congratulations, Daisy, you’ve got yourself a job. Well, for a fortnight’s trial anyway,’ Penny says with a broad smile.

‘What?’

‘Do you mean, “I’m sorry, could you please say that again, Penny?”?’

‘Yes.’

‘You have a job.’

Daisy is lost for words.

'Oh, did you not expect a positive outcome? I love a girl with a strong opinion, just what we need. If you wait for five minutes, you can sign your contract and start ASAP.'

With Penny gone, Daisy swings her feet on the desk and rocks back on her chair. A mug falls over and marker pens cascade off the edge.

Daisy can't believe what just happened.

Who employs someone who hates old people?

Her head replays the other carefully planned answers.

Never learnt to cook, sorry.

Hate working in teams.

Personally, I support euthanasia for the over seventies.

Always late.

Daisy knows she's been set up. She spent ages on Google last night looking at the qualities you need to get a job in a residential home so she could make sure she didn't have any of them for the interview.

Why did Gran dress me up when she'd stitched me up already? Well, she can get me a job but she can't stop me getting sacked.

Her long legs slide off the desk. Papers drop down the other side. A grey filing cabinet leans against the wall covering some of the window and one of the horrible green curtains is folded on the top as it can't hang down. Each drawer has a label with two letters. Penny has A to F near the floor and V to Z at the top. *What cretin creates a backwards system?*

A revolting embroidered thing hangs over her head. 'Don't ask why were the old days better than these. For it is not wise to ask such questions: Ecclesiastes 7:10,' it says in fancy blue writing.

No clue what that means. At the bottom, it says 'To Mum, lots of love from . . .'

Before Daisy can read the signature, Penny returns with two sheets of A4.

Daisy considers pretending she can't write but Penny doesn't look like someone you defy, and Gran is waiting outside. If she can get chucked out of sixth form, it shouldn't take long to offend an old crusty and get the sack.

Daisy scribbles her first name but carefully prints the newly chosen surname she's been using online. STULTUS. She took ages to pick one and, in the end, went for the first word she learnt in Latin. Her new surname matches her new identity. STUPID. She's sunk low but refuses to bring shame on her father's name. Penny doesn't seem to notice.

'I'll see you next Wednesday morning, then.'

'Woohoo,' Daisy mutters under her breath as she scurries towards the exit. If Penny hears she doesn't let on.

Gran's car is outside. 'How did it go?' she asks as if she doesn't know.

'Open the boot.' Daisy doesn't say please. She's stunned Gran doesn't call out her poor manners.

Gran hands over her rucksack.

Daisy pulls off Gran's muck-coloured skirt, the blouse and the jacket and dumps them on the tarmac. In her tights and bra she reaches into her bag to retrieve the cigarettes and lighter she nicked from Tesco's. Whilst Gran watches with wide eyes, she lights her fag, and slowly inhales before blowing out a twirly smoke train.

Dorothy and Daisy both notice the blind slats in Penny's office part into a triangular spy hole. Neither can quite see who's looking, but Daisy doesn't care.

A flung sweatshirt knocks her lighted ciggy onto the ground. ‘Put that on and get in the car,’ Gran demands before slamming the car door.

6

Dorothy

As she drives to Pen's, Dorothy is glad it's Monday, Derrick's golf day.

As always, Owen's letter and his photograph are in her coat pocket. She takes the letter everywhere, it's like Daisy's childhood cuddle bunny. It makes her feel safer, like he's guiding her. Lest she forget.

When Peter died ten years ago, his clothes were in the charity shop a week later, along with his tennis shoes, medical books, and caps. She loved him extravagantly but there's no point hoarding and hoarding them would have broken her heart. Peter would have absolutely agreed.

But Owen is her darling boy and, whilst she knows it makes no sense, this letter represents the last of him, the true him before he totally disintegrated.

He wrote it in the days leading up to his diagnosis. There were already signs, but he was absolutely still himself, the Owen she knew. The Owen he knew.

'Come in, come in,' Penny gushes as the door swings open before Dorothy can knock.

They chit chat whilst the kettle boils. Politicians, an embarrassment. Winter is here, horribly cold. They hate it. Why do men moan so much? Gets on your nerves. The woman next door is agoraphobic. Poor her.

As soon as they relax into recliner chairs, a cuppa at hand, they can talk about what matters.

'How are you?' Penny asks, her head slightly tilted to the side.

'Oh Pen, some days I miss him so much I wonder if I'll survive.'

'I can't imagine, and in such awful circumstances.' Penny pauses. 'And then Ben doing what he did.'

If Dorothy thinks too much about that, about what might have been if Callie hadn't come home early, it'll be the end of her. She could have lost them all.

'It's always hard this week, what with it being the end of the month,' Dorothy says, eyes averted.

'You still having a monthly breakfast?'

'Oh yes, we won't forget him that easily.'

'And Daisy, does she still come?'

'Not always . . . but mostly.'

Dorothy can't remember the last time Daisy attended a remembrance breakfast, but she needs Pen to believe her granddaughter can be responsible.

Penny drains her cup and chuckles without explanation.

'What?' Dorothy asks.

'I was thinking about Daisy's BAFTA performance at interview. She had her answers and reeled them off in quick succession. Her face was so smug, I wish you'd been there.'

'I hope she wasn't rude.'

Penny can't suppress another giggle. That's one of the things Dorothy loves, with Penny she's young again.

'On the contrary, she was exceptionally polite and articulate. I was impressed by her knowledge of our values and the person spec for a care assistant. "What would you do if someone had a fall," I asked. "Well!" your grandgirl said. "My balance isn't good so I might topple and hurt them."'

'Oh, she didn't,' Dorothy chuckles, 'when she's balancing on walls, flashing her pants, her balance seems okay. They think I don't see her dreadful posts.'

'Well, they believe we're past it, don't they? The young ones are surprised I manage the computer system.'

Dorothy's delight is fleeting.

'Am I doing right, Pen? I can't do her more harm. Tell me honestly, is it too much sending her to your place?'

'Let's play it by ear. But I promise I'll watch her closely. God willing, it'll be what she needs. Maybe even healing.'

The door is shunted open. 'I thought the Sussex coven were here, given all the cackling,' Derrick says without a smile before closing the door on his way out. There's a crash from the kitchen and Penny raises her eyebrows.

'Ignore him, he's frustrated that it's too wet for golf.'

Dorothy listens as Penny mimics Daisy's answers:

I can't work around body fluids.

I have asthma and eczema.

Allergic to cleaning fluid I'm afraid.

Penny finishes with an impression of the teenager's face when she found out she'd been successful.

'She thought she was smarter than us old birds, didn't she?'

'And then the little blighter came out and strip-teased in the car park,' Dorothy adds.

As if deliberately synchronised, the two women throw back their heads and laugh and laugh. Dorothy can feel her body release some tension. It's fabulous to find humour when she's mostly in despair.

Penny disappears into the kitchen to make more tea. Dorothy hears raised voices and strains to listen, but her hearing isn't so good and the door is closed.

Her back hurts as she reaches down to retrieve a thick envelope from her bag, the suede one Owen purchased in Italy. She lets the package rest on her lap. The cash is heavier than she expects. Immediately, her mind runs back to the incident that almost killed Ben. She can't speak about it, and he hasn't said but she knows it was that. He's such a sensitive soul. She did wrong but it came too soon after the terrible things that nearly killed her. She was still reeling from all that had happened with Owen. It was all too much. If only she had foreseen the impact of her selfishness on Ben.

When that kid knocked Owen's door, head down, hands deep in pockets, Dorothy couldn't believe it. She and Ben were minding Daisy. Owen and Estelle had gone for a long weekend to Dorset, it was to be their last weekend break. Owen's behaviour was already erratic. Before they left the house, Owen had lobbed a faulty toaster, narrowly missing Estelle's head.

Daisy was at school and Ben was washing up, they had enjoyed a rare giggle over his marigolds. Dorothy had finished washing the floor when she heard an almighty crash at the door. Estelle had purchased an enormous brass lion's head as a door knocker.

The mop was still in her hand when she casually unlocked the door. No doubt an Amazon package for her granddaughter, some new felt tips or another study text. Sheltering from the rain, a youth stood close to the door lintel. She couldn't tell if the young face belonged to a boy or a girl. There was no parcel.

An anorak hood was pulled low over a cap. Long scruffy trousers hung over grey sneakers that were once white. A brown sock exposed by a hole in the toe. Dorothy will never forget those eyes, so dark she couldn't differentiate the pupils.

By the time Ben came running, she was clinging to the door frame, afraid of fainting. Ben listened whilst the situation was retold. At first, he argued, pushed the door so the kid had to step back. It seemed impossible, unthinkable. Ben raised his hand, about to push the door, to stop that grubby shoe ruining the freshly mopped floor.

The kid took that as a cue to resist, to step forward, not back. For a moment those brutal eyes challenged her son. She wanted to run and call the police. She was afraid if she disappeared, a knife would be pulled.

Then, supporting evidence was whipped out of a back pocket and thrust into her face. Ben snatched the undeniable from a hand with filthy nails. A photograph with dates. How could three flimsy scraps of paper ruin so much? How could a visit from a stranger taint an entire life lived well? Without thinking, she let go of the long handle to cover her mouth. As she fought to stay upright the mop crashed outwards forcing the visitor to jump back.

They had no choice. He was demanding money, a lot of money. No doubt he had expected to meet Owen's poor wife, to bully her. Of course, a small-time criminal wouldn't know the big house and flash cars would soon be sold. Without Owen's income, Estelle had nothing. Thank goodness Dorothy had a good pension and a small nest egg for a rainy day.

Dorothy has a great deal of experience thinking on her feet. At work, there were frequent life and death decisions: dither and the moment has gone, a mother or baby in trouble.

She had taught her students to scan for evidence and make quick assertive decisions.

That day, the agreement was made too fast. Ben was stunned. Panic written across his pale face. She, his mother, should have known better. She should've shown the wisdom of age. She should have sent the stranger off with a flea in his ear. This wasn't something to be discussed on the door. And it wasn't her place to act as judge and jury. She should have called a family meeting, sought advice from Estelle and her parents. This would affect them all but especially Daisy.

Instead, she gathered herself. Back straight, she pushed Ben back and herself forward. She could smell the stench of cigarettes as she got closer. She refused to be intimidated like a frail geriatric. She struck an impulsive and stupid deal. Worse than that, her hypocritical guilt forced Ben to mop up the aftermath. Her betrayal was costlier than thirty pieces of silver. She betrayed Owen, Estelle, Daisy, but most of all she betrayed Ben. She has denied it but when she stares into the mirror, the ugly truth stares back. The mirror on the wall screams at her. It rightly accuses Dorothy of infecting Owen and almost killing Ben.

On her return home the following day, the bulging envelope had gone. She was so flooded with relief that it was over, over for her, over for Owen and over for Daisy that she didn't see Ben. She couldn't look at his ghostly skin, the dark circles, or the sadness in his eyes. She turned away from the tears brimming over those long lashes. Lashes wasted on a boy, her boy. The debt was paid, the dirt swept under the carpet.

When the kitchen door reopens, and Penny returns juggling cups and saucers and a pack of bourbons. Dorothy is suddenly aware of her racing heart. Her dropping dead is the last thing the family need.

‘Sorry, so sorry, Derrick wanted to chat about some staffing issues,’ Penny explains, her face reddening as she searches to place the refreshments.

Dorothy pushes the newspaper to one side and pops a couple of novels on the floor to create space on the coffee table. No one could accuse Penny of being house proud.

Dorothy can’t inhibit her thoughts for another moment. As soon as Penny sits down, mug in hand, Dorothy gabbles what she’s been ruminating about all week.

‘Penny, I know I’ve put you in an awkward position. I’m so grateful and I want you to have this . . . by way of compensation.’

Dorothy clutches the beige package. Her palms are damp. Will her friend feel insulted or patronised by her gesture?

If this bulging bag of cash had been ready on that day, she could have sorted out the appalling mess and saved Ben. She can’t bear to think about what might have been if Callie hadn’t found him. She will sort out Daisy’s mess if it kills her.

Penny is staring at her, waiting. She’s never quick to speak. When Dorothy can’t bear it any longer, she springs up. Surprised by her adrenalin-fuelled energy she takes two strides, thrusts the beige package at her friend. As the package lands, Penny leans back and stares at the lump on her tartan pleated trousers.

Dorothy rushes to her chair and grabs her mug. She ignores her trembling hands to reach for a biscuit.

‘Oooh my favourite biscuits,’ she says, taking a bite.

Penny looks puzzled. Dorothy can’t cope with the slowness, the deliberate way her friend sets aside her drink to open the sticky flap of the envelope. Dorothy watches as recognition widens Penny’s eyes. She knows what she’s taken.

'Oh no you don't,' she says skimming the bulging envelope across the floor to her friend's feet. The mug judders in Dorothy's hands and a few drops drizzle onto her lap.

'Please, I want to help, I know things are tight for you too,' Dorothy pleads.

'Well, I'm not taking your money. I'll give Daisy the trial we agreed. I've persuaded Derrick to give her a month, promised him he might be surprised. She's clearly a bright girl.'

They finish their tea in quiet companionship, both women pondering the decision they've made and wondering if they'll each regret it.

In the safety of her car, Dorothy secures the money into her glove box and shoves the container shut. She retrieves a fading envelope from her coat. This crumpled A5 rectangle is beginning to show its age. Dorothy wishes she'd copied it and kept a pristine one. She could ask Ben or Penny, but she can't bear the thought of them reading it.

She takes out the cream sheet, typed in an unusual font on headed paper and unfolds it onto her lap. She loves hearing his voice.

Dear Mamma,

I'm writing this on Daisy's birthday. How did our girl get so grown up? Thank you for sacrificing so much to support us. I don't know how long I've got.

Already, I see the look on your face. When you furrow your brow to cue me in, it's the stare you gave when I was small. It stopped me in my tracks when I was tempted to back chat, kick a ball indoors. I was always scared of that look. It still stops me in my tracks. How long before that look gets ignored? How long before I'm what the consultant called behavioural? How long before I'm hurting you, or worse, harming Daisy? I am already a man I don't respect and often despise. So, I need you, the only person who truly knows me, to stand by what you promised yesterday. This letter formalises what we agreed, so you won't dither when the time comes. So, here is what you promised.

When the time comes. When I

Dorothy hasn't read the rest since the day she received this paperwork. With the letter came a short report completed by a solicitor to confirm Owen had capacity to outline his preferred wishes. The solicitor hadn't referred to Owen's wishes. Did he even tell him? Unfortunately, his last wishes clashed with hers, and everyone else's. In the end she had no choice, she had given in and done what he asked. When the time came, sooner than anyone had expected, she had kept her part of the bargain, against her better judgement.

Dorothy skims over the middle paragraph. It's too black and white. She can't read of her promise. She skips to his closing paragraphs.

When it's done, I need you to do two further things.

Firstly, help Daisy to remember me. The me I am and not the me I'm becoming. When I've gone, insist she keeps dancing, laughing, reading and writing. Don't let her make me an excuse, don't let her become a victim. I insist she sets the world alight, like we planned. Remind her of that every day. Remind her who she is, who I was and who I want her to be. Remind her she promised to write her journals into a book.

Secondly, when I go, don't look back, just like when I cried at school. I mean that. Go eat breakfast at my favourite café. Swim in the sea and dance to my records. This is your last duty of love. To let me go.

I know you blame yourself. Don't. Ben will take care of you, for us both, your two boys rolled into one. So much love and gratitude to you,

Your Owen

The car seat creaks as Dorothy's body rocks with sobs. Blinded by tears, she stabs the key in the ignition. She sets off home with a renewed determination to drag their family back on track. She'll do anything. She promised her boy.

7

Ben

'Here he is, my baby boy.'

Ben winces as his mum rushes to cup his face in her cold hands. He pulls away, trying to hide his irritation. At least Meadow Stores café is quiet. Callie is right, he can't carry this on for the rest of their lives. His wife was understandably gutted when he declined Simon and Leah's birthday do.

'But you were there when we arranged it?'

'I clearly didn't connect it was the first weekend of the month.'

'I can't deal with that group on my own, it's all so intense especially now Leah is pregnant. You promised you'd be there.'

'I'm sorry, Callie, I can't. You know I can't.'

'Yes, you can. One time. That's all I'm asking.' She sighed, looked at him sadly. 'It's been years, Ben. It's ridiculous. You hate it.'

'I know, but Mum would be disappointed if I don't go. I can't leave her with just Estelle, you know what they're like.'

'And it doesn't matter that I'm disappointed. I'm your wife. I'm your family.' Callie slumped into the armchair, arms wrapped around herself, head down. 'I'm sorry,' she said. 'I know it's complicated, that you want to do what's right but we've not been out together for ages. I need you today.'

Ben gave up. He knows she's right. He wants to be with her. He would love to be with their friends. He could point out how Leah is blooming with health and happiness. It might give them an opportunity to speak properly about starting a family. Instead, he'll be sitting in silence at a misjudged family gathering.

Callie had always said she wasn't fussed about kids. He was sure he didn't want them, especially after what happened to Owen. You can never tell what surprises biology has for you. But recently he's changed his mind. Suddenly he aches to hold his own child. To get something right. To bring new joy into their family.

Since Leah, Callie's oldest mate, announced they were expecting, Callie has been super snappy. She's staying later at work and he's not sure who is avoiding who. They used to be so close, but they've not been out in ages. He's either dealing with Daisy dramas, sorting his mother's plumbing or just cream crackered.

As he slides onto the café bench beside her, Estelle leans in to plant a fake kiss on his cheek. He avoids his mother's gaze. He knows she's scanning for evidence of illness, signs he's going to crack up. Ben plonks his fists on the table not intending to create such a thump. Dorothy grabs his hands in hers.

'How are you?' she gushes. 'You look too tired?'

'Is Daisy coming?' he asks, snatching his hands into his lap. He knows Daisy won't show.

A waitress who looks hungover plonks down a tray before Estelle can answer. She sweeps back a piece of hair that's escaped a hastily scraped ponytail and offers a brief smile.

He knows how she feels. Wishing to be miles away but offering a necessary show.

Pain au chocolat for him and his mother, Owen's favourite. Ben would prefer a bacon butty. A plain croissant for Estelle and coffee for all. He can't believe how thin Estelle is, she's lost the weight he's gained. On top of a day job, she's doing a refresher course so she can practise again as a solicitor. She must be shattered. Everyone is shattered.

'Please could I add a large glass of house red?' Estelle pipes up before the waitress escapes.

Mum looks at her watch. She's thinking, 'Not before the yard arm.'

If a passer-by peered in, they'd see three lost souls with sad eyes, gathered around food they don't fancy, trapped in a ritual nobody can stop. The weekend after Owen went, when they were all grief stricken, Mum suggested breakfast here. This is the café Owen and Daisy visited each Saturday when Estelle was socialising, it was their place until his last weeks.

That first time, they all came. Daisy was fourteen, the four of them sat around, playing squares and squabbling over pastries. Daisy convinced them her music wasn't a noise. Whilst plugging her earphones in two different heads, they all bathed in the sunshine that was Daisy, their grief softened as the pastries and coffee were consumed.

When it was time to go, Mum announced, 'I have a great idea,' clapping her hands and smiling for the first time in weeks. 'Let's make this our thing. On the first Saturday of every month, we'll meet to remember. We can share memories of Owen, bring happy photos, and eat his favourite food. We'll make sure he's never forgotten. Our hero,' she finished, holding an open palm for Daisy to high five.

Estelle looked unconvinced but nodded as Daisy was beaming. It was set in stone, a family breakfast once a month, with Daisy as the centrepiece.

But then Daisy changed. She matured and her maturity whipped away her protective naivety. Suddenly and dramatically, it dawned on Daisy that the FTD monster who stole her father could return to ravage her. She realised that she might lose her words before she graduated. She realised she might be falling over before falling in love and she realised that before her menopause she could be freefalling down a dehumanising descent into a meaningless existence. Day by day, Daisy retreated into a shell that month after month became harder to crack. In their hurt, Estelle and Mum became super scratchy with each other, and now Daisy has abandoned them altogether.

Dorothy seems oblivious. 'Isn't it marvellous about Daisy's job?' she smiles, requesting more pastries.

'I'm not sure Owen would describe leaving college to be a care assistant as marvellous,' Estelle says, picking flakes off her drying croissant.

'No, but it's a start, isn't it, Ben?' Dorothy snaps.

'Who knows,' he mutters, glad he can't see Estelle's hard stare. His sister-in-law used to work hard on her appearance. She always looked younger than her fifty years. These days she doesn't even bother with lippy.

After an hour, one more glass of red and mostly silence, Estelle makes her excuses. 'I promised Daisy we would shop,' she mutters, reaching under the table for her bag.

That's a lie. He doubts Estelle knows where Daisy is. Most nights, she sleeps out. Nobody knows where she is.

When Ben arrives home, he's disproportionately exhausted. Glad that's done for another month, he drags himself upstairs to shower away the feelings these monthlies leave on his skin.

After, sitting on the sagging settee, his feet up on the chipped side table, he finds a footie match to distract him from the emotional cocktail messing with his head. Guilt for hating those family breakfasts. Frustration that Daisy won't save them. Angry that Owen left. Sad he's let Callie down and full of unfair rage at his mother.

A figure outside startles him out of an aimless stupor. A hunched figure in a hooded coat rushes past the window heading for the porch. He jumps up, ties his dressing gown and rushes to the hall for cover. He checks his watch; the postman came ages ago.

Something in his subconscious stirs. An uninvited memory hooks him. He turns around to lean against the wall, get away from the glass of the door. His heart is pumping. Sweat is gathering at the back of his neck. He pushes his feet into the floor, a grounding technique the psychologist showed him.

As the letterbox opens from the outside, Ben tries to stop his hands shaking.

Slowly, a crisp pink envelope emerges through the door mouth. It doesn't drop but hangs half in, half out as tiny fingers are withdrawn and the outside flaps back into place.

Ben edges back to the lounge window, still close to the wall so he can sneak a peek but remain hidden behind the heavy denim curtains.

Huddled in an oversized coat, the figure sprints away.

Get a grip man, she's gone, she went years ago. She promised.

But there's something in the hunch of the shoulders, the strand of dark hair escaping the anorak that tightens his chest. He staggers to his chair, terrified he's having a heart attack like his father, the lightly scented envelope scrunched in his fist.

Ben blows a series of short breaths to regain control. He flips the envelope over and allows a quick glance, a check. His name is handwritten on the front. Maybe it's a mistake, after all, there must be heaps of women who write with flouncy loops and use that perfume.

'Go on, open me, you coward,' the letter chants.

It can't be, she promised.

Without giving eye contact to the offending item, he feels the thickness. It's slim, one page. He turns it over and slips his thumb under the fold, ready to open but changes his mind. He can't know. He shoves it deep into his dressing gown pocket and runs upstairs. Yanking opens his underwear drawer, he buries the letter as far towards the back as it'll go. For now, that's where it's going to stay.

8

Daisy

This afternoon it's raining, not chucking it down, just dribbly cold rain that makes you shiver and feel sadder than you should. What sane person sits on cold concrete in November? When Daisy used to walk home in her blazer and a satchel stuffed with assignments, she'd noticed people like them. She'd see them on street corners and in this park and wonder why. Who would sit on cold grass when they could be studying or watching Netflix with a mug of hot chocolate? Who would choose to be alone when they could be snuggled on the settee, writing a story or chilling with bessie mates? Now she knows. The cold, lonely park was better than home.

Mum and Gran won't let up about the FTD test. It's getting in her head. They're desperate to know if she has the faulty gene, the gene that besmirches their perfect family. They pretend it's for her, so she can plan, have certainty. Daisy knows it's them who need to know if she's next. They talk like they get it, like she has choice, like it's a routine blood test. Daisy doesn't wanna know if she'll live or die. No wonder she spends all her time here. Yeah, it's miserable but less miserable than being with them.

Kiera and Ryan reckon this abandoned cricket pavilion next to the rec is the best thing ever. They yack about it like it's some fancy house in the trees with a log fire and millionaire shortbread in the fridge.

'Here he comes.'

Daisy is yanked back into the life she hates. If only she'd known how lucky she was back then. If only she'd known one day she'd be sitting among litter, smoking fags that make her sick with people who make her sick.

The familiar old man is hobbling up the path. His back is bent and his stick wobbles as he leans. Keira and Ryan can't wait. Ravenous wolves salivating at the thought of bleeding meat. Daisy hates them both.

As the man gets closer, she sees his knuckles are swollen and out of shape. He grips the top of his stick like his life depends on it, maybe it does. His grandad cap covers his eyes.

'Oy, corpse man,' Keira shouts, 'you should be dead.'

Daisy flushes red, she stubs her cigarette on the ground and snatches up her hood clinging to the fur on each side. Ideally, she'd like to disappear in a puff of smoke.

'Yep, dead man,' Ryan yells, in response to a sideways gut punch from Kiera. Daisy is glad Ryan is between them.

The man hobbles away, unable to run or speed up. She hopes he's deaf, unaware of the hooligans shouting at him. Hooligans. That's what her father would call them. People who have no manners or intelligence. Daisy is now a hooligan.

'What's up with you today, Chain?' Keira leans forward to sneer at Daisy.

On the first day they met, Ryan introduced the girls.

'Kiera, this is Daisy.'

Kiera stared without speaking for what seemed like ages. Daisy had felt small, scared but desperate to be accepted.

Taking a long swig from a can, Kiera had laughed, a nasty laugh with half-closed eyes.

'What, Daisy as in chain?' Kiera then burped so close that Daisy could smell the beer.

Daisy had stood, awkward. Should she take that as cue to leave? She hadn't known how people like Keira play. Now she knows.

Ryan struck a match and lit her first cigarette. Her first downward step into an unfamiliar world. A world she hadn't wanted to be part of. She'd wanted to throw up. It wasn't the nicotine though. The thing that made her sick was remembering Dad's voice, '*Whatever you do, Daisy, don't let yourself down, stay true to who you are.*'

That was the day she left herself behind. Daisy has no clue who she is now. She hates this so maybe there's some small bit of her left. She's terrified that one day she'll wake and inside be as dead as Dad. She's terrified one day she'll be here shouting disgusting things and mean what she's saying. She wonders if then she'll feel whole again. Right now, she is a misfit everywhere. Too bad to be with family. Too good to be with friends. Too young to be at The Orchards and too old to be on the swings.

Keira readjusts her pose. She slides up the wall, her upper body against the old wood, her legs bent as if there's an invisible chair. Daisy knows trouble is brewing.

Kiera pulls Ryan up by his coat. Daisy stays on the floor, head down, tracing lines in the dirt with her finger.

A girl stumbles up the path, pulling a boy behind her. She stares ahead, the play area her obvious goal.

'Hey, you,' Kiera shouts.

The girl picks up speed, dragging the kid behind. The little boy has enormous eyes and turns his head to stare. Three filthy teenagers surrounded by cans and stale butts. The girl knows to get to the play equipment she has to pass them.

Daisy has not seen her before. They're here most days, they know their targets.

'Is ya head cold love?' Kiera sneers, mocking the scarf she's wearing.

The boy offers a cautious smile. Trusting. He doesn't know what the real world is like. She remembers holding Dad's hand. With her hand in his, she could do anything, face anything. He was her hero, her refuge. But now she's on her own.

'Looks like the kid needs a wash, a bit dirty isn't he,' Kiera cackles and kicks at Ryan's shin. His cue to join in, add a comment, kick a can. Daisy knows they won't do more than that. Keira's two oldest siblings are in prison. She knows how far to go, enough to hurt and intimidate.

Kiera lunges forward and shouts, 'Boo!' The girl startles. She tugs on the boy's hand to drag him past. He cries out, hurt, confused.

Daisy sighs with relief. They've made it. Keira is too lazy to go any further. Kiera slides back down the wall with a thump, deliberately shoving Ryan into Daisy. She leans across Ryan and takes two cigarettes from the packet resting on Daisy's lap. Ben gave her a fiver yesterday and she nicked a few quid from the pot in Gran's kitchen.

'Thanks for your support, Chain!' Kiera sneers. 'What's wrong with you? Too good for us, are ya?'

Daisy lifts her head to look up. She offers a thin smile.

'Sorry, got my period, my head hurts.'

'Next time. Try or you'll be out,' she threatens.

Daisy doesn't care. In a few days, she has her induction at The Orchards. The thought of being there, dressed in those rank overalls makes her want to scream but at least she won't be here.

Kiera stands up, eyes Ryan from a height and holds her hand out. That's the cue for her puppy to walk at his master's heels. Ryan puts on his cap, turns it to one side and follows. He doesn't say bye but when they're far enough away, he flicks his head around and smiles. She knows he's not like Kiera, not evil, just trapped and scared like her.

Daisy brushes the back of her skirt, swearing at herself for wearing her best one.

The quickest way home is to cut through the play area but then she'll have to walk past the people Kiera abused. But the long way will take too long, and she won't have time to get Gran some lemon sherbets.

She pulls her hood forward and keeps her eyes to the floor as she strides over the tarmac. Out of the corner of her eye she can see the boy being pushed on the swing. Daisy would give anything to be five again.

When she's almost at the exit gate, a small voice calls out.

'Excuse me, auntie.'

Daisy can't see any other adults. Where's his auntie?

'Excuse me, auntie.' The little voice gets louder and closer to her heels.

She knows it's him, that little boy with the beautiful eyes and sweet smile. She spins around and pushes back her hood.

He's standing with his hands on his hips looking up at her.

'Yeah,' she smiles.

'What's a Paki?'

His mother rushes over and grabs his hand to get him away.

Daisy is horrified. Her eyes fill with tears as the kid waits, resisting his mother's tug. Daisy adjusts her skirt, kneels down, two bare knees on the damp ground, and looks him in the eyes. He deserves that. She searches for words to answer his naive question. Dad's disappointed opinion blasts into her head. '*Bystanders are cowards, worse than the bullies*.'

Daisy speaks carefully, articulating each word, wanting to say the right thing.

'It's a word used by stupid people, because they don't know any clever words.'

When she stands up, his mum is listening.

'I'm sorry for my friends,' she confesses unable to look the mum in the eye.

'You should get better friends,' she replies, her eyes down.

'Yeah probably,' Daisy admits.

Daisy looks at the kid. It's hard to tell but if he's hers, she must've had him well young. She looks the same age as them, like she should be at school or college.

Daisy can't have kids. Not long before Dad went, they all went to see the consultant. Her family were like that. Gran went. Mum and Dad. Ben and her. Callie was working but Daisy got a day off school to go to the specialist hospital in London. Mum had already told her, but they had to visit the ugly doctor with those metal glasses and a wonky tie. They semi-circled around him like he was on a theatre stage. He told them that Dad had Frontal Temporal Dementia, the genetic version. That's why he got it so young. Then, the speccy doc with no hair looked at her, just her and said, 'This has implications for other family members,' and her mum started sobbing until Gran stuck a hankie in her face. Then, she shut up.

That was four years ago. She was glad that she wouldn't be made to squeeze a kid out her backside. But in this moment, looking into this cute face, she feels less certain.

‘I’m Sachini,’ the woman says, offering a soft hand for Daisy to shake.

‘Daisy,’ she says tentatively reaching out.

‘I’m Haizeh, auntie,’ the boy says with pride.

‘Nice to meet you, Haizeh,’ Daisy says before speaking to Sachini. ‘Why does he think I’m his auntie?’

‘It’s a cultural thing. Our children use auntie for adult women as a sign of respect.’

Daisy notices how she exaggerates the word, *respect.* Daisy is not worthy of Haizeh’s respect. His mother is right.

She talks to Sachini about the horrible weather and moans about the lack of stuff to do in Storrington whilst Haizeh races a girl across the park.

‘It looks exhausting,’ Daisy says when they race back asking for drinks.

‘It is,’ Sachini says, ‘especially when you have no help.’

The sweet shop is closed by the time she ambles home but she’s glad she met Sachini. For a minute, she felt like herself. She smiled. She played and she felt affection for that family she’d only just met. Everything has changed and she rarely feels herself these days, whoever herself is. She might even restart her journal. She’s not updated it for ages. When Dad was about, she rarely missed a day.

Daisy looks in the windows she passes, small houses with small lives. Their other home was in a nice road with nice people. Everyone had a wide drive, room for four cars. They had a big garden with a large wooden gate that opened when her father pressed his key.

The leisure room had coloured bean bags and table tennis. In the summer, the doors opened to let in the outside. They ate burnt sausages on the patio and splashed together in the pool.

Daisy's room had a sink and a slide from the bed to the swirly purple rug on the floor. She cries as she remembers Dad piggy-backing her around the kitchen whilst her mum warned it would end in tears.

Well, Mother, it did end in tears, didn't it? He's gone and we live in a soulless half-house squashed in a row of identical half-houses.

Daisy lets her coat zip scrape against the small dirty car. It's parked in their small dirty drive, outside the small dirty house she hates. All her mother lost was her beloved Mercedes. Daisy lost everything, the house, the school, and him.

'Hello, sweetheart, how was your day?'

A collection of obscene words escape her mouth. The words Gran wants to wash away with soap.

This is the greeting ritual they perform every day. Daisy unlaces her high boots and chucks them at the back of the front door.

Her mother is where she always is at the weekend, not at the spa or the nail salon. Not at the gym or lunching with friends but studying law at the table where they eat. In the week, she serves in a cheese shop. How embarrassing is that? In the old house there was a study.

Daisy brushes too close to her mum as she marches into their small living space.

'Why are you being so nasty, Daisy?'

'Why are you being so stupid?' Daisy snaps, giving the hefty legal text a shove.

It tumbles off the table onto the floor. A calculator, a cheap pen and a glass of fizz follow.

Daisy knows she's a bully, who shouts, swears, pushes and sometimes even spits at the single parent she despises. No one knows what to do about her, especially Daisy.

9

Dorothy

For the first time in weeks, Dorothy dabs rouge onto her sallow cheeks, flicks mascara through her sparse lashes and restrains her rebellious hair into a neat bun. Ben is picking her up. They're going to his gallery and the arty bar next door for supper. The prices in that place are extortionate. The decor makes her dizzy and the staff make her feel ancient. But to get alone time with her son is a rare privilege, so she thought she'd better do as she was told for once.

Shivering in her underwear, she avoids passing the long mirror inside her wardrobe door. Nothing fits. She's put on half a stone since Owen. She thinks about wearing her tailored trousers but, in the end, she settles for a dog-tooth pencil skirt and black kitten heels. If she has to meet his new assistant, the right combo of style and confidence must be displayed.

'See it as a good excuse for an afternoon out and a decent glass of red,' Ben said when she had first declined the invite to mark Peter's death anniversary. She can't see why she'd want to remember. She'd rather pretend it's an ordinary day. It's the young ones who have to acknowledge every damn detail, talk everything through.

'Dad would smile knowing you were out with his only son,' he grinned, hair drooping over his eyes. Owen was so similar to his stepfather, she forgets Ben is indeed Peter's only. Throughout the years Ben rarely disclosed Owen as his half-sibling. He adored his successful older sibling, but something has changed. Now, Ben frequently describes Owen as Peter's stepson, his half-brother. She hates it. They weren't a broken family. They were complete. She still talks about 'us four'.

Ben will be late, so she has time to push the hoover around and slosh some bleach down the toilet. By the time she retreats to wait at the window, coat over her arm, it's twenty minutes after he was due to arrive. He's lucky she's so patient. When his ancient car draws parallel with the lawn she races to lock up. She doesn't want those sloppy trainers on her carpet.

Ben gets out and kisses her cheek before manoeuvring his unicycle into the boot. Immediately, she senses something is off. When she slips into the passenger seat, she narrowly avoids an envelope. It's brightly coloured and crumpled. Ben whips it out from under her as if it might scorch.

'Sorry. Was that something important I almost crushed?'

Ben starts the engine and mumbles.

'It's an RSVP from a guest.'

'Oh, have the invites gone out then?'

'Most of them, yes. I'm saving the family ones to give by hand.'

Dorothy gathers orange peel from the centre console and pops it in her pocket.

'What's troubling you, then?' she asks patting his thigh.

Ben stares at the road as he replies, 'Nothing. I'm tired, that's all.'

She daren't ask about the letter or why he's running so late. With Ben she has to pick her moments.

The gallery is finally open but barely. She hasn't seen a picture he's created in several years. After he left university but failed to settle, Ben wanted to set up by himself. He dreamt of a shared community space where anyone could create and exhibit. His father dying was catastrophic for Ben. But Peter had ring-fenced some monies for his son's gallery dream so at least he got that.

She found him this space. It was a disused chapel and needed a lot of work, so the price was perfect. Ben wasn't sure, but he never is. Callie and she dragged him to the auction. Dorothy had raised the final hand. It has taken two years and some help from an old contact of Owen's, but it finally opened three months ago. Four artists work here and there's a waiting list, but the space left for Ben's art remains devoid of content. He says creativity and misery don't cohabit.

She links her arm through his as they take the three deep steps to the front door. The frontage is mostly glass, so the main room is spacious and bright. She hasn't been for a few weeks and can't believe the transformation. So different to when they purchased this depressing space. As she pauses to appreciate the smell of bergamot from a carefully placed diffuser, a petite young thing, perched on dangerously high shoes, gushes towards them.

She kisses Dorothy on both cheeks and clasps her hands like they're old friends. In an accent Dorothy thinks is Polish, she gushes, 'You must be Dottie, I have been so looking forward to meeting you.'

Dorothy forces a smile.

'Yes, I'm Dorothy. Remind me of your name, I'm sure I've been told.'

Ben raises his eyebrows at his mother and frowns.

'Kasia,' she confirms, giggling inappropriately at Ben.

Dorothy notices Ben's megawatt smile, she hasn't seen that in a while.

'So, Dottie, what do you think?' Kasia asks, spreading her arms as if introducing a world-famous orchestra.

Dorothy wants to hate it. Every part of her wants to say something cutting. She wants to criticise the wonderland of carefully curated art and uniquely crafted gifts created by twenty talented local artists and makers. But it is simply beautiful, breath-taking even.

'You've made good use of the space,' Dorothy compliments with a thin smile.

'Oh, come on, Mother, it's mind-blowing what Kas has done. I couldn't have achieved this in a million years.'

'Yes, that's probably true,' Dorothy says watching Kasia totter back to a perching stool near the jewellery display cabinet. Her youngest son could charm the bees from the trees. From pre-school he had women falling for him. It's that idiotic grin and those twinkly eyes. Visually, he's so like his father, a scruffier version.

She follows him down a short hallway into a less glamorous space.

'Ben,' Kasia calls after them 'The exhibition invites are ready to be collected from the printers today, if you have time later.'

Ben strides ahead without responding. This area is out of bounds to the public and needs a lot more work. The floors are bare wood, several half planks are missing. Dorothy steps over the holes and inhales the smell of paint mixed with cannabis. There are two artists working. She suspects the smell is the scruffy yob in the corner. The open plan area is freezing and darker than ideal.

'Hey Ben.'

'Hi Ethan, loving that vibe, the pastels are really working for that landscape.'

On closer inspection, Dorothy can see Ethan is very young. Shouldn't he be at school? she thinks, imagining Daisy in the park. She wonders if this kid was once a good boy, flowing with potential. She wonders if his single mum is home weeping over school photos of a child with glossy hair and rosy cheeks.

A woman nearer Dorothy's age is seated close to a narrow window. The top pane is divided by a crack. She ignores them as Ben points out a squirrel scurrying along a high fence. Ben laughs as the ratty creature falls just before the end.

'A bit like me, hey Ma, never quite reaching the finish line.'

'No comment,' his mother quips too quickly but with a mischievous smile.

Dorothy often ponders her parenting. Did she put too much responsibility on Owen? She was so keen to be an independent wage earner, to make a career so Owen wouldn't suffer as the child of a single mother. Perhaps she over compensated? If she'd known Owen's life would be cut short, she'd have copied Estelle, given up work and spent time with her boy. In her heart, she knows that's probably a self-delusion. She loved work, it was the place she felt in control, most at peace.

Dorothy has a twinge of guilt as she sees a rolled-up cigarette under the pensioner's chair. It is her who is puffing at illicit substances, not the lad in the corner.

Surrounded by piled-up box files and aging carrier bags, she asks her son, 'How's life then, sweetheart?'

She wonders what he does all day. If he's not painting, surely, he could project manage the renovations and get this back part finished?

'You know, same old. Callie's loved up with her new role. She's in early, home late so don't see much of her in the week. I'm doing all the house stuff.'

Before Dorothy can ask how a rectangular semi can take so much time, Kasia bursts in holding a flask of coffee and a brown paper bag.

'At least you have your new assistant at work,' Dorothy says as the heel click fades away.

'Yep, Kasia is a very committed manager. She sorts all the everyday nonsense.'

'Marvellous, you can crack on with your art, then? After all, Dad's legacy was for you, so you could live your dream.'

Ben pours the strong coffee into two solid mugs and retrieves a hefty slice of lemon cake from the bag. Dorothy watches her son. He doesn't change, she can see him frantically searching for excuses, excuses to avoid growing up, commitment, and taking responsibility.

'When Kasia is more settled, I'll do a course I think.'

'But you've got a B.Sc. and a Masters, darling.'

'I need something to reignite my passion. I'm a bit dry on the creative front.'

Dorothy sighs. Ben drove Peter mad. His father was a scientist, he couldn't understand all this arty-farty nonsense. Bizarrely, Peter shared more qualities with Owen than his biological offspring. And all the time Owen was climbing the career ladder, it seemed acceptable that Benji, her little chap, was messing about on his wayward journey but now . . .

'It's great that Daisy has started work, isn't it?' she offers, changing the subject. Penny reminds her she mustn't interfere, that Ben is a middle-aged man.

'Seems catastrophically misguided to me.'

‘What do you mean? It’ll be good for her to have a focus, stop hanging about taking drugs.’

‘She’s not that stupid. Working there is going to make her mood even lower. Anyway, she could’ve worked for me.’

‘Are you kidding? She’d have called in sick, arrived late and you’d have paid her overtime.’

Ben doesn’t argue. Dorothy reprimands herself. She mustn’t put him under pressure, be negative.

‘Yeah, but that place,’ Ben sighs.

‘Penny and I have discussed it, she’ll be closely monitored, working with the more able patients. You never know, she might enjoy it.’

‘I’m still not sure. She’s vulnerable. We made promises to Owen.’

Dorothy feels terrible watching her son fight his emotions. He’s trying hard to be the father Owen was, but he’s too soft, not sufficiently adult to parent a wayward child.

‘It’ll be fine. Trust me.’ She smiles, patting his hand and gesturing to go. She’s freezing and needs a proper chair. Ben leans back and then forward, twiddling his fingers like he’s done all his life.

‘Mum.’

Dorothy inhales a deep breath. She knows where this is going. He refuses to leave it in the past where it needs to stay. She’s adept at avoiding thoughts she doesn’t like, feelings she doesn’t enjoy. Maybe this is what’s been playing on his mind.

‘Do you think about what we did?’ Ben asks, looking at her under long lashes.

‘I try not to Benji, sometimes that’s best. We can’t change what’s done.’

Dorothy wonders what he'd say if he knew all she can't think about. The regrets she has about meeting Jonny, the mess she made of her mothering and what she did for Owen.

'It wasn't our decision to take. I go over and over it in my head. What happened? It keeps me awake. Surely, we should've talked to her, talked to Estelle, made a joint decision, one we could look back on and be glad we spent time reflecting, from all angles.'

Ben looks down. She knows he wants to say more but hopes he doesn't. There's a look in his eyes she can't read. A faraway look that terrifies her.

'Daisy was too young to fully understand and Estelle was in no fit state to carry that burden. We did the right thing. It was a tough call, but we made a decision and that's that.'

She stands. Ben doesn't move. He is tapping his fingers, fidgeting. A mother can read her child. He wants to argue but she doesn't want to think about any of it, such a painful, unpleasant time for everyone.

She pushes an image of her granddaughter out of her mind, and she sends her adult son to the toilet like he's five. With him out the way, she sweeps the crumbs from their cake onto the floor. 'Better,' she thinks as the wonky table is restored to perfection.

10

Ben

Ben has been staring at a blank canvas for more than two hours. Thankfully he's alone in the studio so nobody's judging the lack of progress. The canvases and new charcoal came last week and at least he's unpacked them. He wants the exhibition to do Owen proud but every time he puts an idea into paint, it doesn't work. Ben can't disentangle the brother he loved from what he was told on his brother's doorstep. He's tried, but the smear has clouded everything.

When Owen was managed out of his senior position at his law firm, his last shred of pride went too. Ben is still unsure what happened. Something happened there and he wasn't told what it was. As far as he knows, only Estelle knows.

The letter remains in the envelope, unopened in his clammy hands. The smell evokes a familiar nausea. Whenever he tries to forget, two details elbow into his senses. The dark hair, impossibly black lashes, and thick perfume. A smell so heavy it made him want to pull back.

Trapped in a hospital ward, Ben had promised Callie, 'No more secrets.'

He meant it.

Overwhelmed, Ben had buried his exhausted head and wept. What had he done? The softly spoken consultant was desperate to section him. Mum had rudely challenged him whilst trying to call an ancient family friend for a second opinion. Callie sat hunched near the foot of his bed studying her restless hands. She wouldn't meet his eyes. At least Daisy wasn't invited to the after party. A youthful doctor had hovered near the door, saying nothing.

Callie looked vulnerable, and alone. In that moment the burden of guilt descended as a mighty weight, bearing so hard on his chest he couldn't breathe.

Neglected tears cascaded to Callie's chin. Ben willed her to look up, to reconnect and rescue him from them but she wouldn't.

Just as the doctor reached the edge of his patience, Callie stood. She moved at such speed, it stopped his mother in her tracks.

Waving her arms, Callie screamed, 'Go. Just go.'

Much to Ben's surprise they did. His softly spoken, hesitant wife threw out the doctor and his mother. Out of the room and out of the hospital.

They had sat on the end of the bed for what felt like hours. The desperate pair had cried and talked and cried some more. He spoke of the dark thoughts that had haunted, the feelings that had crushed in on all sides until he felt numb. Fear and grief for the brother he had found repellent and guilt for being relieved when he went. Sadness for Estelle and Mother but mostly for Daisy. Terrible paralysing grief for Daisy. He told Callie everything; everything except one thing.

Finally, they'd both slept. When Callie awoke, she shuffled onto her belly, head resting in her pale manicured hands and made Ben promise to never again keep secrets. Naturally, he promised. He had promised he wouldn't bottle things up. He had promised to accept help. He had promised to tell everything from that moment on.

He got the help. He no longer hoards feelings, and he's told her everything since that day. He couldn't tell her the thing that broke him but fortunately, it happened before the promise so technically he hasn't broken the covenant, has he?

The envelope is second hand. The writing on the front says his name but another addressee has been disguised with a black marker. There's a squiggly line under Ben. It's the writing of someone young, optimistic, Daisy's style before she dropped out.

No more secrets, Ben promised Callie, yet before he smuggled it here, this letter was hidden in his sock drawer inside Daisy's tired baby album. A deliberate act of deceit. For two days, he convinced himself it was an oversight. Callie's always late home, busy. There's been no time to talk.

Closing his eyes, he turns it face down. Maybe it's not what he thinks. Look away and it'll change, block your ears and it's not real. He opens his eyes and flips over the letter. The addressee remains, Ben Bowen-Jones.

He slips it into the back and flicks to the front of the photo album. The pages are sticky from Daisy's phase of daily examining her younger self. The album has an open-mouthed dolphin on the cover. Inside Owen has carefully titled the pages 'Daisy's first weeks' and inscribed her date of birth and weight. Either side of a torn spine hang a cascade of plastic pockets. The first pocket is just hanging on, carelessly flicked over so many times. Owen gave him this album, weeks after his diagnosis. He had been tirelessly sorting his affairs, writing letters, finalising his will and letting everyone know his commands. Ben knew this photo album symbolised a passing over of responsibility.

A photograph of the three of them: Estelle, Owen and baby Daisy dressed from head to toe in pink. In the next, Owen sits upright, his tiny girl under his chin, Ben close, a finger pointing at her thick hair. A new family, ready to create memories. The following pockets hold more of the same. Owen and Daisy on the swing. Estelle in the communal garden of their first flat. Ten pictures of Daisy in the bath, taken the same hour; only parents would notice a minuscule change in each.

Every family has an album like this.

The very last photo is the first family trip. They know how to do family. There's Owen, Estelle, and her mother. His parents. Ben, with the best position. Hands tightly gripping the white rubber support, peering into the chariot. A glorious family crowded around their jewel in the crown, Daisy. A royal child could not have been more celebrated.

In the back of the album a square is taped to the inside cover. It's flimsy with a small rip on the bottom edge.

A black and white grainy image labelled as Daisy's twelve-week scan. Estelle didn't have a curve to her slender figure. No one could know. This square was handed about many times. Champagne was spilt on it, salty fingers passed it on, admired it and smiled at it. That small square represented so much. It showed so clearly a much-wanted, much-loved child.

How come? How come when the author of this letter showed an exact same image, his mother's verdict was 'barely there'.

Who knows what happened to that scan photo. Was it discarded when the money was paid? Is it in a purse or a wallet or pinned to a clip board? Ben will never forget those two days. After that rotten kid had barged into their lives, claiming all sorts, he and his mother had tried desperately to make everything feel normal when Daisy bustled in from school. His mother had cooked lasagne whilst he played crib with his niece. They chatted over supper and Daisy had complained the garlic bread wasn't as good as Owen made.

It was only when he was certain that Daisy was asleep that he collapsed on the sofa next to his mother. She switched on the news, and he switched it off. At first, she refused to engage or even look at him. The kid was coming the following afternoon, but Ben was desperate to retract the promise they had made. He had wanted to call someone. If only his father had been alive, he would have talked sense into the old bat. But, no, Mother insisted it was too late, that they should deal with the mess and protect everyone else from further hurt. With that she had retreated to her room and left him alone with his thoughts and an overwhelming sense of fear.

The next day he had watched as the clock chimed two p.m. After an early-morning dash to withdraw the cash, his mother had disappeared. She reckoned she had an appointment that couldn't be postponed. Daisy was due home in less than an hour and Ben wanted him gone. He sat clutching the bulging envelope sealed with tape. He had longed for it to be over.

When the gentle knock came, he stood tall before he opened the door. He wanted to be strong, to step up. He wanted to deal with this thug as if he didn't care. He wanted to hand over the money not caring what it was paying for.

But it wasn't the man with the cap and dirty hands. It was a young girl, hardly older than Daisy. Eyes to the floor, tears gathering on her bottom lashes. A fresh purple bruise above her eye. They spoke for less than five minutes but he could repeat every word.

'Please,' she asked quietly, constantly checking the Volvo parked outside. 'Please help.' For a fleeting moment, he held her gaze whilst gripping that sordid package. She had whispered her name and begged for his consent. He had nodded. 'Yes. Okay.' She had mumbled a promise to stay away, to never come back, to never tell what he had let her do.

With tears tumbling off her chin, she had pushed a scrap of paper at him before disappearing with the package tucked under her sweater. The waiting driver had flung open the passenger door and pulled away before she had closed it.

The corner of paper she had given was inked with girly writing. A pretty name and a mobile number. Trying to erase those elfin features and childish hands from his mind, Ben had screwed up the number and burnt it in the log fire. Her face and neck were covered in purple bruises and her lip was split and bleeding. How could he turn away a child begging for his help when she looked like that?

He had slammed the front door and flung a mug of cold tea at the wall. Soaked in misery, he had mopped up and wrapped the broken china in the *Guardian* his brother could no longer read. Finally, he had slumped over the expensive oak table and sobbed.

Less than an hour later, he had heard a key in the door. Expecting Daisy, he had wiped his eyes and plastered on his Uncle grin. But it was his mother with a pack of biscuits to share. She cleaned the house from top to bottom without comment.

Ben twists the letter over and over. Open it for goodness sake. No more secrets.

He rips open the envelope. He unfolds the letter. The writing is neat and obviously female. The page looks too empty, just five lines of writing.

Dear Ben,

I'm so sorry I can't keep my promise. I had to return; my grandmother has dementia. She needs nursing care. I'm living on the outskirts of town. I won't tell anyone what happened.

He can't read the signature. He wishes he could use that as excuse to cast it aside, pretend it isn't for him. He notices a familiar feeling in his chest, panic rising. He can't breathe. He falls back on his bed in an attempt to slowly exhale like Sandra showed him. He seeks five things he can see, five things he can hear. Calm.

Calm down, Ben. Don't catastrophise. Ben's hands do an unconscious dance as sweat builds up on his palms.

The screwed-up letter in his hand looks like a historical artefact, crumpled with fingerprints. *Oh, Daisy. I'm so sorry.*

11

Daisy

When Daisy rings the bell, Penny slams the green button to release the automatic doors and tugs Daisy into the entrance hall by her sleeve.

'Quick,' she said, 'those doors shut fast. If you're not careful, you'll get a nasty shunt up ya backside.'

Daisy catches Penny checking her watch. Daisy is bang on time.

Daisy looks around in disbelief as she follows Penny to the staff room. Small, diminished people hover about like extras from a bad zombie film. The walls are peach, like Gran's old bedroom, the one she shared with Poppa. She misses her Poppa and Dad. She wonders who'll be next and then remembers it's her. But these empty zombies weren't forced to face their fate at eighteen. What if that was a thing for everyone? How would people like that? How about if everyone was assaulted with a needle on leaving school? How about if their blood was taken before they got a chance at uni, at life, at marriage or kids? How about if everyone was forced into a big reveal? Maybe there could be a party? A cake? A death reveals instead of a birth one? Everyone could crowd around. Instead of pink sponge for girl, blue for boy. It would be yellow for life. Black for death.

How many people would enjoy that? How many people would bail before they knew? Her family go on and on. 'It makes sense,' Mum says, 'to find out, to know your choices.' Gran agrees: 'Perfect sense.' Yeah!! Perfect sense to them 'cos it isn't them. If they had to take the test, they'd know. They'd know what it feels like to be in a game where the outcome is lose or lose. Don't have the test and live too terrified to move. Find out and know. Game over. End here, shrivelled and almost dead. Normal teens get a car or a party when they make adulthood. When she makes eighteen, she gets a special test. A test that'll tell her if she'll live or die. If those suckers think she's gonna do that, they can think again.

'Daisy.' Penny is holding up a triangular dress with poppers down the front.

'Yeah?'

'I asked you what size you are, but you were daydreaming I think.'

Daisy stares at Penny in disbelief. It's bad enough having to work here but to wear that . . . she's glad Kiera and Ryan won't get to see.

'This is a medium, but I think it'll be too big.' Penny pulls out a second dress from the cupboard and thrusts both at Daisy. 'This is a small, try both and I'll be back in five minutes to give you the grand tour.'

When Penny comes back Daisy is wearing the medium, her hands are shoved in two roomy front pockets. You never know what you might wanna smuggle in or out.

Penny is wearing a black trouser suit. Daisy feels this is pretty unfair given how awful she has to look, although she'd rather die than wear stretch clothes with an elasticated waist. And it's pretty spiteful dressing up in coffin clothes when the inmates are nearly dead. She wonders how old Penny is. Maybe older than her mum but younger than Gran. Daisy is obsessed with assessing people's age, and how long they have left.

‘We have forty rooms within two wings. In Sunflower many of the rooms are doubles. We have twenty residents down there at the moment . . . Oh no, nineteen. Sophie died yesterday – a ballet dancer.’

‘I can’t be blamed for that, I wasn’t here,’ Daisy mutters.

Daisy still can’t believe she has ended up working here. She truly believed if she begged Ben and whined to Gran, they’d take pity on her, find her another school or give her some money. After all, it’s pretty embarrassing for them too, that their youngest relative has ended up in this hell hole.

‘Dad wouldn’t want this for me,’ was her final try with Ben yesterday.

‘Well sadly he’s not here,’ Ben said without smiling.

She couldn’t believe it. He used to be a right laugh. He’s rubbish at being Dad. Now, she’s lost Dad and her bessie mate. He did say sorry when she looked upset. She hates upset. She likes feeling angry. She’s angry all the time. She rages at people; they cower in her presence. The kid who rolled his ball into her foot. The pizza delivery bloke who got the wrong topping. That idiot in TK Maxx who called her skinny. She rages at them all. No one gets to make her feel scared and small. She’s done with that feeling.

Penny rabbits on like Daisy is interested. ‘I’ve been a nurse since not much older than you. I started on the wards before moving to the district. I loved seeing people in their homes. You wouldn’t believe some of the things I saw.’

Penny opens a door for an old man, shuffling around in his slippers. His ears are enormous and the triangular bushes above his eyes are an exact match for his crazy white hair. He looks a lot like a small, fat version of the BFG.

‘Bill.’ Penny taps his arm to get him to look. ‘This is Daisy, she’s starting work here.’

'Daisy, Daisy, give me your answer do. I'm half-crazy just for the love of you.'

Daisy is horrified when her eyes tear up. Dad sang that song at bedtime, even when she was way too old.

The hunched man grins far too close to her face, he has no teeth, which is gross. He claps his hands and laughs like a clown. Small drops of disgusting spit spray from his mouth as he points at the ear buds hanging round Daisy's neck.

'Music,' Penny says, her eyebrows lifting in disapproval.

Hard luck, woman, I'm not being paid until lunchtime.

'If music be the food of love . . .' Bill mutters.

'Play on,' Daisy automatically finishes his Shakespeare.

'Daisy, Daisy,' he sings long after he disappears around the corner. This place is proper wacko but it doesn't stink. She can smell cake and would love a slice.

'This is one of two dining rooms. As you can see, I've tried to make it homely.'

Homely! Epic fail. Doesn't she know about Pinterest for inspo. The hall reminds Daisy of the school canteen. Small round tables with salt and pepper in the middle. Also, plastic flowers and sugar bowls with cute tongs. Not so much like school. The wall has a serving hatch. She suddenly wishes she was eating school dinners. She wishes she'd never met Kiera and Ryan. She wishes she was stressing about assignments and spots and venting to her old friends about normal seventeen-year-old stuff. Instead, she's dressed like a saddo in a psycho zoo, terrified she's next.

'Do you think they care?' Daisy demands. 'The ones I've seen look pretty out of it. Don't they break your stuff?'

'My residents will never eat off cheap plates the colour of mushy peas. We can replace breakages.'

Penny pushes her glasses back up her nose as if that proves she's right.

As they walk back down the corridor, Daisy watches Penny from behind. Every few minutes she lifts up her jumper to yank up her elasticated waist. Every terrible time, Daisy gets a peek at Penny's horrifying dough-ball folds. If she doesn't have children at least her body will stay toned and smooth.

She feels damp patches creeping into her armpits. This is always the first sign, that transparent feeling is coming, like she's not here, staring through a misty window. At A&E, they said her brain was fine. She's not convinced. If they'd known about her genes, they might have looked harder. She's read in two scientific papers, feeling detached is the very first sign. Then memory goes. Then you wet yourself. Then down into loony, away from your family. Throw away the key. Dead. She's not waiting for that to happen.

Penny pushes her onto a chair.

'What?' Daisy asks.

Penny is right in Daisy's face with her glasses up on her head. 'You look unwell. You went very pale. Come and sit on the memory bench.'

For a second Daisy had forgotten where she was. Penny is squinting as if trying to solve a puzzle. This could work to her advantage; this could be her escape.

'Yeah, sorry, forgot to tell. I'm not that well. I get sort of dizzy spells. The hospital said it might be a tumour. They're doing tests.'

Daisy sits forward and puts her head between her knees doing some massive sighs.

'Oh dear. Your gran didn't mention funny turns.'

'I haven't told her. I don't want to worry her.'

'How thoughtful.' Penny rubs a hand on Daisy's back which feels vile, but she needs to play along.

'I told you at my interview I couldn't be around hot food or frail people. I might drop stuff or fall on them.'

'I remember,' Penny says again. 'We'll have to make sure you have extra supervision, won't we?'

Penny's tone has changed from school nurse to head of year.

Penny pulls off a piece of lavender from a plant pot and takes a sniff. Reminds Daisy of Kiera snorting her powder.

'Breathe that in. It'll clear that dizziness of yours before you know it. Let's finish our tour before your legs give way.' Penny chuckles.

Our tour. She makes it sound like a fancy trip to the museum. Silly cow.

Daisy did heaps of museums with Dad. The science museum, the childhood one in Bethnal Green. The Louvre in Paris. She'd give anything to be back there. Holding his hand, stopping to look, chatting, laughing, and then onward to see more. Daisy and Dad, they were the team.

'So, we have two main wings. The colour of the floor is different in each so the residents don't get lost. The blue corridor leads to the Cornflower wing and this yellow one indicates it's Sunflower wing. You'll cover the rooms in Sunflower where our most straightforward residents live. They'll be no need for you to go near Cornflower, that's for nursing staff only. The patients are bed bound.'

Sunflower corridor has a bright yellow floor and coloured doors in a neat line. It's like being inside a sweet factory, but not in a good way. Penny pauses outside a pink door with a matching knob.

‘Each door is painted a different colour. This helps our people to identify their own room. The photo on the door is a picture of them in their younger years. Just think, Daisy. One day we’ll be their age.’

Daisy wants to smack Penny’s shrivelled face. She clearly knows nothing about their family. Daisy’s not going to get that old.

Penny makes a gentle knock on the pink door with the back of her hand, but no one responds.

‘Charles,’ she calls, and slowly opens the door. ‘Staff are not allowed to be in a resident’s rooms without permission from me or the occupant,’ Penny says, as if Daisy’s gonna burgle bedrooms to pinch tragic clothes or sniff pee.

The black and white photograph shows a couple sitting on a motorbike. His hands are on the wide handlebars, he looks super pleased with himself in a clean t-shirt and braces. Behind him the girl is sideways, flashing her leg to the camera.

‘Charles and Selvi live here. Selvi has dementia and is increasingly distressed.’ She sighs. ‘It’s sad to watch. Charles does his best, but she’s become very tricky of late and Charles isn’t coping so well. Poor chap. Thankfully, their granddaughter is nearby.’

Does she think I don’t know how quickly good-looking people shrivel and die?

As if reading Daisy’s thoughts Penny turns to look at her. ‘I’m very sorry about your dad, love.’

Daisy pretends she hasn’t heard.

Mind your own business.

‘Oh my, it’s lunchtime. I promised I’d help – we’re short staffed today. Did you leave anything in my office?’

‘Nope.’

'Great, if you go back to the staff room. I'll send someone to find you. You have officially finished your induction. This week you'll shadow other staff until you've learnt the ropes.'

Daisy dithers about looking at each photograph on the bedroom doors. This place is an utter hell hole. She follows the yellow corridor back to the solid blue door. She peers through the glass panel. The floor is painted sea blue. The doors are white. Daisy thinks of the Seagulls. Dad's team. No rainbow colours in the almost dead corridor.

'Sad,' Daisy thinks as she tugs at the chunky silver handle. It's locked. The sign on the door says 'No Entry' to visitors or staff without a blue pass. She slams her side against the edge but there's no wiggle room to break in. The slot above the handle requests a key card. Her mind ponders that. Behind each white door is a warm space where staff make predictable visits. Behind each white door is a resident who can't see or hear. Behind each door is a victim who has no idea what is happening in their room. Dark thoughts stalk Daisy's sharp mind. What if next time she was cold and lonely, she had a quiet space to hide? What if when she was tired, she had a warm chair to read her books and a secret place to stash her belongings? Penny had explained the system at her interview. Sunflower corridor is open to all but Cornflower is managed by trained staff. Daisy noted the Cornflower rota on the back of Penny's office door. The residents in coma corridor are left to rot for hours. What if . . .

Before she can think further, a nurse appears at the far end of blue corridor. There must be another entrance from the outside. Daisy turns from the looking glass before the nurse spots her.

'Food for thought,' Daisy thinks, shoving a cough candy in her gob. Thanks, Derrick, for leaving them out.

12

Dorothy

'Over here.'

Dorothy is delighted to spot her friend, but less delighted to see she's brought 'him'.

She can't calm her nerves. She's certain Ben's hiding something, and she needs to share her worries with her friend. She's permanently terrified he might try again to end his life. Ben promised he wouldn't, that it was a blip resolved by therapy, but she can't be sure.

She plasters a smile on her face as she navigates the overcrowded café. Penny reckoned the garden centre would be quiet as it's midterm. A toddler crashes into her ankle. The mother makes no effort to apologise. No manners. Probably a single parent. It's been drizzling and overcast for days so she can't stomp off her agitation in the park. The conservatory café even feels dark.

'Hello,' Penny says, reaching for a hug.

Derrick pours the last dregs from the silver pot into his cup.

'Don't worry,' he says. 'I'm just the driver. I'm off to grab some plants for The Orchards. I'll leave you two to natter.'

Dorothy hopes her irritation isn't obvious. Much as he irritates her, she needs him onside.

Dorothy joins the queue to buy the coffee. She ought to save herself for lunch. Her trousers are far too tight and they're a size bigger than she ought to be in.

'Here you go,' she says, carefully placing the tray on the table. It's on a slope and the coffee spills as the tray settles. If Peter was here, he'd have shoved a serviette under the leg. Sorted it out.

'Oooh, sticky toffee cake. How lovely,' Penny enthuses, taking a forkful. 'So, come on. Spill the beans. What's up?'

Dorothy hesitates. She's always kept her own counsel. Even when Peter died, she had put on a work face. This kind of friendship is new.

Penny waits. Her overworked hands cup the warm mug.

For a minute Dorothy fears she might cry. 'It's Ben,' she says. 'There's something the matter. I can feel it in my bones.'

'Oh dear. Do you think it's the gallery? Or is the exhibition too much pressure?'

'I just don't know. He's avoiding me. And that's what happened last time . . . and . . . it's . . .'

'Here you go.' Penny hands her a tissue and waits.

Dorothy feels such a fool. Thankfully all the nearby tables are empty. She hates indulgent snivelling, especially in public.

'At breakfast the other day he wasn't unusually preoccupied. But when he collected me on Peter's anniversary, something was off. And that was before he crowbarred an awkward topic into the conversation. On Sunday, I popped in and he looked awful. Dark circles under his eyes.'

For reasons she doesn't understand, she omits to tell Penny about the pink letter. The obvious explanation is an extramarital affair. *Please no more hurt.*

'Oh, how worrying for you. Did he say anything?'

'Nope. He wouldn't look me in the eye. He was closing the door before I had my foot out. He claimed he was busy. Something has happened. I know it.'

Dorothy is glad Penny didn't ask about the awkward conversation. She's certainly not going to confess to being bullied into blackmail. What a fool!

'It must be very hard managing it all on your own.'

'It's when I miss Peter most. He would know what to do. He'd know what to do about Daisy. He'd know what the matter with Ben was.'

Dorothy drains her cup and pours them both a refill. It's a relief to chat.

'I don't know much about Peter,' Penny says, sensing Dorothy needs to talk. 'With all that's gone on since we met, we've not spoken much about your marriage. Where did you meet?'

'At work. He was a locum at the maternity hospital. I was reassuring a distraught mother before her caesarean when a dramatic knight dressed in pale green scrubs burst in. "Ladies and gentlemen. Good evening," he announced as he gathered the surgical tools he needed. He was stupidly dramatic. We were used to a quietly spoken consultant, but she had been taken sick. He stepped in for six glorious months.'

Penny laughs and offers a gentle touch to the back of her friend's hand.

'Tell me more,' Penny encourages. 'I love a fine romance.'

Dorothy hopes Penny doesn't notice the blush as she remembers the quiver of desire that took her by surprise. It had been at least a decade. She took an instant shine to him. She loved his Yorkshire accent and the unprofessional tuft of hair poking from his theatre gown was rather nice. But it was the twinkle in those blue eyes that stopped her in her tracks, the way the corners wrinkled when he smiled. Ben has Peter's eyes, and they melt her heart, even when he's being a pain.

'We gradually became friends and one day, out of the blue, he asked me for supper. When he said he would be cooking, you could've knocked me down with a feather!'

'He sounds like a keeper. I wish Derrick could cook.'

'Peter loved cooking; he was especially fabulous at the old-fashioned food I love. His spotted dick was something else.'

Penny doubles over in hysterics even though it wasn't Dorothy's intention to be crude.

'Let's have a mooch around the centre,' Dorothy suggests. 'You said you needed to buy a Christmas present for your daughter-in-law.'

'Oh no you don't. We'll shop when I've heard the end of this story,' Penny says, elbowing Dorothy like they're sitting in the back row of a school class.

'There's not much more to tell. Peter was older, a widower. I was over the moon. It was so unexpected. Owen was much less enamoured.'

'I hadn't realised Owen wasn't Peter's.'

'Probably because he was more like Peter than Ben. I stupidly got myself in the family way just before I qualified. Owen's father was long gone by his first birthday. By the time I met Peter, Owen was practically taller than me. He considered himself the man of the house. In his opinion, I didn't need another.'

'That must have been tricky?'

'Actually, it wasn't, or it wasn't for long. Peter quickly won Owen over. Before long they were the team. Off to football, cooking together and leaving me feeling like the third wheel.'

'So, Peter is Ben's father?'

'Yes. Peter had wanted children, but his first wife hadn't. Given my age we weren't sure I would conceive but it was surprisingly easy. Peter presented the news so Owen believed it was his idea. Fun to have more boys.'

Secretly, Dorothy had longed for a girl. Typically, Ben was late. Owen was desperate to attend the birth and a colleague facilitated a home delivery. Most twelve-year-olds would've been distressed by the gore but the son of a midwife knew more than most. Wide brown eyes met screwed-up blue ones. It was love at first sight. Many things changed as they matured but her boys stayed as close as siblings could. No wonder what happened to Owen broke Ben's heart.

The story over, Penny and Dorothy set to shopping. 'Jingle Bells' is blaring out from the speakers making Dorothy's hearing aid scream in protest. Penny picks up different products, sniffs candles and reads the small print on boxes of chocolates.

'Haven't you got any presents left to buy?' she asks as Dorothy follows her about the garden centre, unable to muster any Christmas enthusiasm.

'Got most of mine,' she lies. 'I'm happy watching you and holding the basket.'

Since Owen went, Dorothy has been consumed with a fury she detests about Jonny, Owen's father. She was so fragile and needy, desperate for male attention when she first left home. If she hadn't been pregnant, her affection for Jonny would've been as fleeting as his commitment.

Within weeks of sleeping with him, she was vomiting. Nothing like the labour ward to make you face reality. Jonny was delighted. Delighted to have inseminated her. Delighted to smoke the essential cigar but less delighted to practise fatherhood. Before Owen's first Christmas, Jonny was out more than in. She knew one day he'd go but not come back. If she'd have known the sinister legacy he'd implanted, she would've taken a shotgun and blown out his senseless brains. It's a good job he's long dead.

'Why don't you get this for Estelle?'

Penny holds a chunky fuchsia candle under Dorothy's nose. 'Who doesn't like a fancy candle?'

Dorothy has no idea what Estelle would like. They hardly speak. Sad, given they're both grieving for a husband and child.

As they exit the tills, Penny remarks, 'Derrick has gone. I presumed I could grab a lift home with you?' Dorothy helps her with two carrier bags of tatt. She's amazed by how much Penny can spend in half an hour.

'Isn't that where Owen got married?' Penny asks as they pass St Mary's church.

Dorothy can't believe how much Penny remembers. She's such a special person.

'Indeed.'

'What was Owen like before he got sick?'

'Oh, Owen was everything!' Dorothy laughs 'Clever from birth, focused and responsible, everything Ben isn't.'

'Were the changes sudden?'

'No. Very gradual. I was still living in Dorking so wasn't seeing him as much as Ben, but in my heart I knew. His shoulder hunch was one of the first tells. I knew something was up but didn't want to see. Didn't think I would cope with any more loss. In the end Ben made me face it.'

Dorothy drops Penny off and waits while she finds her key and opens the door. She wishes they'd ended their time on a happier note. It's hard to revisit that time. Thankfully, she was living an hour from Owen when his symptoms first started. She recognised something was amiss before anyone but chose to stay blind. In the end, it was Ben who forced the issue.

'Mum, Owen is not right,' Ben had said, handing her some leftover wine after a family gathering. 'His speech is odd. He's irritable, stumbling about. And those sweets. He's scoffing children's sweets. It's weird.'

'It's stress,' she argued. 'Estelle says he's always working.'

'But he called me in the middle of the night yesterday and asked to borrow a CD. He swore when I refused to drive it around.'

'When I worked shifts, I got muddled, the days blur,' she had snapped defensively.

'But he doesn't work shifts,' Ben had responded, his tone even. He rarely got irritated then.

'Ben, I don't want to discuss this, it's been a long week.'

Ben had taken her glass to set it on a side table. He shuffled close and put his arm awkwardly around her shoulders. He spoke quietly so she had to look at him.

'You said that three months ago, Mum. There's a serious problem.'

When Ben's eyes misted over, she gave in. She knew. Owen had been out of sorts for several months. He had food on his suit and frequently overslept. Sloppy was so not him.

The most peculiar change was the sweets. He had bags of them, in every pocket, in his desk and in the car. He couldn't explain, he had never had a sweet tooth. They later found out that's often one of the first tells for Frontal Temporal Dementia

Her knees had given way and before she knew it, she had collapsed into her son's embrace and sobbed and sobbed. She didn't tell anyone but there was something in his emerging character that reminded her of Jonny.

Instead of returning home, Dorothy does a three-point turn. She ignores the honk of a hefty van and drives towards the gallery. She parks a few roads away, locks the car and fires up her umbrella. In her bag she has a book, the *County Times* and a few biscuits wrapped in cling film. She's timed it so Ben can't leave the gallery without passing her. She'll take a window table in that wine bar she hates and whatever time he leaves, she'll be waiting. Waiting to find out what has taken the light out of her boy's eyes. She's lost one son. She refuses to lose another.

Dear Daisy girl,

I'm so grateful I took time out in your early years because in the blink of a tired eye, you were off to school. On the first day I wanted to pack your Scooby Doo bag, but I got a sharp shove. 'By myself,' you declared. You're still fiercely independent but these days you've reframed that sentiment into something more mature. Now, when I step over the unseen line, I get a shove, but you say, 'Take a chill pill!' or simply, 'Leave it, Dad.'

Time kept flying. People kept saying, 'Before you know it, she'll be taller than you. Before you know it, she'll be leaving school. Before you know it, she'll have a boyfriend.' Daisy, the world is constantly propelling you forward. Stay present. Live on purpose or things will keep happening to you before you know it.

I never stopped loving our time together. After school we built Lego, or I built Lego whilst you created a story or painted a picture. Gran said, 'Spend as much time with her while she's young,' and I did. Despite often being dangerously low on sleep and dropping balls at work I lived for those hours playing with you. I'd pretend to be a monster and chase until you screamed. At night, you'd sit on my lap, listening to stories from Gran's old book. The book with the outdated stories, all containing a prince and a happy-ever-after.

When you could recite them word for word, I panicked. Did you believe you needed to be rescued by a man? I was chuffed when I discovered the feisty girl series. They were a far better fit for you, and me. Girls who climbed trees, outran the boys, and punched when anyone pushed their luck. Do you remember Blaze? She was the most like you, the one with long hair and big boots and determination of steel. Set the world alight, my Blaze.

On Saturdays, Mum's day off, we'd go to the music shop and share a hot chocolate. When the weather was fine, we'd play in the woods, light fires and toast marshmallows. By the end of the day, you were too shattered to walk so I'd piggy-back you home chatting about the big stuff like litter, and bullying, and who would be prime minister when you got to uni.

After your bath, I'd watch you drift off to sleep and stay put for an hour to admire the length of your lashes and the curve of your mouth. Some nights your mum would come home and find me sleeping by your side.

Daisy, there'll be times in your life when you feel sad and lonely, But there's no need. First try salted caramel ice cream, that often works when I lack the strength to go on. If the ice cream fails, it must be bad. In those moments, grab a blanket and snuggle down. Close your eyes and tell me what's up. Know that I'll always listen. Never feel alone as I'll be there. I'll be there sleeping by your side.

Goodnight, precious girl, goodnight.

13

Ben

'Hello Amanda, It's Ben Bowen-Jones. The FTD association gave me your name as someone who might be prepared to speak at an exhibition I'm organising in my brother's name?'

'Hello, yes of course. Anything to help raise the profile of this dreadful disease. Can you email me the date and what you'd like? I'll text my email address. With so much going on, I've become dreadfully forgetful. Sometimes I fear the dreaded beast is stalking me too.'

Ben reminds himself that Amanda's husband has FTD. 'I know what you mean,' he says. 'My niece is terrified of it; she keeps checking into A&E and asking for scans as she's convinced she's got fatigue and dizziness.' Ben pauses, wanting to give Amanda a moment. 'Just so you know, the theme of the paintings will be emotional distress.'

'A pretty fitting theme. There's distress for everyone. I don't feel anyone understands. It's like he's dead but here. My husband, but not. I miss John so much and yet he's in my bed and lounging on the settee. When he's asleep, I watch him and apart from some odd twitching, he looks like him. But the moment he opens his eyes, I see it. He's gone but who the heck is the person in his body, shouting and carrying on.'

Amanda obviously needs to talk. He gets it. FTD is the weirdest thing. When his dad died, it was awful, and it hurt but he was alive and then dead. What happened to Owen was intangible. It was subtle, hard to know when he transitioned from his old self to the version he became. Harry Potter's dementor had sucked out his character and left an empty shell.

'Can I ask if your husband will come? I mean . . . is . . . he good . . . well enough?'

'I'll see. He'll want to come if he gets wind of it. He's always liked an excuse for a drink but now I have to watch him like a hawk. The things he does . . .'

Her voice tails off and Ben can hear that she's crying. Hearing her upset makes Ben's lip quiver. For a moment they pause to get past the emotion, both knowing what this is like. Ben can remember those days with Owen, it was truly horrific.

Owen was Ben's go-to, even when his father was alive. Dad could be a bit old school, a bit black and white. Owen knew Ben like nobody else.

When Ben was in college. Owen had collected him from footie training, even after they'd had Daisy. Ben had felt so proud when Owen strolled across the pitch, his work jacket slung casually over his shoulder as if it wasn't important at all. Owen would take Ben to his local. He knew everyone, but he focused on his kid brother. With Owen, Ben was always the main event. With his parents he often felt like an irritating side show. He knows Owen made Daisy feel like the centre of the world too.

By the time he finishes his call with Amanda, it is almost dark outside. He hates these endless short days. To top it all, it's raining, not a decent downpour but a slow pointless drizzle accompanied by a freezing wind. On these dark days, the pain he feels at losing his big brother is catastrophic. He'd give anything to look up, and see Owen, with his shoulders back, grinning from ear to ear with his arm slung around Daisy.

The next best thing would be Daisy wanting to be close again. He's so sorry she's lost faith in him. He's failed to live up to Owen's expectations.

Drowning in a raging ocean of dark thoughts, he startles to a halt almost knocking a teenager off a bicycle. Mother is in front of him, dressed in a yellow mackintosh and holding a Mary Poppins umbrella with her legs wide apart as if in a star jump. Just as he thinks she's lost her mind she launches into a terrifying tirade.

'I won't let you pass until you tell me what's going on. I've had enough. Something is the matter, and you'll tell me or I'll stand here all night,' she spews. 'I mean it, Benji. I'm not moving until you tell me.'

Ben hates it when she calls him that, treats him like a child. All his life he's been the baby. Owen and his father were the men who demanded an audience. Benji and Daisy forever the children.

Ben has no idea what to do. A huge part of him wants to explode. He should grab his mother by the shoulders, plonk her backside into a puddle and tell her exactly what the matter is. He should scream into her face like he did as a teen and tell her that it's *her*. She's the matter. He should yell that she's controlling and manipulative and that by forcing him to pay off that thug, she ruined his life, his marriage and almost killed him. They eye each other, a metre apart. Passers-by have to divert to miss them. He's glad it's dusk. Wearing his woollen hat pulled over his ears, he's hoping he looks unremarkable. When he was a teenager, he and his mother had frequent stand-offs. She's impossibly stubborn. Owen was her perfect son until he wasn't, but Ben struggled. His father was effortlessly calm, but she screamed like a banshee when he was late, or messy or refused to give in to her demands. Here they are again but now the mediators are gone. It's just him and her in the ring, no referee.

Whilst he stands, struggling to suppress a familiar blend of rage and humiliation, a man in a sharp grey suit exits a cab on the other side of the road. Both him and his mother are thinking alike: it could be Owen. He knows she wishes it was him who degenerated not her precious firstborn.

A career-driven alpha male. The perfectly proportioned bloke leans in to pay before turning around to reveal an athletic build and chiselled jaw. Even his briefcase shouts luxury. Ben knows this man has it together just like his brother.

If this man had a secret problem, he'd sort it out.

He wouldn't hide a letter from his wife like a trembling Bambi.

'Callie,' he'd say, 'something I didn't tell you. My mother commissioned an evil thing. But, hey, my mother doesn't know how it ended. No one knows. It might ruin our lives. It might ruin everyone's lives.'

Since that letter, Ben's head has been all over the place. Yesterday he missed the speed camera. Callie was furious.

'Seriously Ben, it's at the end of our road. Who gets a speeding ticket somewhere they drive every day?'

The rain stops, the suited man disappears around the corner and mother deflates her umbrella. He lets her link her arm through his, but he doesn't bend when she stretches to plant a kiss. She brushes her lips against his shoulder leaving a pink smudge. They walk. He knows what she's up to. It's Dad's side by side tactic. Less confrontational.

'Spit it out,' she says.

His mother sighs when he retrieves his phone in response to a bleep. A text from Estelle. As if he isn't stressed enough already.

Ben, you promised to give us a date.
Sorry, but the three of us need to talk
about the test. She's eighteen in less
than a year.

Ben sighs. He had promised he would gather information, look at the research so they could support Daisy to make an informed decision. He didn't agree to facilitate a meeting behind her back, take on the issue and resolve the problem as if it's his. Ben fires off a text to her.

Soz, will call next week.

He does feel sorry for Estelle even though they've never been close. Owen's demise left everyone in dire straits and although he knows it's irrational, he's angry. When Owen was eventually diagnosed with Frontal Temporal Dementia it was horrific but a relief. He was beginning to wonder if Owen was taking steroids. He was so aggressive and rude.

'Will you listen instead of playing on that phone,' Mum snaps, pulling at his jacket like a sullen child.

'Sorry, what?'

'That's what I'm asking. What's going on? You're preoccupied, avoiding me and you look dreadful.'

A car speeds too close to the pavement splashing them both from a filthy puddle.

'Cheers,' Ben says, not knowing how much to say. Does he make an excuse or tell what really went on that day? Should he tell how the boy went but a girl returned? A girl with less acceptable terms? Should he tell her that girl got her way? Should he tell her that her guilt is misdirected? Her money went but her problem didn't.

‘I’m worried about Daisy and the genetic test. What if she’s positive, I can’t bear it,’ Ben blurts out a partial truth. He is worried about Daisy. Every time he looks at Daisy, he remembers what he did and can’t bear it. A secret that devastating can never see the light of day.

‘There’s nothing to worry about. I’m sure she’ll be fine. She looks much more like Estelle the older she gets.’

Mum pats his arm. There, there, nothing to worry about. Ben wrenches his arm away and steps closer to the kerb.

‘That makes absolutely no sense,’ he snaps. ‘A neurological disease can’t be seen. No one knew Owen had that ticking time bomb.’

His mother sighs. She needs to reassure, make it better, and tell him it’ll be alright in the end. She refuses to accept things that can’t be swept under her cream carpet even if it is freshly hoovered.

No one knew Owen had that bomb until it exploded leaving everyone fragmented and diminished. More than any of them, he wants to protect Daisy. As Owen deteriorated, he became increasingly irrational and absent. His colleagues were as flabbergasted by the personality changes as his family. Ben still doesn’t know what he got up to in those crisis months. Eventually, the senior partner at Austin’s contacted Estelle. They said Owen wasn’t engaging with a disciplinary process she knew nothing about. Owen denied everything and had refused to discuss what didn’t concern him. Ben still doesn’t know what the accusations were about. He’s unsure if his mother knew the full details. She wouldn’t let on if she did. In the end Owen was ‘let go’ using some fancy legal terminology that in simple terms meant ‘not good enough’. That was all he was told. His astonishing career was over.

'Estelle wants to talk about Daisy's test but it's not her life and it's not mine or yours. Only she can make that decision,' Ben says, holding her eye.

Ben can feel his temperature rising. Is he angry at his mother or is he defending against the guilt he feels for doubting his best man? There were rumours in the pub. The longer life goes on without Owen, Ben doubts his judgement. Was Owen really the hero he had made him out to be? And if he wasn't, was that the illness or is dementia like alcohol, it just reduces the cover veneer? These are the stories that torture him when he should be creating a masterpiece.

'Well, I can't see any reason she'd be stupid enough to resist finding out. To find out makes total sense,' his mother says, accidently stomping in a puddle like Daisy in a mood.

'Blast,' Dorothy moans, brushing water from the edge of her coat.

Ben can't be bothered to argue but refuses to leave it there.

'It makes sense to you,' he says, his tone becoming edgy. 'I let you pressure me, and it's cost so much. I won't let you gang up on Daisy.'

'Oh, don't be so dramatic.' His mother is less keen to talk about his feelings if it means she has to examine her own actions.

Rage from nowhere erupts within. Ben flips around to face her and leans closer to his mother's shocked expression.

'Somehow,' he pauses to find the breath. 'Somehow, I don't think anything can be more dramatic than paying for someone to die.'

14

Daisy

Derrick insists hair is scraped back. One of many stupid rules enforced at The Orchards concentration camp, but every time Daisy squashes her hair into a knot, straggly bits escape. They must arrive fifteen minutes before they're paid. Daisy told the others they're treated like skivvies, that it's probably illegal. But they're either too thick or ancient, or both.

'Hurry up, ladies, I need you ready to start handover.' Penny claps her hands like a primary teacher and turns over the sign on the main door: 'Staff meeting in progress, please call 01903 567764 for attention.' She follows Daisy into the dining room.

Derrick is perched on a stool, holding a clip file with his agenda. Daisy hates him. He reminds her of the man who lives next door. His jumbo brown cords bunch up like an oversized nappy when he sits. His checked shirts get tucked in, usually it's blue or red. Creepy weirdo with his psycho glasses balanced on his head.

'Thanks for getting here on time,' he says to the people already sitting. Daisy meets his eye, dares him to challenge as she methodically finishes her hair.

'If we have to be here early, you should pay us,' Daisy mutters loudly. The room stays quiet.

Derrick pulls down his specs and looks at her over the top. 'It is not unreasonable to be ready for your shift, young lady.'

He nods at his wife. Daisy has no idea why Penny married him, she's such a wimp. The other staff become more interested in the state of the grey carpet tiles. They're pathetic too.

Penny turns to Patsy, the deputy manager. She's awful and vile to the ancients. 'Can you please manage handover while Daisy and I have a chat in my office?'

'Of course.' Patsy takes the file from Penny's gloved hand. Penny marches towards her office. Daisy walks close behind, copying her walk, trying to catch someone's eye. Gary the chef gives her a cheeky wink.

'Close the door,' Penny demands.

Uninvited, Daisy sits on Penny's office chair and allows it to swivel a half turn. Penny stands with her hands on her hips eyeing her up and down. Daisy wishes she'd remained standing.

'That will be the last time you challenge Derrick's authority in a meeting. If you have a complaint, you can request a private chat like everyone else. We are not unreasonable people. If you have as much sense as your grandmother tells me, you'll change your attitude. You are being paid more than someone your age will get elsewhere. If you push me, you'll be working on Wrighton's factory line.'

Wrighton's is where all the dropouts end up. They start there after school and stay until they die. Daisy's mind replays Dad.

Stay focused, or you'll end up in the factory.

Dad was obsessed with the rewards of a good education. 'Find a job you love, and you'll never work again,' he'd say.

If he caught her on a screen instead of studying, he'd throw out a factory one-liner.

A yellow nylon dress wouldn't suit you.

Shall I buy you a blue hair net?

But that was rare as she was a clever girl. His good girl who studied hard, desperate to follow him to Cambridge.

Daisy considers Penny's evil stare. Her head chirps some responses.

Stick your job.

You can't order me about.

Do one.

In her last term at school, Kiera described one girl in school, the only one Kiera was scared of. Donna Massey was a vicious bully. Donna and two of her sisters work at that factory.

When Daisy doesn't answer back, Penny goes out, leaving her in the office.

You see, Dad, you were wrong, the slackers do win, laziness does pay, rudeness does work. Shame you spent so long being good, look where that got you. And while I have your attention Dad, these are the other lies you told me.

You can stay in your school.

You'll never lose your bedroom.

It won't always feel this bad.

One day you'll understand.

The digital clock on Penny's desk shouts coffee break. If she gets to the staff room before the briefing meeting ends, she can sneak one of the resident's chunky cookies and unpack her bag. Daisy slides off the chair with surprising grace and rushes out colliding into mad old Bill.

‘Daisy, Daisy, give me your answer do . . .’ The old man grins and grunts at the same time.

‘You’re half crazy,’ she sings, adding some inappropriate words.

He keeps snorting long after he’s passed as if she’s made the funniest joke. He does this every time they meet, sometimes ten times in an hour. It drives the other staff mad. They try to shut him up. He makes Daisy laugh and Daisy doesn’t laugh much these days. Bill is the oldest resident, he has Parkinson’s. Daisy has looked it up. He walks as if he’s ice skating in slow motion. When he’s not clapping, he has a moody face, but the website said that’s a Parkinson’s mask, so he can’t help it. She told Sharon in the office that ’cos she knows nought about the diseases in this place. With her hands deep in the pockets of a vile checked dress, Daisy watches him. All the way along the bright yellow corridor, he stops and starts. When he reaches the end, he shuffles around and starts back towards her; watching him is kind of relaxing.

Even Daisy’s skinny butt can’t fit on the narrow stool in the break room. It’s one of three against a high table with a crazy patterned plastic top. She’s informed Penny it’s the law for staff to have a decent place for breaks. There are still no comfy chairs.

Silviya, the girl from Bulgaria, is struggling to balance on the plastic pinhead, her backside hangs down either side. She is so boring. Daisy retrieves her bag from her locker. Before she leaves today, she needs to stash her tin of letters and the classics she’s smuggled from home into her new hiding place.

With a mug of hot tea and a warm cookie, she can relax for ten minutes. Determined to avoid eye contact so Silviya doesn’t speak, Daisy grabs the scruffy A4 book from the far end of the shelf. On the front, in black, 'The Orchards Staff Manual', underneath in smaller print, 'Do Not Remove'. Who'd want this as a bedtime story?

She flicks through, page four falls open. Right at the bottom, she finds the most amazing gift. She can't believe her luck. In the tiniest print, it says: 'If evidence is provided, time off to attend health visits is acceptable at the discretion of the management.'

It's time to accept Dr Staples's kind offer of weekly psychology sessions, or at least pretend. Daisy hopes Penny won't look too hard at the appointment card. She wouldn't want anyone to know she's wacko enough to be seeing the mental doctor.

Her rucksack is thankfully lighter. She's ordered another stash of books from the FTD society. Three new research papers have been released this week in the *BMJ* and there's a random article in the *Guardian*. She has to read it all and she must get through *Pride and Prejudice* this month. She might not have long on this planet, but she doesn't want to end up thick.

Daisy glides out the staff room with a broad grin, Silviya follows but Daisy forgets to hold open the door.

15

Dorothy

Dorothy is finalising the dining table with condiments and sauces when she hears the rattle of Ben's engine. From behind the curtain, she watches him get out of his battered Fiat. Why on earth didn't he use his inheritance to buy an updated model?

He made her wait for a week but yesterday he accepted her call and agreed to come for a cooked breakfast. Having suffered another sleepless night, she was glad of a reason to leave her bed at five a.m. She has cleaned the house and baked gratitude cakes for Penny. She's so indebted and, so far, Daisy is complying. Penny said she's punctual and despite her attitude is showing a kindly way with the old folks. Dorothy forgets she could now be described as an old folk.

Ben rings the bell despite having a key. Her darling, darling boy. Those dreadful teenage clothes, pockets bulging with phone, wallet, and no doubt a notebook to jot ideas for paintings. Ideas that won't reach the canvas.

She watches as he paces on the spot, checks his phone, runs his hand through his hair. She longs to be sure he's stable, not teetering on the edge of crisis. She must know she hasn't ruined him.

She's reticent to let him in. she doesn't want to fight. There's only the three of them now. Her, Ben, and Daisy. They have to stay close.

Dorothy pulls her face into her best smile as she pulls open the front door.

'Hello, darling. Sit yourself down while I finish the food. It'll only take a few minutes to do the toast and eggs.'

Dorothy moves slowly, she studies his mood. Hands buried in deep pockets, Ben leans back in Peter's high-back winged chair and closes his eyes.

In the kitchen, she pops the sourdough in the toaster and adds salt and pepper to the mashed avocado. As the water heats to host the eggs she leans against the fridge door. It's cold on her back and sends shivers down her torso as she considers what she commissioned Ben to orchestrate. She knows it wasn't right. It's Peter's face that jumps to mind. All her career she was pro-life. She's seen terminations and however early they were, a child was visible.

Not long after they met, she and Peter discussed the issue. 'I admire you. Keeping Owen took courage. Many would've opted for a termination to avoid the shame.'

Abortion created one of their final debates.

'At the ethics meeting today, Clive Janson, that new embryologist, was spouting some nonsense about a new-fangled idea – personhood theory.'

Peter ranted as he leaned back into the settee, sweet and sour dripping down his chin. Eating a take-out in the lounge was a rare treat. Usually she retrieved crisp white napkins, full cutlery and insisted on food at the table.

'Not heard of that?' she said distracted by the headlines moving silently across the television screen.

Peter wanted to go on. He had a video clip of conception on his phone. 'See. A flash of light appears when a new human is formed.'

She felt her temperature rising, she remembers picking the crumbs off her skirt wanting the conversation to end but feeling powerless to derail it.

'You see?' he kept on, pointing at the screen. Prodding with his finger at the tiny spark of light. Miraculous. She couldn't deny.

In the end, she snatched his phone and kissed him. Usually, it would be a peck, but she was desperate. She planted a firm smacker on his lips until he lost his train of thought.

She truthfully agreed with him about the sanctity of human life. She truthfully agreed with him on so much.

Night after night that first year, lying in bed, as intimate as two could get, they told each other everything. But she hadn't told him that thing, that one thing that made her shiver, that one thing that broke her on the best of days. She's so glad he isn't here to find out what she made their son do, that was even worse.

She's brought back to the present by the unnecessary ping of the toaster. The water is boiling, fast and furious.

She pokes her head around the lounge door to tell Ben, breakfast won't be long, that she got momentarily distracted. He's fast asleep. A gentle snore escapes after every out breath. His brow is furrowed, and his skin looks sallow. Dorothy's heart sinks as she notices his tortured features. Both her sons have suffered too much. Is this her punishment?

'I'm sorry,' she whispers as she rushes back to the kitchen to retrieve the poached eggs.

She piles two plates with yellow and green and decides to eat on laps.

When she pushes the plates through the door, Ben is upright and wide eyed.

'For what?' he asks.

She gives him his breakfast and lays her own on the side table to retrieve the cutlery.

'What are you sorry about?' he repeats.

'You know what?' Dorothy answers, glad to have the distraction of eating and not face to face.

'Do I?'

'Come on. You've not spoken to me properly since we argued in the street.'

'But what are you saying sorry about?'

'For doing what you said I did.'

Ben swallows a last fork of toast, sets down his plate and twists to look at his mother. He exhales a long sigh. Her heart races as she waits.

'It's not so much what you did,' he speaks slowly, carefully. 'It's what you bullied me into doing, the way you said I had no option, made me feel guilty for wanting to pause. You took away my choice as well as . . .'

Dorothy can't listen any longer. She can't bear to see the pain in his face, the shadows under his eyes, and the tremor in his fingers. She reaches to still his hands in hers and he doesn't pull away. His hands are cold.

'I just couldn't bear any more pain.' She knows it sounds pathetic, needy.

'But it wasn't about you.'

'Well, it was. I'd had enough. I wanted an end to drama in my family.'

'But it's my family too, and Daisy's. Not just yours.'

Dorothy bows her head and pulls back her hands. She knows he's right.

Ben continues. 'And it wasn't just what you made me do but how you treated me afterwards. When you came back, you couldn't look at me. You didn't ask about me. You thrust custard creams in my lap as if a biscuit made everything right, as if I was a child and didn't deserve to be heard.'

'I didn't think it would help. Going over things, making it harder. I thought it was best.'

'Best for you, Ma, not for me or anyone else. Best for you.' He pauses. 'It wasn't our decision to make.'

For a moment she thinks he's going to storm off.

'And what made it worse was that I couldn't tell Callie.'

'I'm sorry,' she repeats. She is so sorry.

Ben gets up, comes behind her, squeezes her shoulders and says, 'I've gotta go. Finish your breakfast.'

He waves as he strides past the window.

She puts her full plate of food on the carpet. Her appetite is non-existent.

She waits at the window until Ben is in his car. Worryingly, there's a yob hanging about by the lamp post. When she catches his eye, he pretends he's on his phone. She hopes he's not sizing her up, checking she lives alone so he can break in at night.

Ben's engine roars away. He's given the best he can right now. She hopes she's given him what he wanted, enough to move forward.

With her hands cupped around a cold mug of tea, she looks up to the framed photo of her beloved Peter.

'You should've chased after him for a hug,' he'd say.

Peter never compromised on important issues, especially if it involved family.

That's the reason she couldn't tell him about that fragile girl with the lanky hair wearing a flimsy hospital gown too short for her long legs. She couldn't tell him about the metal table with the cold against her collarbone. She couldn't tell him of a bright circular light above or the harsh face of a man with eyes the colour of his scrubs. She couldn't tell anyone that.

She should have learnt. But despite all that Peter poured into her, all that happened to Owen. When she had her chance to get redemption, she failed. When it truly mattered, she acted as judge and executioner without consulting the jury. She harassed their son into co-conspirator. That pushed him over the edge. She could be. Should be. Held accountable for the loss of two lives.

16

Ben

Standing in the psychology waiting area, Ben flicks awkwardly through a women's magazine pretending he's as relaxed as the next bloke.

He hadn't intended to be this early but didn't want to miss Daisy. She's not asked for him in ages.

Having spent the last year raging at him for failing to be Owen, she's now accusing him of being just like her father. He knows there's no chance of that. Then, on Thursday, his phone had flashed up with her picture.

'Hey Bubba.' That's what she used to call him until everything went wrong. Then it became Ben or unmentionable labels. 'I need picking up, Monday.'

Before he could gather his thoughts to speak, she had gabbled at top speed, her words blending together. He wondered if she'd been drinking but heard a child's voice so she must have been at the park.

'I'm going to your psychologist again. I've gotta go lots 'cos I'm proper bad. I've gone downhill since I last saw you guys,' she finished.

'I'm sorry to hear that,' Ben had offered, not sure whether to be sad or suspicious. He hopes she hasn't got worse. When he first booked the appointment to see Sandra, it was after he'd seen cuts on her arm. He knew instantly what they were.

Daisy had been sitting on the back step at their new house. For a moment Ben had been delighted. He could see a glimpse of the real Daisy as she sat scrolling through her phone but snapping the occasional photograph of the birds. The real Daisy, who was kind and gracious and who loved nature. It was reassuring to see she was in there somewhere.

Unusually, Estelle had invited a few friends including him and Callie, but Daisy was refusing to join for supper. He had handed her a Pepsi and asked to see the photo she had taken of the crow perching on the garden wall. Much to his surprise she had passed it up to him. Her sleeve shrank back and exposed four distinctive marks. Two cuts were raw, but the others were older. Daisy realised her mistake and yanked her sleeves over her hand. He said nothing but he saw in her face that she knew he had spotted the incriminating hurts.

He had left her to go back inside. Mum, Callie, and Estelle were in the kitchen drinking tea.

'Estelle has had another call from school,' his mother had said.

Ben had put his finger to his lips. For goodness sake, Daisy was in earshot and this wasn't helpful. Callie shot him a look that said, 'Stay calm, it's not worth it!'

It came as no surprise to Ben that Daisy was self-harming to soothe her pain. They're all doing something. His mother cleans the dirt away, Estelle drinks herself into oblivion, so why they judge Daisy for acting out, he'll never know. Before he left that evening, he had gone in search of Daisy, who was in bed. She still sleeps with that mouldy old bear Owen got on a business trip.

He had sat on the edge of the bed like he used to, and gently pulled up her pyjama sleeve. She hadn't said much but had agreed to see Sandra, the psychologist who had helped him. He had made an appointment the next day, which turned out to be her last school day.

When the clock in the reception area hits six p.m., Sandra opens her door but before she gets it to full width, Daisy barges past. Sandra raises her eyebrows and offers a fleeting smile.

'Hey, how's my fave relative,' Ben says attempting an upbeat tone. The eyes that used to be filled with adoration are brimming with hostility. It's hard not to retaliate.

'I'm not five,' Daisy spits, eyes narrowed.

'You will always be five to me,' Ben offers, wishing he could think of something constructive to say.

'And you will always be old and stupid,' she says, seeking the eye of an older man by the door. She offers a trout pout and the creep winks back. Ben would love to punch his smarmy face and yell that she's a vulnerable child.

Instead, he slips his arm around her shoulders as they walk towards the exit. 'Go on, give your Uncle Bubba half an hour, and make an old man feel special. Callie's baking pizza.'

'I've stuff to do, people to see.'

Ben used to be able to read her like a comic but now he has absolutely no clue. Is that the truth?

She slams the exit button as if that's to blame for everything.

For a millisecond, he thinks she's going to cry.

Before he can clear his throat to respond, elbows push him away and she slams through the automatic door, races down the steps and into a power walk.

'I can come for half an hour, then I'm meeting mates,'

The door shuts in his face. No doubt the winking man is having a right laugh.

‘Deal,’ Ben shouts, running out to catch up. Daisy doesn’t respond.

Her tiny skirt makes it impossible to climb into his van, so she hitches up the blue denim as if for the school sack race. He looks in the rear mirror to check no one is watching. Once she’s in the seat, she jiggles the skirt back. When she’s not forcing a scowl, Ben glimpses the little girl who danced in Peppa Pig knickers not caring who was looking. How might she react to that memory? Ben can’t suppress a fleeting chuckle.

When Daisy attended St Cuthman’s, a prestigious girl’s school, funded by Owen’s income, she loved being collected in Ben’s van. When Owen went, so did the luxuries, and some of the basics too.

The first time Ben drove to Steyning Academy, his heart sank.

But everyone thought Daisy would fly whether at Eton or the local comp. After all, she was a good girl, a science geek, destined to succeed. Owen’s mini me.

Even as a toddler, she had a strong sense of self. In her first year, Owen had proudly shown off the year group photo. All the girls wore a pinafore dress or a neatly ironed skirt with their small hands resting in their laps.

‘Look,’ he said. ‘That’s my girl.’

Daisy was in the front row, the only girl in trousers with her hands on her hips.

Estelle was always Owen’s girl until Daisy arrived. From then on Daisy was ‘his girl’. Two peas in a pod; apart from their size and gender, they were the same. Stand-out people, with style that can’t be taught and oversized brains designed to change the world. Kasia would probably describe them as influencers.

‘Hey Callie, we’re home,’ Ben shouts as he unlocks the door. He can’t remember the last time Callie was back before him but he’s grateful. She knows he’s struggling. When he told her he was collecting Daisy, she took a half day to cook supper.

Ben nods towards Daisy’s muddy boots. Without comment she kneels to unlace them.

Callie comes out to meet them, wiping her hands on an apron that used to belong to her mother.

Callie waits for Daisy to straighten before pulling her into a firm hug. Ben expects Daisy to retreat but she stays in Callie’s arms for longer than necessary. It’s as if that cuddle is just what she needs.

‘So glad you’re here,’ Callie enthuses. ‘I need an opinion on a pair of dungarees. I’m not sure if they make my butt look huge.’

‘Daisy can’t stay long. She might have some tea with us if it’s ready, but then she has to go.’

‘Sure. If you put the pizzas in, Ben, I’ll steal your marvellous niece to my closet for ten minutes.’

When they come back down, Daisy is carrying a bundle of clothes.

‘Hand-me-downs,’ she laughs. ‘Stuff that’s too cool for wifey.’

‘Watch it.’ Callie grins, gesticulating a double slap on Daisy’s cheeks.

Callie puts the huge pizza on the kitchen table and persuades Daisy to taste a chunk of the homemade base.

‘It’s her new thing,’ Ben tells Daisy, ‘homemade pizza.’ Daisy allows her uncle a rare moment of shared smiles. Callie doesn’t do homemade anything.

‘Don’t forget we don’t have long,’ Ben reminds everyone.

Talk of time forces Daisy back into role. She doesn’t see the high five Ben slips Callie as Daisy darts into the utility room for privacy. She leaves the door open a crack, so Ben can see her purple nails press random numbers on her phone.

‘Hi Kiera,’ Daisy says in a loud clear voice. ‘I’ve been held up.’ She leaves a timely pause before throwing in some maybes, not sures and whatevs. Ben makes some heavy footsteps in the hall. Daisy says goodbye in an exaggerated tone.

‘Sorted.’ She wanders nonchalantly into the kitchen still checking her screen. ‘I can stay longer.’ Callie catches his eye, tomato sauce dripping below her lip. Ben enjoys a whisper of desire. Tonight, they’ll enjoy some overdue connection. He hasn’t even asked about her appraisal last week. Hopefully when Daisy goes, they can check out the newest features on Netflix. A film and a couple of beers followed by an early night is exactly what they need. He’s been so consumed by the letter, and Daisy, and conflict with his mother. He’s let his marriage slip. No wonder Callie’s always at work. What’s the point of coming home to him?

Daisy transforms, her shoulders drop, and her mouth relaxes as she pulls out her scrunchie to let her hair fall loose. The lengthened hair covers the shaven bit at the back, so she looks more like her old self.

The three of them squash round the minuscule table that came from Callie’s parents. They scoff pizza followed by Häagen-Dazs.

Daisy argues that strawberry has always been her favourite even though everyone knows it was salted caramel, the same as Owen.

Meals like this have become rare, no arguments and clean plates. Daisy helps Ben clear the table without complaining.

‘Right,’ Callie says. ‘It’s film time.’

As the two girls plonk themselves on the carpet, Daisy spots a tired hardback on the bookcase.

‘I didn’t know you still had that,’ Daisy says, crawling on hands and knees to retrieve it.

She sits with legs stretched out and lugs it onto her lap. ‘Wow, I’d forgotten how heavy it is.’

The scruffy cover has suffered sticky hands over several generations.

‘*Adventures for Girls*,’ Daisy reads, following the title in now-faded brown letters with her finger and grinning with pride as if it’s the first time.

‘Did you know this belonged to Great Gran?’ Daisy asks.

‘Yes, and Mum read it to Owen and then me.’ Ben laughs.

‘Oooh she’s so gender neutral,’ Daisy laughs.

‘I remember your dad reading it to you,’ Ben says. ‘How cool is that?’

Owen read it so often Daisy could recite each tale by heart. Then a colleague gave him a more up-to-date series they both loved. And this old thing was discarded and forgotten. Ben had swiped it when Mum moved to Storrington. By then, Owen had lost his job and she had given up the family home to move closer to the family.

The book swoops Ben back to a time when he sat on his father’s knee and listened to tales that made no sense. That book meant comfort, cuddles, and hot chocolate. Sometimes Owen would sneak behind the chair and listen, pretending he wasn’t. Even though his father died ten years ago, suddenly of a heart attack. He misses him every day.

Tears irritate Ben’s eyes as Daisy carefully flicks each page, studying the old-fashioned pictures with girls in pinafores and boys in short dungarees. No picture complete without the dog and an apple tree.

Ben hates sadness and fear. But with that sweet-smelling envelope hiding at the back of his subconscious, he's constantly fearful and agitated. He just wants everyone to be happy.

Giggles from the chair drag him back. Daisy has taken the book to show Callie and is snuggled close to her aunt on the settee. Daisy is petite for her age and watching them read, she could easily be their prepubescent child. Callie is great with her, so natural – like he used to be. Now he analyses every word hoping not to push her further away. His heart aches for this intimacy to stay. Callie catches his eye over Daisy's head and smiles. Is she thinking the same? What if we had a daughter of our own? Surely most women eventually crave a baby, don't they?

'Ah no, please not this one! Us girls don't need a strong prince,' Callie teases.

Daisy has chosen a tale about a handsome soldier who saves the day. If Ben had shown her such an outdated tome, his niece would've created a terrible fuss, accusing him of being sexist, last season, outdated and pathetic. But with Callie there's no hint of distaste as she gives in and reads the story.

'The end,' Callie announces firmly, and they both descend into fits of laughter mimicking the book.

'Please, Mamma, may I have lemonade?'

'We'll ask Papa when he's home from his important work.'

Ben needs emotional respite for half an hour and uses the excuse of work emails. By the time he returns to drive Daisy home, his wife and niece are sharing the comfy couch in matching fluffy socks.

Dressed in one of Callie's old jumpers, Daisy is in no hurry to leave. Her head rests sideways on the arm rest with her legs hung over her aunt's lap. Here, she can believe the world is a safe place. Her chest slows to a gentle up and down as her eyelids give in. Callie gestures that she's desperate for a wee but stays trapped. This moment is too precious to sacrifice.

Perhaps there's still hope.

17

Daisy

Dressed in ironed trousers and an old school blazer Daisy struts into New Look. She feels the most miserable she has felt in ages and has nobody to talk to about it. Chilling at Ben's last night, she had felt like her old self, like she had a family and like she was a child. In the end she had stayed over and slept great, but now she feels even more empty and lonely than ever.

She flicks through cosmetics and accessories, searching for easy wins. In and out. As she marches out the revolving doors, she grins flirtatiously at the store detective with her head high. Sucker!

With her St Cuthman's beret perched on her head she carries a roomy leather bag stuffed with fifty quid's worth of stuff. Both Kiera and Ryan have been caught but she never has. Private school girls don't get stopped. Nicking stuff is one of her few remaining joys. It's retail therapy without the queue. Half an hour, and only three shops, she's bagged some cool stuff for her and some bits she can give as Christmas presents.

'Watch where you're going,' Daisy shouts at a smelly hag pushing a trolley loaded with black bags. The woman swerves to miss the teen but Daisy's not budging.

Daisy smiles when passengers point from the windows of a passing bus. She knows her elbow made the bags topple to the floor. She heard them split.

The bitter cold smacks her right in the face as she hurries away. She's freezing and tired. The Orchards is modern-day slavery. She starts before seven a.m. They get a measly ten minutes at coffee and half an hour for lunch. She's started a petition, but no one cares.

'You are lucky,' Silviya keeps saying. 'In Bulgaria we get no breaks until we've worked three months.'

Scrubbing toilets and changing beds doesn't feel lucky. She grabs the ends of her new scarf and tightens it around her neck.

What would it be like to die?

Daisy's mind stalks her like a foul-mouthed tramp. The bad thoughts won't go. Wherever she goes, however fast she runs, the thoughts overtake. She can hear him limping to catch up as she heads towards the park. He's cursing, threatening. Screaming the truth. Disgusting. Ugly. Die, yeah, just die.

Even an evening at Ben and Callie's hasn't helped. Nothing helps. So, she's here again. The park. It is usually quiet at this time of day especially in the winter. On Mondays, Daisy is desperate for Friday, her half day off but now it's here she hates it.

If only they still lived in their spacious place. She needs somewhere to hang out, to be undisturbed, alone, and to have thinking time. At the moment she's being careful with the room. It's so exciting to have a hiding room within The Orchards but if she gets caught, it'll be game over, so this alcove at the back of the cricket pavilion is the next best option. It gives her some privacy and shelter from the wind. Keira and Ryan sit around the front. So far, she's not seen anyone here. This side, she gets alone time overlooking the humongous recycling containers.

Her body contacts the cold ground, and she unpacks the small rucksack where she keeps her private things. The sizzle of burning on her arm is awesome. She never realised you can hear the burn. The relief is like descending into a warm bath after snowboarding. Daisy leans against the brick wall inhaling the high. For a while the pain inside feels better.

Last time, she was here, in the park, Keira upturned her bag, and the photo booth pic of Dad went missing. With a sickening smirk, Kiera invited Ryan to body search her for the missing photo. But he didn't find it. Daisy ran all the way home. She crashed into Ben and Callie's without knocking. Ben held her and wiped her tears with his sleeve, but he doesn't smell like her father. No one smells like him. It's one of the things she misses most, the smell that came with the safe feeling.

Tears flow as she remembers getting that photo. Dad could still walk straight and didn't slur like a drunk psycho. His eyes looked at her and not at the ceiling. He was normal and kind and he didn't have beer and custard down his shirt. He wasn't disgusting.

Spinning the seat with one hand so both their faces could fit in the square, he had pulled her into the photo booth in the shopping centre. When the light flashed, they stuck out tongues and made faces like toddlers.

Then they went to his favourite café for hot chocolate. Her family insist on meeting for breakfast at that café, once a month so everyone can sob and bitch at each other.

Here, she can see the footpath without being spotted. Ryan is heading home. His cap is on backwards and his trainers are too big. He makes her smile as he swaggers off with his hands in his front pockets.

Ryan is the nearest thing Daisy has to a friend. Shame he hangs about with Kiera so much. Daisy's mum refers to her friends by description.

Kiera is 'that nasty girl with the wayward brothers'.

Ryan is 'that grubby kid from the estate'.

Daisy met Ryan on her first day at Steyning. He had pinched her skinny bum. She felt the sting before his mates chorused animalistic noises. Her heart was thumping so hard she thought the teacher would see it under her neatly pressed jumper.

Without thinking she kicked back in time to catch his shin. Out of the corner of her eye, she saw him flinch and wondered if he'd thump her, but he had slouched to a chair at the back. The next day he had winked at her. She tried to ghost him, but a smile slipped out. After that he disappeared from school. He had been expelled for stashing weed in his locker.

Ryan wants to be terrifying with his piercings and tats but is easy and kind. Daisy knows if she shouted, he'd wait. But today Daisy doesn't want company. She watches him disappear out the gate at the far end of the footpath and then she lights another cigarette to burn her ankle. There it doesn't show, there it looks like she's hurt it on a door at work.

Before she does the deed, she hears a voice. When she looks up there's a chubby face peering between the containers. She can hardly see him.

'Hello auntie,' he shouts without moving.

She stubs her cigarette into the grass, then walks over to peer into the gap between the shoe recycling hub and the brown one for cardboard.

His cheeky grin instantly makes Daisy want to laugh. He doesn't expect anything from her. He doesn't care what she looks like or what she's been up to. He's not cross or judgy.

‘Hello Haizeh,’ she says, reaching into the gap with her fingers outstretched. He returns the gesture and giggles. His fingers tickle hers. They do that several times before she hears a frantic female voice calling out.

‘Over here, Sachini. No panic,’ Daisy reassures.

Sachini runs out from behind the pavilion. Today she’s dressed in jeans and a puffy jacket and her black head gear.

Sachini looks around but can’t see her son. Daisy points between the containers.

‘There,’ she says, ‘he’s hiding there.’

Sachini is shining with sweat and out of breath. She runs behind the bins and returns holding Haizeh’s hand, his head is down.

‘You could’ve been taken. Anything could’ve happened,’ Sachini shouts.

Did Sachini think he might’ve been hurt or even taken? By Kiera, by *her*. For a moment the two females consider each other.

Daisy breaks the silence.

‘I recognised him from the other week,’ she says, ‘he’s such a cutie.’

‘Not when he runs off and leaves me terrified.’

Haizeh escapes Mum’s hand and runs to the swings. Daisy is glad she let Ryan go. Glad she bumped into these guys again. She’s thought a lot about the day she met them in the park.

When Sachini walks to the bench and sits to watch her son, Daisy follows and sits with her. She’s not sure why, but something about Sachini makes her want to talk. So she does. She tells her the good bits about hell hole. Makes her laugh about Bill and his sayings. Tells her about the delicious food and scrumptious cookies. She tells her about her uncle, the artist, and her mother who's retraining as a lawyer. She rabbits on and on. Nineteen to the dozen, Gran would say. She doesn't mention Dad, the amount her mum is drinking or how awkward she is. Daisy doesn't know why she's yapping on like a loony. All she knows is she doesn't want this moment to end. Her and Sachini on a bench watching a little boy swing to and fro, to and fro.

When finally, Sachini calls back her son, Daisy's heart sinks.

Sachini kneels to zip up Haizeh's coat and put on his woolly hat.

'Here,' Daisy says, pushing towards them a wind-up mouse she nicked in the pound shop.

He holds out his palm and she gently drops it on his hand. He looks so happy. It makes Daisy wanna cry.

'Wow,' Sachini says, 'thanks so much, he loves that sort of thing.'

Mummy and son hold hands. Ready to go. Daisy feels bereft in a way she can't describe. Before they get to the exit gate, Sachini turns back and shouts, 'Would you like to come back for a cup of tea? We're a bus ride away but it's only one pound forty.'

Daisy doesn't know these people, this woman could turn out to be an axe murderer or a psycho, but she doesn't care.

'Yes, please,' she says and sprints to catch up.

Haizeh puts his mouse in mummy's basket and takes Daisy's hand in his.

She hopes he won't look at her as the tears are coming thick and fast. #embarrassing

18

Dorothy

'Come on,' Dorothy orders, tugging at Penny's sleeve. 'If we hurry, we'll have time to grab a coffee.'

Arm in arm, they run up the stairs to Victoria mainline as if they're twenty years younger. At the top, clutching her chest Penny makes a sudden stop. For a ghastly moment Dorothy panics its heart pain, that it's going to be Peter all over again. She couldn't cope with that.

Then she realises it's a frantic fit of giggles.

'Look at us,' she laughs. 'Derrick would be horrified.'

Dorothy is relieved that there's no queue for the Starbucks booth.

'Come on,' Dorothy prompts. 'We can't miss it at last base.'

The station guard waves them through. Two old birds racing to catch the last train out of London, puffing and panting after their day trip. Penny is laden with Primark bags, bargains for the grandkid's stockings. Dorothy juggles a handbag and two take-out cups.

It's been a long day. The plan was to do lunch and a matinee but Penny couldn't resist a quick shop so they ended up in a crowded theatre with bags under their seats and at their feet. Dorothy purchased one tasteful scarf from Hobbs. Perfect for Christmas.

They heave a synchronised sigh as they find an empty booth with a table. Penny reaches up to secure her many bags onto the parcel rack. Dorothy can't help silently tutting at her friend's exposed midriff. She hopes she hasn't gained that much.

'It's when you land, you realise we're not thirty after all!' Penny smiles as she takes her coffee and leans back into the upright seat. 'This will keep us awake. Derrick won't be best pleased if we miss Pulborough and end up at Barnham.'

The warmth of the cup is a welcome pause.

'Daisy's doing well with us. Is she any better at home?'

'Nope,' Dorothy answers, recognising she's using a Daisy word.

'Are you still writing, darling?'

'Nope.'

'Is work any better?'

'Nope.'

'Have you thought any more about the test, or your future?'

'Nope. Nope. Nope.'

'She'll come right,' Penny assures. 'She's doing great with some of our residents.' Penny peers over her spectacles and adds, 'Don't worry, I'm keeping a beady eye.'

Two exhausted friends look out the window in companionable silence. Not much to see apart from a few Christmas lights flashing in the darkness. They are both too shattered to natter.

Dorothy waves from her front window as Derrick pulls away. She has never been able to work that man out. He's so loyal and helpful to his dear lady but always disgruntled. Penny is waving like a schoolgirl.

Dorothy feels very lucky to have Penny. She's such a dear chum but so different to her.

As Dorothy hangs up her bag and unwraps the scarf from the unnecessary tissue paper, she longs to climb into bed fully dressed. She's exhausted and exhilarated at the same time. What a lovely day. When Penny suggested they went to a panto in town, she thought she was joking. Then she thought it would involve taking Penny's awful grandkids. 'Oh no! For us, just us.' Penny revealed she went every year. A delightful reward to herself.

Dorothy had thought for a moment. What a preposterous idea. Two grown women at a Christmas panto. But, as usual, Penny's childlike enthusiasm won out. The next day, a confirmation email had dropped into her inbox. Two tickets for *Puss in Boots* at the Dominion. Dorothy had blushed at the thought of Michael Ball as the handsome baddie. She had always rather fancied him.

The living-room clock chimes midnight. Tomorrow, she'll regret not giving in to sleep. The day's excitement has left her bone tired but mentally awake. Deciding to allow herself a wind-down hour in front of the television, she reaches into the fridge for an elderflower sparkle and a slice of cheddar.

Coming back from the kitchen, Dorothy stops in her tracks. There's a definite shadow outside the front door. She can see it through the upper glass. With Daisy keeping such unsavoury company, she's an easy target for a break-in.

Quickly discarding her refreshments on the stairs, she grabs her chunkiest umbrella. Keeping her back to the wall she moves nearer the glass. There's a man outside her door and he's getting closer. She can hear Peter's warning: 'Don't even think about it, you daft woman.'

Standing tall, she pushes back her shoulders to open the door, hoping the element of surprise will give her the advantage. She's older but she refuses to be a vulnerable old lady. She'd rather be found murdered than cowering in her dressing gown in a pool of her own urine. She's not dead yet.

She inhales deeply. If one of her mothers was having a difficult labour, she'd prepare and then go in for the fight.

Dorothy yanks open the front door with full force. She's faced with a spotty youth in a backward cap. For a horrible moment she thinks it's him. The lad who intruded at Owen's. The one who blackmailed them with photographs and threatened to smear her wonderful son when he was vulnerable and defenceless.

'Alright, Grandma?' the little blighter declares.

Dorothy stares open mouthed. She recognises this kid as the one who always scowls on Penny's instawhatsit. Penny uses her account to see when Daisy's skiving with a hangover rather than at the psychologist like she claims.

'I beg your pardon. I don't believe we've been formally introduced.'

'Sorry, I was . . . er . . . was just . . . hoping Daisy was here,' he says showing teeth that haven't seen an orthodontist.

'It's midnight. Why would she be here?'

'She's not been round mine or Kiera's for weeks.'

'She doesn't live here.'

'Her old dear chucked water at me when I went there.'

Dorothy can't help smiling at the thought of Estelle treating him like a stray cat. She's pleased her daughter-in-law is regaining some gumption.

Covered in tattoos with a cigarette balanced on his lip, he's trying hard to be a man twice his age. He's shivering in a flimsy summer t-shirt and can't be older than sixteen. He has a black eye, and his ear is bleeding into his fair hair.

'It's Ryan, isn't it?' Dorothy asks.

She doesn't feel able to close the door. It's freezing and he's skin and bone.

Ignoring her inner wisdom, she asks, 'Do you want to come in?'

He takes off his cap and nods. It's a much younger child who rushes in, takes off his trainers and sits before Dorothy closes the door.

She makes him a hot chocolate and hands him the remote and the wi-fi code. She hopes she's reading him right and that he doesn't steal her bank details.

By the time she returns from making a sandwich, he's fast asleep, breathing like a contented pet. She doesn't have the heart to evict him. Gently removing his cap, she puts it on the floor and covers him with a blanket. She takes a damp flannel and gently wipes the blood from his hair. Who is looking out for this kid? Who gave him those cuts and bruises? She can't go to bed with a stranger in her house. He is sleeping like a baby but what if he wakes and steals all her valuables or suffocates her with a pillow. She might feel sorry for him when he's asleep but she's not stupid.

She retrieves the sleeping bag Daisy uses when she stays and props herself up in the chair. When either of the boys were unwell, she'd stay up and watch them. Years of night duty trained her well. She can still switch onto alert when she needs. Watching this boy, she ponders her mothering. Was she enough? As an only child with suffocating parents, she had tried to learn from their mistakes. She hadn't wanted to hover over Owen, diminish his confidence. But honestly, that gave her the excuse to work too much, neglect him. She knows that she left him alone so she could climb the career ladder. When Ben came, Peter's income had allowed her more freedom. So how come she had carried on full time?

Did she make Owen too responsible? Was that why he did what he did? Did the pressure of being good, perfect even, finally crack him open? Was it really the illness or did the illness enable his true self to emerge?

The sight of this vulnerable adolescent slumbering in the warmth breaks her fragile heart. For the first time in weeks, she openly weeps. She weeps for her boys, neither of whom she could save. She weeps for Daisy, and she weeps for this lost boy asleep on her settee.

Before she turns out the light, she prays he'll wake early, and that the cannabis smell will fade before the neighbours arrive for bridge.

19

Ben

Ben is outside 'Little Bears' wondering why on earth he thought this a good idea. He pretends he's on his phone as he walks past three mothers blocking the footpath. He bets they were the popular girls at school. No wonder Kasia hates pre-school pick-up.

Poor Robbie, he's not a typical boy who loves to kick a ball or rough and tumble. Ben doesn't know who Robbie's father is, Kasia hasn't mentioned the subject, so he hasn't felt able to ask. Kasia describes her boy as sensitive, but Ben suspects those mothers would describe him as an oddball or maybe even a brat.

He dials Daisy, might as well do something useful.

'Have you remembered you're babysitting Robbie on Friday night?' Ben shouts to be heard over the static of poor signal. The exhibition is five days off and he needs Kasia there. He hopes he hasn't made a mistake asking Daisy to childmind. He was so hurt when she had refused to help with the exhibition and now Callie can't come either. He wished he could forget the whole thing.

'Seriously, you're asking me to suffer a naff show full of desperados?' she said.

He knows it's the topic she's avoiding, but it still hurts. He thought they could bond over the prep, be a team like old times. At least it means Kasia can come.

Ben has managed only one canvas but it's his best in a while. Ethan has done three beautiful paintings and a couple of well-known Indies are exhibiting. He needs more to make it worthy of media attention. He hopes to make five grand at least. That's why he's here. Kasia promised if he collected and occupied Robbie for a couple of hours, she would secure two further artists via a gallery in Hove.

'Yeah, have you remembered it's double pay after midnight?' Daisy quips.

'Unfortunately, yes. Don't tell Callie, or Gran.'

'You know me. The most trustworthy family member,' Daisy laughs.

'I'll pick you up at six,' Ben says.

'Okay. I'm at the mental department until four but I can wait. Get me from there.'

'How come? You saw Sandra last week, didn't you?'

'Yeah, I'm on weekly now.'

Ben doesn't know what surprises him more, that she's still employed or that she's engaged with therapy. Last task for the day is to get a date night with his wife. Ben can't put it off any longer. He needs to fess up. He'll tell her what happened at Owen's. He'll tell her how scared he was when threatened by a boy half his age. He'll admit to his rage towards his brother and how guilty and confused that makes him feel. He'll tell her about that small kid with the purple bruise above her eye. He'll tell her that he looked her in the eye knowing she was probably being abused and that he was trying to do right.

Callie replies instantly:

Love to go out. Thanks. Tell me I haven't missed something?

How does he respond to that question? Yes, darling, you have missed something. A letter from a young woman I shouldn't know.

Ben types back a half-truth.

Ha Ha. You haven't missed any anniversaries! About time we sat in the same room.

Great idea, where?

Don't mind. Fish factory? Pizza Express? Not much in the bank, needs to be cheap.

How to make a girl feel special, Mr BJ.

How does she do that so fast? It takes him twice as long to write a short text. Why didn't he just phone?

Let's go fish.

Ben looks at his watch and wonders whether he has time to make another call. Before he can decide, his phone rings.

'Ben.' His mother's tone is similar to Ethan's when he's asking to borrow a tenner.

'Can it wait, Ma? I'm collecting Robbie.'

'I promised Estelle I'd get a date for us to meet about Daisy.'

'I've messaged her,' Ben snaps.

'Oh, have you? Okay. Thank you.' Ben hears the sadness in her voice and feels guilty. Then she's gone before he can say sorry.

The side door opens, and an older teacher emerges with a caterpillar of children in tow. Robbie is holding her hand. Is that a privilege or a punishment? Plodding along, head to the playground, book bag swinging.

Robbie spots Ben and pulls on his teacher's sleeve. The teacher smiles but holds her finger to her lips.

Ben watches the other children. Such beautiful diversity. He imagines painting this scene. Each child dressed in different colours. Some tall, some less so. Some still. Some unable to be still. Three girls in a line of boys. The curly-haired girl is pointing to a tree. Who knows what she has seen or if it is anything at all. But she has the attention of the other girls and a few of the boys. All looking up. She'll be the prom queen in secondary.

But all white, mostly middle class. Ben would want their child to go to a school with real diversity. They would probably have to move to Brighton to get that. Here in Storrington, there's no chance. It's then he notices the single non-white child at the back of the line.

A serious-looking chap with black hair, brown skin, and a wonky fringe. Probably a home cut like he got. Poor blighter. He's the smallest of the children and walks slowly with his hands behind his back as the caterpillar swirls into the playground. An intelligent face. Destined for great things. A consultant. Or a lawyer.

But as the little boy catches Ben's stare, Ben makes a sudden turn to follow the little boy's gaze. Who is collecting him? A few metres away, there she is. A mirror image of her child. An image assaults his mind, and he shakes his head to dispel it.

Her head is bowed low. A scarf covers most of her hair. The few wayward strands twitch in the wind. His heart thumps so hard. He's convinced a theatre beam has spot lit him so everyone can see. All these parents dressed in their heavy coats and winter scarfs with woollen gloves know.

Ben turns away. Focus on Robbie, the acceptable target. But he can't. His eyes keep sliding to the child with the serious expression, and his mind drags him back. Kicking and screaming but right back there.

He doesn't care if the bell has to ring. He needs to get out and he needs to do it fast. Ben swoops towards the caterpillar, mutters something incomprehensible to the teacher and takes a startled Robbie's hand. He walks away furiously, before breaking into a run, until his chest is too tight to breathe, and Robbie's cries are too loud to ignore.

Dear Daisy

When you reached double figures, I wanted your growing to slow down. I longed to savour each moment, bottle it and lock it away for safe keeping. I dreaded that day, the day you'd replace your old dad with mates and boys and even TV. It's hard for me to imagine that you'll soon be a teen and that's saying something as I have, like you, an above-average imagination.

I'm utterly thrilled I've had a front row seat for the astonishing production that was your childhood. At twelve, you've got a sensational smile and fabulous cheekbones. With each advancing year, I see the awesome, funny, strong woman you will become.

Not only can you formulate grammatically correct arguments, but you use them to defeat me like I dreamed you would. I wish I could watch when you annihilate your opposition in court. The judge will be blown away by your verbal talent and offer you his position without further ado.

You dance like there is no tomorrow.

We still hang out at six p.m. every night. These days you don't need a story but sometimes you indulge me with a few chapters of Dickens or Hardy. I'm thrilled you share my passion for literature. With a book, you can always escape into another world when you've had enough of this one. I'm no longer allowed to stay in your bedroom and watch you fall asleep, that's now creepy as opposed to comforting. Fair point, Daisy girl. Before I'm chucked out there's usually time for you to illustrate my personality flaws. At the moment, I'm too clingy and my world views are a little off. You refuse to discuss my dress code – apparently, it's beyond repair. Your mum agrees. I'll take that, especially if you promise to keep reading the classics.

This curse has stolen our future. We were supposed to visit the Colosseum, climb the Eiffel Tower, and run up Snowden. When I least expect it, feelings of despair catch me out. It's usually when I'm watching you poring over an algorithm or explaining FaceTime to Gran. Leaving you behind – how will I cope? I worry far less about you. You aren't easy to mould or brainwash. In fact, I'm fairly certain my brainwashing period is completely over. If I've done nothing except inspire you to have a happy, successful life, then I've done my job.

I'm not sure what I did to deserve you and much of what I say is indulgent nonsense but always remember this, from the bottom of my heart, I love you. If my elementary knowledge of human anatomy is correct, near the bottom of my heart is my spleen. I would ascend Chantry Hill and shout my love for you from there but I'm quite wobbly and terrified of heights. Also, you'd die of shame so my clumsy words will have to suffice.

I love you now, and forever.

Daddy x

20

Daisy

'Hello Daisy, you're early. Dr Staples will be another quarter of an hour. Would you like a drink?'

'Nope.'

A man comes out from the psychologist's door. Daisy pretends she's not looking. He cracks up the quiet with his loud voice. Dad was like that. If he was in a room, he was the star, people looked up, gave him attention; Mum hated that. She's such a wimpy useless mouse.

'Thank you so much, see you in a fortnight,' the man says, looking behind him.

'Bye Mike, keep up the good work,' Sandra's voice shouts from behind a closed door, there's no sign of her body.

'You can go in now,' says the reception woman.

When Daisy enters the clinic room, Dr Staples is standing with her back to the door, flicking through her filing cabinet.

'I'll be two minutes,' Dr Staples says without looking around. She has a peachy bum, that's where Ryan would be looking. Daisy wishes her bum was round like that.

Daisy hesitates. Then an exciting thought comes. Should she? That'll give this old cow something to analyse. Holding her breath, an urge builds in her belly. Feeling thrilled she plonks herself into the therapist chair. What's Miss Peachy gonna do now?

Daisy reaches under the chair for the pale brown file. Daisy Bowen-Jones is written on the spine. That surname is a great Cambridge name. It's the name of success. It belongs on the door of a room in St Catharine's College. Daisy is very pleased with her new surname, it's a far better fit for a crackpot in a shrink's office. She's gonna make reception change it on the file. When she's eighteen she will legally change her name. Ryan's changed his to erase his father's name. He said it was easy.

Daisy clutches the file to her chest. She doesn't wanna know what's written inside. Probably 'crazy girl with blood curse'.

It's alright for Gran and Ben to say she's too young for FTD, that she's being stupid, they don't have a ticking death bomb charging through their veins.

'Ah, we've swapped places, that'll make a nice change.' Sandra chuckles as she sits in the patient's chair. 'What would you like to ask me then?'

Daisy lets go of the file. It slips on the floor, spilling some papers. Dr Staples doesn't seem to notice. She stays quiet, her head cocked to one side.

'What's your full name?' Daisy puts on her proper voice. Crossing her legs, she tilts her head to match. It feels a bit wonky on her neck.

'Dr Sandra Staples.' She sounds like that quiz programme Dad watched. Daisy wants to say, 'What's your specialist subject?' Dad got loads of answers right. He was super clever. The worse he got, the less answers he knew. Then he started breaking things, angry at his own stupidity. Daisy gets that.

'Why are you here, Doctor?' Daisy smirks.

'To help people who are hurting.'

'Don't you think some people are too mental for help?'

‘I think everyone can be helped if that’s what they want.’

‘Bit arrogant, aren’t you?’

‘I didn’t say I can help everyone. But I believe no one is beyond help.’

When Sandra smiles, her eyes wrinkle. Daisy’s been studying people at The Orchards. When does your skin start cracking? Gran is way more crinkled lately. This woman defo looks better from the back.

‘So, Daisy, that was fun, but we should probably do some work. I’d hate to waste your family’s money. Stay where you are, I’m quite enjoying the view from this side of the room. What are you noticing from over there?’

‘Not much.’

‘I wonder if today we can chat about your future. What kind of future do you want to create? You’ll soon be eighteen, an adult. What do you want from the next decade?’

How can she ask that? She saw Ben. She knows what happened to Dad. She must know what’s coming for me! Is she getting her own back ’cos I stole her chair? That’s it, I’m done. This stupid, stupid cow has blown it.

Daisy bites hard on her lip to stop the tears until the taste of blood spreads into her mouth making her feel nauseous.

‘Some people . . . are cursed, and you can’t help them and—’

Daisy springs up. She stamps hard on the file leaving a perfect boot print. *That’ll teach her. If she wants a game, she’s picked the wrong playmate.*

The door feels too heavy for Daisy to yank open. Her arms are getting weak. Is this the start of her disease? She shoves with all her might using both hands. Daisy runs for the exit gasping for air. The doors whoosh after her.

She runs and runs. Faster. Into a sprint until she can't picture the therapist's face or hear her squeaky patronising voice. *Eighteen. Eighteen. Eighteen*, screams like a psycho in her ears. She fumbles with her air pods and turns up the volume to drown out the pounding voices. Her. Dad. Mum. Gran. Uncle Ben's. Everyone is shouting. Words firing like relentless bullets. Die. Test. Pointless. Hopeless. Bad girl. No future.

She stops running when the crossing glares red. She's tempted to run into the road. That'd serve her right. That'd serve them all right. She imagines a black newspaper headline shouting 'Sick Girl Dies After Stupid Therapist Screws Up'.

Daisy's music is still screaming in her ears when her phone vibrates.

The watch she found at The Orchards says it's 3.20 p.m., that she's done 9,000 steps and her heart rate is 124. She has over two hours before Ben is collecting her. She doesn't want to babysit. She wants to go to the exhibition. Looking down at her dragging feet, the tears return. This time they refuse to stop. The test they want to do will show what everyone knows. She's FTD positive and she's going to degenerate and die.

The sound of a low engine startles her. The vehicle is getting closer. It's slow. She's on the edge of a park with no coat and she can't hide the fact she's small. Why did she head for the rec rather than town where there are bright lights and people? A girl was attacked two miles from here just weeks ago.

More newspaper headlines scroll in her head. She sees Gran arriving with the police to identify her corpse.

Her heart is pounding so hard she can feel it despite the music in her ears. It's a van. She can see it out the corner of her eye, copying her pace, creeping along behind. She speeds up. The van matches. Why didn't she do as she was meant to? Why didn't she do her session, wait for Ben? What's wrong with her?

She wrestles her door key from her pocket and grips ready to do harm. *Be brave, Daisy, you're on the way out anyway.*

She spins around, holding her key like a knife, prepared to burst an eye.

'Who you runnin' from?'

She doesn't recognise this throaty male voice, but the face looks familiar. He has greasy hair and a bushy monobrow. His hood is pulled low, and his arm is slung over the window rim, so his elbow is touching her boob.

She pulls back, about to run.

'Hello auntie.' A small voice speaks from inside. Her whole-body eases with relief. Sachini is in the passenger seat with Haizeh on her lap. Her friend offers a hesitant smile and leans to release her seat belt.

'Wait there, I'm coming out.'

Sachini disentangles herself and opens the door.

'H said you were a friend,' the bloke says, a cigarette poking out the corner of his foul-smelling mouth.

Daisy moves back but stays close enough to hear what Haizeh is trying to say.

'My uncle came. Mumma's going to work, we've got sweets and crisps.'

Haizeh rests his feet on a box of beer. There's something about this man she doesn't like. The way he leers. The way he stinks of beer and is driving with a small kid. The way he shoved Haizeh when he tried to move closer to her.

Before Sachini reaches the pavement, the stranger thrusts his foot on the accelerator and wheel spins off the kerb and onto the main road.

Daisy wanted to say goodbye to Haizeh. What's she thinking leaving her kid with him?

When she went to their flat before, Daisy was shocked. It was so small. Everything in one room. But no bloke stuff. The shower was broken and there was a bucket in the bath. Haizeh's dad disappeared when he found out his mum was knocked up. So, who is this guy?

'You reckon I need better mates?' Daisy chirps to break the silence.

'Yeah. He's not the best but I don't have choice like you. I've bagged a few hours cleaning at the offices in Church Street. I need money to feed us.' She stops and looks closely at Daisy. 'You've been crying?'

'Nah,' Daisy lies.

Sachini pushes her friend backwards until she's under the glare of a streetlight.

With a touch that feels too soft, she wipes away Daisy's tears with the back of her thumb which sets off another sobbing fit.

'You need a hug?'

Daisy wants to say, *No. Nope.* Of course, she doesn't. She's tough and strong. She doesn't cry like a stupid weak baby. She wants to shove this girl and tell her to mind her business, that she has loads of friends and doesn't need the pity of an idiot who gets abused by people like Kiera and him, whoever he was.

Instead, she crumples like an idiot, with her mouth open, and her eyes low, snot from her face and nods. 'Yeah.'

Sachini holds Daisy while she cries and it's nice. Daisy remembers when she got hugs all the time. Daddy cuddled her. Her mum. Her grandparents and even Ben. She was the family's cuddle mascot. Now she keeps them away.

Sachini's hair smells of lavender. When Daisy opens her eyes, she can see a black ponytail glossing under the light. Finally, they pull apart.

Daisy strides ahead, feeling embarrassed for losing it.

'Hey, wait. I'm going that way too.' Sachini hurries after her.

They fall into step again. 'So, who was the git in the car? Is he the bloke who dumped ya when you got preggers?'

'No.'

Sachini shoves her hands into the pockets of her long black coat.

'Who then?'

'He's my cousin. He doesn't live local now. He's here for the day. I didn't have anywhere else to leave Haizeh.'

'Where's ya mum and dad?'

'Mum is in Sri Lanka with my brother. My dad died when I was fourteen. They sent me here 'cos there wasn't money for all of us.'

'Ouch. Thought my folks weren't up to much but . . .'

'They thought it'd be better for me. England is seen as good. People get to go to school. My mum loves me.'

'Was it better?'

'No. My mum and brother don't know I have a son. Not even my grandmother knows. That's why I hide in a damp, broken flat. I am an outcast. My father would be deeply ashamed'.

'What about Haizeh's dad?'

‘He’s long gone. It wasn’t really a thing.’

‘Ha. A one-nighter?’

Sachini stops. She pulls Daisy around to face her. ‘Daisy, sometimes you are a stupid girl. A spoilt girl who has everything.’

At that, Sachini storms off. Daisy runs to catch up.

‘I’m sorry. You’re right. You have had a rubbish time and you’re always kind to me, not mean.’

For the first time in ages, Daisy is sorry. She wants to make up. She wants this friend. With her she feels connected, more alive, real. She offers a lemon sherbet from a paper bag. She got them for Gran but then Gran was a dick, moaning on, so Daisy kept them.

Much to her relief, Sachini takes one.

‘Tell me what happened with Haizeh’s dad. Did you love him?’

‘No. I didn’t even like him. It was him. He wouldn’t stop. I didn’t know how it worked. What men were like. He said I wanted it as much as him.’

‘That’s horrible, why didn’t you tell?’

Daisy can see Sachini deciding whether to go on. Her mouth pounds the sherbet, her eyes are wide, tearful.

‘He was my . . .’

‘Your what?’

‘I’ve never told anyone this before. How do I know if I can trust you? How do I know you won’t run off and tell those horrid mates and shout stuff at me next time I’m out?’

‘’Cos I’ll tell you some bad stuff about me.’

Sachini looks at her watch and then takes Daisy’s hand dragging her further into the park.

‘I have half an hour before work. Let’s sit on that bench by the duck pond.’

Daisy tells Sachini things she hasn’t told anyone. She talks about Dad. How he talked, the music they danced to. She tells about Ben and Gran and how everyone is ganging up on her. Finally, she tells her about the ticking time bomb and how it makes her feel like a freak, a loon. How she wonders what she did to get a curse that means she’ll crumple and die before she’s done much. She even tells what she does for pain relief. When Daisy says that she cries and Sachini joins in. This time she doesn’t feel stupid. When her friend reaches out to hold her hand, she grasps it and notices the warmth and joy that this small hand is giving. She fears she might never be able to let go.

‘So, that’s all my stuff. Now, tell me. Tell me about Haizeh’s dad.’

Sachini takes back her hand and bites at her thumb nail. Then she lays both hands in her lap and looks down.

‘My grandparents needed my help with money. They are old and my aunt is sick and there were nine of us needing to eat. Me and Chez, the boy in the van. We got jobs. He didn’t care but I wanted to study. My parents sent me here to study, go to university and get a good job with money and a life they didn’t have.’

Daisy is unusually quiet and so Sachini keeps going.

‘A neighbour said he could get me a job in a law practice. I wanted to be a solicitor, to study law. He said this would be experience and when I was older, I could get qualifications. He took me for the interview, and I got the job. It was only filing and calling people, but I liked it, the people were kind. We laughed. I worked more hours than I was paid, and they gave me more responsibility.’

‘Sounds better than scraping vomit out the carpet,’ Daisy says.

‘Yeah. I knew I was lucky. But then it all went wrong. One of the lawyers . . . he . . . liked me. Well, you know. Anyway, I got pregnant and then I left and that’s it.’

Suddenly, Sachini stands up, turns around and rushes off without saying goodbye.

Daisy doesn’t know what to think but she feels better, less alone. Better knowing she’s not the only one struggling.

She has just ten minutes before Ben will arrive outside the clinic. For once, she gets a move on. She sprints through the high street, across the mini roundabout and arrives with minutes to spare.

21

Dorothy

What on earth should she wear for this evening's extravaganza?

In the end she settles for her purple trouser suit with the clutch bag Owen bought. At the last minute she grabs the silk scarf Peter gave on their last anniversary, for courage. She slips on matching shoes and a hint of lip gloss. She hopes to do Ben and Owen proud.

But as she strides through the door and spots that everyone else is bright and beautiful, she feels old and dull. She can't see anyone she knows well enough to relax with. Callie was devastated when her manager booked her a place on a French conference. But Ben knew Callie was desperate to hear the key note speaker in Paris. Her boy has a loving heart. Even though she would miss the exhibition, he had insisted she went away.

'Dorothy,' a moustached man with onion breath gushes, 'how lovely to see you again.' Embarrassingly, she can't place him. Is he one of the sponsors from Austin's or a colleague of Peter's?

When Ben explained about the art exhibition and that it was to raise money in Owen's name, she'd been relieved and delighted. It would be fabulous to have good come out of darkness. And surely it would give Ben a kick up the backside to produce some actual art. How hard can it be to load a paint brush and flick some colour on a piece of paper? As a teen he was so creative, he showed such potential. Then he started this habitual overthinking.

'Mother.' Ben takes her by surprise. She flushes as if he can read her mind.

'Thank you, darling,' she says, taking the large glass of red.

'Good job Austin's paid for all this alcohol,' he says nodding towards a group of men in suits from Owen's law firm. They have full glasses and are crowded around the bar she sourced.

As much as Ben's expression pleads for his motives to be understood, she can't support his decision. Most of the details surrounding Owen's dismissal were not disclosed to her, nonetheless Dorothy is certain about her feelings towards the vile Michael Austin, the senior partner, and towards the traitors who called themselves colleagues. They had shamed her poor son when he was most vulnerable. More than a decade of sacrifice was conveniently forgotten when he grew unwell. They couldn't wait to show him the door. She couldn't understand how Ben was willing to overlook that. *She* will never forgive them.

Estelle had dealt with Austin's during Owen's illness. Owen was too far gone to contribute. She had asked Estelle to let her help sort things out on several occasions, but Estelle had claimed she was protecting not only Owen but also Daisy. She had said there were details that wouldn't be helpful for anyone, especially his mother.

Of course, she protested. She hated being excluded and Owen was *her* son. She hadn't thought Estelle would stand her ground in the face of a fuss. But with regards to Owen's dismissal from work, she wouldn't budge. She knew Estelle went for a number of meetings as she saw them pencilled on the calendar when she cleaned. Over the years, she and her daughter-in-law had enjoyed an easy relationship. Until then, she would have described her as a friend. However, Dorothy had felt shut out at a time she craved intimacy. She knows there were several occasions when her resentment came out. Her relationship with Estelle hasn't recovered and now, things are increasingly tense because Estelle and Ben don't see eye to eye about Daisy and the test. Estelle is desperate to know for her own peace of mind. She says she can't cope with forever watching Daisy for signs. Ben says to leave Daisy alone and Dorothy is uncertain.

The same day Ben suggested the fundraiser, Dorothy found 'Bottoms Up', a company specialising in gallery events. They organised the canopies and programme and kindly agreed to host a discounted bar as it was for charity – but it would still be a large cost, that would need to be covered by sponsors. In the weeks leading up to this evening, Ben had a multitude of opportunities to disclose the identity of the sponsors.

He finally let it slip a few days ago. Dropped it in when he carried her shopping to the door on Wednesday as if he was chatting about the weather.

'By the way, Austin's have offered to pay,' he had said with his face hidden behind a large box of cornflakes.

She couldn't believe her ears.

'I presume you told them where to stick that offer?'

Ben said nothing but she saw that sheepish face. The guilty downward gaze she remembered from his school days. Ben has always been an inefficient deceiver.

'They offered a massive budget. It means the event will be worthy of Owen's name. It means we can give a large sum to the FTD support team even if we don't sell a single picture.'

Dorothy was speechless. She wanted to scream the home truths he hates. She wanted to say it's a drip of the payout Owen deserved. She wanted to say it was too late, that if they wanted to help, they should've paid for nursing care or Daisy's education. She wanted to call Ben disloyal and a traitor. She wanted him to share her hurt, her disappointment and misery. But she didn't. For once she held her tongue. She has ranted to Penny, but she has kept quiet with Ben. For Owen's sake.

Pushing the thoughts to the back of her mind, Dorothy meanders around the art trail drinking in each portrait. She can't paint for toffee but has always adored art. When she first had Owen, she indulged herself with a study of art evening class.

Ethan has contributed four small square canvases. They're bright and modern. He's combined clay and wood to create a 3D look that doesn't make any sense to her. They're titled 'Descending into the Abyss'. That doesn't make much sense either. The next wall holds black and white photographs taken by an older lady called Daphne. She was once a psychiatric nurse, and the photos clearly depict emotional pain.

Finally, she's alone in front of Ben's work. Admittedly she hoped for more pictures but this one is spectacular. It's a tall narrow piece and it's breathtakingly beautiful, yet horrific at the same time. The canvas shows an upright man in a suit and tie. Within him is a series of Russian dolls with increasingly diminishing demeanours. The smallest figure is torn apart and barely human. He has claw like fingers that are yanking out matted strands of hair.

Before she can escape to regather her composure, a couple approach from behind.

'That's really something,' the woman says. 'It tells the story perfectly, doesn't it?'

When Dorothy turns around, she's faced with Amanda. Dorothy remembers her from the diagnostic clinic. In her mid-forties, Amanda is well turned out, but the pain behind the open smile is tangible.

'Amanda,' Ben says putting his glass aside to give her a hug. Dorothy is relieved to be rescued by her boy.

'Mum, you must remember Amanda and John,' Ben says.

'Of course, hello again. So glad you could make it.' Dorothy offers a tentative smile.

'Amanda and John are going to say a few words about the impact of FTD,' Ben tells her.

Amanda's husband is extremely close to Ben's masterpiece. If he whipped out his tongue, he'd taste the paint. Dorothy feels conflicted. She senses Amanda's shame. She remembers when Owen started behaving in ways unlike himself.

The first time was in an upmarket restaurant. Owen had developed a habit of standing too close to strangers. When the waitress invited him to give his order, he had stood up, peered into her cleavage, and offered a bra size estimate. That was so not her son. He was a private, polite man. A little uptight even. The colour drained from Estelle's face, but she said nothing. On the way home, it wasn't discussed. It was the first of many social blips.

Amanda grabs John's hand to pull him away but he yanks his hand back.

'Who do you think you are? Ordering me about like a child.'

Ben diffuses the situation.

'Hey John, what do you make of this one,' he asks, resting his arm over John's shoulder and steering him across the room.

‘Sorry,’ Amanda says, gulping a large mouthful of red.

‘Don’t be, my dear,’ Dorothy says, patting her hand like Penny does.

She wishes she could leave. It’s too much. Amanda’s pain, the pictures, this whole event – they are all stimulating a flood of avoided memories. She remembers Owen shoving a crate of beer off the kitchen side on her birthday, Owen raising his fist at the cinema and finally that noise. The noise she won’t ever forget. The noise of Owen’s large, capable hand colliding with the softness of his teenage daughter’s face. The look on Daisy’s face as she realised she’d been slapped, and by her daddy. Her precious, gentle, soft and funny daddy had raised his arm and slapped her. Dorothy will never forget that moment. She can’t decide which was more horrific. Daisy’s face as it drained of colour or the look of disbelief on Owen’s face when he processed what he’d done. He knew. She knew. They knew this was the moment they had talked about. The moment when the FTD beast was stronger than him. This was the moment when she had promised to step in. She had promised Owen. She had promised him that when this moment came, they’d end it. And she had kept her promise even though it broke her heart and it broke Daisy. Dorothy frequently experiences flashbacks in the dead of night. Just as she’s trying to drift to sleep, she’ll startle into sitting with her nightie drenched in sweat. The dreams assault her with all she supresses in the day. The worst night terrors replay the day Owen crossed the line, the line they agreed could not be crossed. Taking her beautiful son from his home, his family, and his precious baby changed her irrevocably. Could she have found a different way? She’ll never know.

Dorothy is glad when it is time for speeches; the evening must be drawing to a close. She’s had enough. She simply hasn’t the resilience for this.

John and Amanda make their way to the front to the sound of clapping. John pauses to pick crumbs of his clothes but gets distracted and chats to another guest about a washing line.

Dorothy finds it unbearable. John reminds her too much of Owen. So competent and normal but so odd and unlike himself.

An older lady wearing a leather skirt retrieves John and guides him to the microphone next to his wife, Dorothy can't watch this spectacle, it hurts too much.

Ben hands Amanda the microphone to distract the audience from her obvious tears.

Amanda swallows and carries on. 'When we went to the doctor that day, I knew our lives would never be the same . . .'

Dorothy can't leave the room, that would be a poor show when Amanda is showing such courage. In that moment she knows she could not have stood in her place. Ben didn't ask her because he knew she's a weak coward.

Dorothy tiptoes to the side of the room to quietly clear away the discarded plates and glasses. She's helping her son, doing her bit for the evening. Long ago she learnt to block out the voices she didn't want to hear. She is deeply relieved when the audience bursts forth with enthusiastic applause. It's over.

She races for the cloakroom, desperate to retrieve her coat and go. She'll call a taxi and text Ben from the car to say she's safely on her way. But as she's hurtling towards the studios, Michael Austin catches her eye. For a moment they both freeze. The last time she saw him she should've slapped his arrogant face. Estelle had asked her and Ben to collect Owen's things. Estelle had said it was all over and she couldn't face his colleagues, those peers who had once been her friends.

Ben had offered to go. He had insisted Dorothy stay home, arguing it would hurt her to see the office. As usual she hadn't listened. She had wanted his colleagues to squirm, especially Michael Austin.

She had wanted to say goodbye to the son who had sat in that spacious office with his pristine suits and his beautiful writing. She had needed that. She had needed to remember he wasn't a bad man. He was a good man with a bad disease. She wanted to dismantle his office and take time to appreciate each item. The landscape Peter had gifted Owen after a promotion. The clock Estelle had given for their tenth anniversary and a childish picture Daisy had done before she got so big for her boots. Michael didn't allow them five minutes.

When they had arrived, Michael was waiting in the door of Owen's personal space and gesturing to a box on the floor. Everything that represented Owen had been thrown into a misshapen cardboard box.

When she had opened her mouth, Ben had flushed red, shaken his head, and mouthed, 'Please, no.'

Ben had taken a deep breath and lifted the box, gesturing for her to follow. Michael had held open the main door. They had driven home in silence.

Now that tosser is striding across the room, champagne flute in hand.

'Dorothy,' he gushes, 'lovely to see you.'

Michael's mouth smiles but his eyes do not. Dorothy is pleased he looks old. His hair is grey, and his belly is protruding over his designer trousers.

Lawyers. All shine and surface. Behind closed doors they're no better than common scoundrels. She hopes her son was the exception. She tells herself whatever he did under the influence of neurological disease, it wasn't him. Every day she tells herself that.

When Ben spots her with Michael, he rushes over. The panic on his face says it all.

The two men shake hands. She has no idea how Ben can be so congenial with this man.

'You've got some cheek,' Dorothy spits before Ben can interrupt.

'I beg your pardon,' Michael replies, taking a step back.

'And after all he gave to your company. If he hadn't been there when you started, given his life, worked all the hours . . .'

'Mum,' Ben interrupts, placing a gentle hand on her shoulder.

Dorothy shrugs him off and carries on.

'He didn't deserve that. As if being terminally ill wasn't enough . . .'

'Eric and I did everything we could to keep him. We didn't know he was unwell. But even when he was late, rude to clients or absent, we stayed loyal.'

'You call that loyal, sacking someone at their lowest ebb, you . . .' She knows her voice is raised. The last drinkers are staring but she doesn't care.

Michael raises his palm to stop her mid-flow.

'If you want to have honesty, I'll give you it.'

Ben tries to intervene. He stutters to speak but there's no point. Michael and Dorothy are too far in.

'Even when we thought Owen was drinking, we were kind. We offered help. You're damn right. We all had a long history, and he was our friend as well as a colleague.'

Michael pauses for breath. His face is flushed. There's moisture gathering above his eyebrows.

Ben tries again.

'It has been a long and emotional evening . . .'

Michael regroups. He leans closer to Dorothy. She can smell garlic and Hugo Boss. She wants to hurt this man. She wants to wrench his ugly ears off his face. She wants to slap him hard across one cheek. Then the other. And when he crumples in a heap she wants to kick and kick until he's in the same dehumanised state as Owen. She hates this man.

As if Michael can see into her heart, he takes one step back, inhales deeply and continues. He is not shouting but his voice is clear and steady.

'I wish it wasn't true. But. There are things too grievous to overlook. There are some things you can't pass over. What Owen did was one of them. He crossed a line.'

'Go on . . .' Ben asks.

'As I told Estelle, when a young woman with a swollen body and bruises is dragged in and we're told that happened on our watch, at the hands of a senior employee . . .'

Dorothy wants him to stop. She can't hear this.

'Owen was not . . .'

Michael cuts her off. 'Surely, you don't believe we should've turned a blind eye to that?'

Michael slams his drink onto the table. It shudders like it will fall but remains vertical. Dorothy knows this is the cue to stop, to give up. To save face for her and for Ben, even Owen, but she can't. She never has been able to.

'So, if you were unwell, you'd like to be sacked, would you?'

‘Dorothy, I understand your distress, but we couldn’t . . .’ Michael’s voice has softened. His defeat obvious.

‘I doubt you do . . .’ she interrupts.

Michael puts a hand on the top of Ben’s arm as he speaks.

‘Sorry, mate, truly I am. I wanted to protect you. Your family. But I had no choice. Nobody in this day and age would overlook a serious sexual assault against a teen.’

With that Michael walks out the door leaving a room of total silence.

22

Ben

'This is novel, walking out with my beau in the moonlight. It's been too long.'

'Indeed, it has,' Ben says clutching her hand a little tighter. Callie is relaxed and cheery which makes him sad. He doesn't want to hurt her, to make her sad but he knows he must come clean.

Holding this mess in his head is becoming unhealthy and he's spiralling down again. He must stay strong for Daisy. Yesterday, he broke his promise to his brother. Owen said no hanging about. No prolonged rituals.

But he went to Owen's resting place. Ben knows it's stupid. He knows the real Owen isn't there, but he thought being there might help.

It didn't help. Sitting on a seat surrounded by half-dead flowers made him more confused and utterly despondent. He can't align the competing versions. His best man, who sacrificed everything for his kid brother versus a serial predator, the worst of men.

Since the day he collected Robbie, he's been unable to focus. He can't look Daisy in the eye, not that she would notice. He's avoiding his mother, irritable with Callie and he can't paint. The picture he did for the exhibition was empty. A poor reflection of what he could've painted. Should've painted.

He can't get that boy's face out of his head. He is the exact age her child would be. She begged him to let her go. She promised she would never return. That promise allowed him to push it away, to deny there was a baby with the genetic defect that tore apart his brother.

When Ben saw that child in the school playground, a real-life playground with other real-life kids, it changed everything. He wanted to deny it. A lookalike. Maybe it wasn't. It was four years ago. Could he remember someone he saw once? He's tried to suppress what he saw. Tried to ignore it.

But Ben knows. He knows who he saw. He saw his mother's second grandchild. His nephew. Daisy's brother. He saw his brother's child. The child who shouldn't be. It was bad enough swallowing that. But after what Michael spat out at the exhibition, he has to share this with Callie, or it'll poison them.

'Look up, the stars are beautiful. I'm so glad we moved to Storrington. There's no way you'd see the sky this clearly in Brighton.'

Ben bites his tongue. She was horrified when he first mentioned moving. She'd kicked up a huge fuss about living in the same place as his enmeshed family.

As they walk to the car, Callie has a spring in her step, full of energy; she's understandably excited about an overdue night out. How can he tell her there's a sinister letter hiding in his clothes?

Come on Ben, no more secrets, you promised. You've coped with worse. She's your wife, not a child. Don't let yourself go down there again.

He grabs his wife's hand and pulls it to his face for a kiss.

'Quit the slop, and get me food,' she laughs.

‘We have time for a quick walk along the beach,’ he suggests, wrapping his arms around her thick duffle coat. She pulls up her hood.

The sea smells great as they inhale. He loves the sound of the sea, the raging waves. Ben is glad she suggested this fish place at Shoreham. It’s relaxed, familiar.

He convinces himself they’ll end the evening hands entwined along this same path, able to face anything if together. For better, for worse. After his darkest year, she’d reminded him of those marital promises. Even though they’d been made before a God in whom she disbelieves.

‘Good evening, what can I get you to drink?’

‘Just a blackcurrant and lemonade for me,’ says Callie.

‘Make that two, please.’

The waitress scuttles off without comment.

‘What are we like? And our first night out in ages.’ Callie laughs. She’s got a deep voice, and a laugh to match. That laughter always lightens Ben’s mood.

Callie orders two fish pies. It’s a no brainer here.

They sit in contented silence at a table by the window, enjoying the peace. This parade of restaurants is brightly lit. A family walk past, parents with two children followed by a man in a filthy coat and summer plimsolls. In his hand, he clutches a carrier bag with a bottle-shaped bulge.

His stoop, his sagging walk, reminds Ben of Owen.

Ben knows it’s time. He had made a commitment from his hospital bed with Callie curled up under the blue knitted blanket next to him. He had promised her there would be no more lies, that he would never keep things from her again, however painful.

‘Babe.’

Callie turns to her husband, fighting her desire to keep listening to the argument brewing on a table nearby.

Ben notices her body tense at his tone.

‘What?’

‘You remember when Owen and Estelle went on that last holiday to Beaminster?’

‘Ben. Do you think there’s ever a day I don’t go over and over those last weeks? How ill Owen was, how upset Estelle was and how you seemed to spiral afterwards into a pit of despair.’

‘When we stayed at theirs, something happened.’

‘What?’

‘A teenager came to the house. By the time I got to the door, my mother was as white as a ghost.’

Callie prods her untouched salmon. She pushes the tomato slice across her plate and without looking up says, ‘Go on.’

‘He had pictures. Pictures of Owen and a young girl.’

Callie looks up, open mouthed. ‘What sort of pictures?’

‘Nothing like that, a picture of him walking down some stairs at the office. Her on his arm. Another at a work party, the two of them clinking glasses. Nothing sinister.’

‘Why did that shock your mother?’

‘That wasn’t all. He had other stuff . . .’

‘For goodness sake, Ben, just say what you wanna say. Spit it out.’

‘He produced a baby scan picture with a date.’

‘But it could’ve been anyone’s scan.’

‘It had my brother’s surname on it.’

Ben wants to leave it here. He's told her now. He's told her Owen got someone pregnant. He wants to make up a story of an affair, claim that's what upset his mother. He wants to explain how he was naive and that finding out his hero worship was misplaced so discombobulated him, that he couldn't take it. He wants to say it was just a stupid affair with a woman at work.

Callie is waiting. 'Go on, I know there's more.'

'The boy . . . well, a girl came back. . . she was so young. Hardly older than Daisy. She was obviously pregnant.'

Ben knows he's telling half-truths. He needs this over.

'So, what happened then?'

'Mother was desperate to pay for it to disappear,' Ben says but can't meet Callie's eye. He can't admit that he was complicit in something so serious, that he made choices that weren't his to make.

Callie is still waiting. She knows there's more.

'My mother ran off and left me to pay them off. It was me who had to look into that girl's eyes, knowing I should say sorry, that I should help her. But I just shoved her a grubby envelope and closed the door in her face.'

'Ah, that's the bit she left out.'

'What. Who?'

'Your mother. When you tried to . . . when you were in hospital I wondered if you'd been having an affair or something. You'd changed, been so withdrawn since you house sat. I was searching for explanations, and they were getting madder and I was getting more and more distraught. Then she broke down. Apologised. Said she'd paid for a woman to have an abortion. She said it was obviously a mess Owen had created when he became ill. She said that you'd been there and that upset you.'

‘But she didn’t mention how she left me to wipe up that horrid mess. Or that she refused to speak about it ever again.’

‘No, but that’s her all over, isn’t it? She can’t bear emotional stains especially when it involved golden balls.’

Ben can’t help but smile at that. Callie is staring at her supper, prodding the fish as if it’s to blame.

The waiter has been hovering for a while, uncertain whether they’ve finished. Tentatively he asks, ‘Shall I take your plates?’

‘Mmm, I think so,’ Ben says apologetically.

Ben feels some relief. Callie knew all along but didn’t want to make him feel worse. But she doesn’t know. He needs to tell her about the letter. The boy.

As they walk to the car in the December cold, Ben admits, ‘There’s more.’

‘Go on.’

‘I spoke to the girl. I gave her my address. You know just in case. She said she’d leave. Disappear to relatives miles away and never come back.’

‘And?’

‘She did. But now she’s back. She wrote me a letter.’

‘Saying what?’

‘Just that she’s back. Her grandmother is ill and she has to help.’

Ben can’t say it. It’s too hard to look Callie in the eye knowing the bit that’ll shock and upset her is that the girl left but not to have an abortion. The girl left to give birth to his nephew, and he’s looked that child in the eye and walked away.

'Look, Ben. I know it's all a bit messy. Owen was unwell. He wouldn't have done that if he wasn't. He loved Estelle and Daisy, you know that.'

Ben is unsure of what he knows these days. He has to tell her the truth. He has flashbacks frequently. The victim was crying, and she spoke in a whisper. He was unsure whether it was fear in response to the waiting thug or that she simply had no voice. He had tried to give her the money. The flashbacks thrust tiny hands at him. Hands that trembled as she handed him a piece of paper. It had her telephone number and a name. She whispered two lines. The sing-song nature of what she said, and the quiet tone made him think she was reciting a poem, a prayer. When the words sank in, he heard them with a resounding clarity he will never unhear.

He opens his mouth to tell the truth. He wants to say, 'Callie. I said she could keep the baby. Please tell me I did right?' But before he can formulate the right words, Callie launches in a different direction. She reaches for his hands and fiddles with his wedding ring as she speaks.

'Anyway, babe. It's all worked out for the best. Just think if that girl hadn't had an abortion. I mean, they'd be a kid. A kid walking about looking like Daisy and having the same undetonated bomb waiting inside. It's not nice what you and your mother did. And it's not great that she bamboozled you. You should have chatted with Estelle and maybe even Daisy. But you did what you did. In hindsight that's a damn good thing. Imagine if we had to deal with an illegitimate kid on top of Daisy being a mare.'

As Callie races up their path, keen to get in the warm, Ben's mind is racing faster than he can manage. There's no way he can tell her now.

'There's a downstairs light on,' Callie whispers, grabbing his arm.

‘I definitely turned everything off.’

Ben moves in front of Callie and very slowly turns the key. Gently he pushes the door and pauses. They both listen. The TV is on.

‘You’re early. About to watch another movie, you guys cool with that?’ Daisy says, aiming the remote at their wide screen.

Callie heaves a sigh of relief and smiles brightly. ‘Tell you what, why don’t you and your Uncle Ben watch the movie. I’m shattered,’ she says.

Without a backward glance, his wife heads upstairs. Ben plonks his tired body next to Daisy. For once, she’s the last person he wants to deal with.

‘Press play then.’ Daisy pokes her foot into his leg. She leans back on the deep sofa, snuggling against his shoulder. She swings her legs onto his lap. Ben despairs. Tomorrow, she’ll kick him and say he’s creepy.

Halfway through the film, Ben jerks awake in response to vibrations from a phone under his backside. Before he’s retrieved it, Daisy whips it out of his hand as if it’s dangerous.

He’s amazed her fingers can produce anything coherent at that typing speed but leaning forward he can see words appearing on the small screen. Texts from her mate Ryan.

What you doin?

Watchin film

Wanna come out?

Daisy swings her legs off Ben and gets up at the same time as slotting her mobile in her back pocket. Grabbing her coat, she opens the front door.

'You can go to bed now,' she shouts behind her.

'Daisy, it's gone eleven.'

'And?'

'A bit late for going out. I thought you were staying over.'

'Change of plan. Hope you make up with Callie.'

Before he can open his mouth, she's gone.

He zaps off the screen which leaves him in total darkness. All he can think of is those blasted two lines. Two lines whispered as that young girl handed over a package of money, dirty money.

Tears had streamed down that teenager's face and tears had streamed down his. For a moment they had both held that package of filthy money. If someone was watching, they might have thought they were lovers, handing over a gift of love, captured by the emotion, lost in love.

Before she grasped the money, she had whispered those words and said he just had to nod. That if he nodded, she would know he was consenting to her request. She promised if he gave his consent she would go and never return. She gave her number but didn't ask for his. 'Just in case,' she had said. 'Just in case, one day, you want to know.' She had said as she handed over her number. The bloke in the car was getting impatient. He sounded his horn.

She whispered those two lines. The lines he can't forget. The lines that ruined everything for everyone. She whispered, 'My name is Sachini. I want to keep my baby.'

And he had nodded his consent.

23

Daisy

When Daisy opens her eyes, it's very dark. It can't be morning, it's so cold. There's a metal cage at the end of her bed. Her chest tightens. For a freaky moment she thinks she's done it again. Drunk too much and fallen asleep at Kiera's. Last time, she woke in a pond of her own vomit, half dressed with her leg trapped by the shower doors. One of Kiera's brothers had been standing over her with his flies undone. She totally freaked but he was having a pee in the sink 'cos the bog was broken.

When she hears a sneeze from the cage, she remembers. Last night, Ryan had gone home in the early hours. She had thought about going to her room at The Orchards, she's stoked that she has that option. But she had felt overwhelmed and alone. She needed to yack with someone who understood. She had regretted not going to Dad's exhibition. Why is she such a cretin? Why does she say no when she means yes and yes when she means no? She wants to make Dad proud, but she no longer knows how.

She had thought Sachini would be in bed, but she had called anyway. Sachini sounded happy to hear her voice. She said so. Sachini had opened the door a crack with her finger over her lips. She had pulled Daisy by the hand. Silently, Sach had guided Daisy over Haizeh's metal cot, whispering directions in the dark so as not to wake up the maggot.

Eventually, they had landed here, on the saggy bed in fits of giggles.

The curtains are flapping from the cracked window and the room is lit from the streetlights. Daisy wonders how they can live in this minuscule dive. She and Sach lay side by side staring upwards. There are fluorescent stars on the ceiling. She had those in their old house. Dad had put them there when she was little. Daisy feels tears run sideways off her face.

Out of the silence, her friend whispers.

'My father was killed in Sri Lanka. There was fighting and he hated being part of it. After he went, everything changed. Mother cried all day. She couldn't cope. We lost our flat.'

Daisy can't imagine being homeless. For the first time she can see her situation isn't all bad. Ben and Gran still care. She has places to sleep, and she might be alright for twenty years.

Daisy shivers and Sachini tugs the duvet until it covers their shoulders. The room is freezing but the flowery bed set is heavy and smells like Gran's washing.

She can hear Sachini's shallow breathing, but it feels like she's talking to an invisible presence. A presence who isn't judging or blaming for everything she's messed up.

She had planned to listen, to ask details about Haizeh's father and why Sach was sent away from her country and family but when she opens her mouth, all her secrets came tumbling out.

'My dad got sick. Not sick like cancer but sad, then angry. He smashed my stuff, his stuff, anything, his precious records, toys, everything.'

'I'm sorry,' is all Sachini says.

Daisy cries as she remembers him lying exhausted on the floor, sobbing into his hands like a baby, rocking backwards and forwards saying, ‘Everything is broken,’ as if he hadn’t done it. She hated that the most.

‘Like beauty and the beast in reverse,’ her mum had said. An amazing, clever, prince gradually turned into an ugly beast.

‘Imagine watching your father turn into a raging animal, that’s bad. Then imagine realising the monster will return and do the same to you. Yeah, that’s what I get for my eighteenth. Not a car, not the theatre and drinks out. I get to visit a real-life vampire set. It’s so real that the vampire sticks me with his sharp needle and steals my blood to crystal-ball my future. That’s what my family want. It won’t help me. Just them.’

Sachini stays quiet. Daisy pokes her arm to check she’s still alive.

‘What?’ she asks without moving.

‘Nothing,’ Daisy admits and continues her monologue. She’s not told anyone this stuff. Not Mum. Not Gran and not even Ryan.

‘When I was in juniors, my parents left me with Ben and Callie. I knew something was off as I got to throw a fake sickie. All Dad cared about was school. That was when the feeling started in my stomach, a watch out, stuff is going wrong feeling. It’s still there. When she came back, Mum was on her own, no Dad. I watched her. She was like a robot, picking stuff up, going from room to room, and packing my bags but with no talking. I held her hand to make her look, but she didn’t. Then we went home, Dad was in his chair trying to get comfortable. Then he went mental ’cos we didn’t laugh and then he smashed his mug on the oven. When he'd gone upstairs, Mum made me hot chocolate with marshmallows. She did that when my cat died.'

Haizeh interrupts her flow with a coughing fit. His cot is like a dog crate without a lid and he's too big for it. His chubby legs touch the sides, and his head is bent at an angle.

Sachini strokes his head and then crawls back up and under the duvet.

'Go on. Tell me what your mum said.'

Daisy feels exhausted, done with it by then. She can remember it all as if it were yesterday.

'Sit on the settee,' Mum had told her. She sat close and had put both arms around Daisy. She can replay it as a film, Mum's face very, very still as Daisy had looked into her teary eyes.

'Daddy hasn't been very well lately, has he?'

Daisy didn't admit that.

'He is very cross and sad sometimes, isn't he?'

Daisy had said nothing. She'd waited, willing Mum to smile and say, 'But now he's going to be okay, no more bad Daddy who hates his little girl.'

'Daddy has a disease that is making him cross and not himself, it isn't his fault.'

'When will he get better then?' Daisy had asked.

'We don't think he will, sweetheart. I am very sorry.'

'Is it cancer?' She had felt so grown up knowing about that.

'You won't have heard of it but Dad has something called Frontal Temporal Dementia. Some people call it FTD.'

For years, she had thought it was called Temper Dementor. She thought someone with a temper had stolen

Dad and replaced him with a monster. No one had mentioned the monster would return for her.

There are no buses before six thirty, so Daisy has to walk. She searches for 'Dad's songs' on her playlist. Dad had promised when she reached eighteen, they'd go to a live gig.

A Madness song starts. He loved Suggs. They used to dance like mental peeps to this song.

Yeah, it really turned out bad. As bad as it gets. These days the tunes that play in Daisy's head are not fun, these days her own lyrics are louder than her music.

Everyone wants me dead.

I wish I was dead.

I wish they were dead.

I have no future, might as well be dead.

A familiar tug jerks Daisy from that horrible film, the automatic doors have swooshed shut, trapping her bag. Wiping her eyes and nose with a jacket sleeve she spots the reflection in the glass.

They'll think I'm hungover like always. Best thing about working here is no one cares what you look like.

Penny is at reception, she looks at her watch ready to say, 'What time do you call this, young lady?' but stays quiet as Daisy is thirty seconds early.

'Can you get changed as quickly as you can, please?' Penny asks while Daisy signs in as slowly as she can.

Every day her first job is to clean 'her' rooms.

'Charles, Charles, Charles,' Selvi screams. Daisy stands in the doorway.

'Ignore her luvvy, she can't help it.' His voice is steady, kind, but he is gritting his teeth. Maybe he wants to bite her.

‘Don’t shout, Selvi, love,’ Charles whispers, close to her face.

‘I have to shout, or you don’t hear. Who are you? Where is Charles?’ Selvi’s even smaller than Daisy. Her nightie is too big. Her small bony feet are poking out. They look more duck than human.

‘I am Charles, love, your Charlie, look here at the photo.’ He points to an ancient piccy of two young people, the man is in uniform, the girl is wearing a long dress, a little bag is hanging from her elbow. She is looking at the man like he’s famous. Selvi bends to squint at the photo. She looks back at Charles, the white-haired old man in front of her, and back to the photo. She picks up the frame and brings it close to her nose. Daisy is also struggling to play snap.

Selvi discards the picture on the floor. Making unintelligible noises, she pushes her husband. It’s a pretty good push for someone so small. He doesn’t move.

He is a better-looking old person. He has smooth skin, nice teeth and eyes that are big. He stands tall instead of stooping like the other men.

‘Get out, get out,’ Selvi snarls with no teeth.

Selvi opens her wardrobe and tugs out an old green raincoat, her purple ankle wellies, and a black floppy hat. She puts the coat and hat on but treads on the boots leaving them at the bottom of the bed. A skinny old lady dressed for bed with outdoor clothes and a broken umbrella.

Selvi pushes past Daisy and into the corridor. Penny will take off her coat like Sach does for the maggot and bring her back to Charles.

Daisy has almost finished hoovering when Selvi returns. She’s alright now.

‘Hello, love,’ Charles says as if she hasn’t been a monster.

Selvi goes to Charles and dribbles on his forehead.

'I've made you a cuppa and found your teeth. Put them in and we can do the crossword.'

Selvi plonks herself into her plastic-covered armchair and nods off.

Daisy watches Charlie's sad eyes. Selvi is quietly snoring. It must be cool to forget you're so messed up.

'It's Daisy. Give me your answer . . .' Daisy avoids looking up, she's so not in the mood for Bill, it's hard enough getting the hoover into the corridor without him in the way.

Penny raises her eyebrows as he follows Daisy singing the Daisy song.

'Mmm, given she's dishevelled and ten minutes behind schedule, maybe she could do with a bike for two, Bill.'

Penny is okay, it's hard to dislike her. She reminds Daisy of her reception teacher, Miss Rutter, always the same, old-fashioned, strict about stupid things, but fair. She loved first school. She was top set all the way through.

Derrick is standing by reception; he claims he doesn't miss a trick.

'Where you off to, young lady?' He looks at his watch. Then, squeezing out his constipation face, he uses both hands to inspect the appointment card. It says clinical psychology. Daisy hates him knowing, but the shame is a reasonable exchange for time off. She has psychology twice a week this month, she's getting way worse.

Derrick doesn't spot the extra dates are scribbled in a different colour.

'Three hours maximum, a minute more and you'll lose it from your annual leave,' his voice barks after Daisy. She doesn't point out her shift will be finished by then.

'See you tomorrow, Derrick,' she shouts without looking back; he'll have already walked away.

24

Dorothy

Dorothy plonks the phone into the handset. She's been awake since the early hours. How did her sweet family become such a mess? Her house is spotless. There's a cake in the oven and she was ready for the long-dreaded family gathering. But now Penny can't come. She was going to be their mediator, should they need one.

When that filthy creep made those accusations at the gallery, Dorothy felt sick to the stomach. If it wasn't for Ben, she would've clobbered that Michael with a hefty ornament. She had refused a lift home and declined Ben's calls. A taxi had been called by Kasia. Dorothy wanted to seethe alone but as soon as her front door was locked, she collapsed. Face down, sobbing into her settee, she wondered if her heart might break.

Fortunately, young Ryan turned up again. Dorothy isn't sure what she makes of him, but he gave her an excuse to mop up those ridiculous tears and do something useful. She should turn him away, but she can't. He reeks of the unwashed with a hint of dope, but he's so young and needs a sensible adult. Ben would go ballistic, as would Daisy, for different reasons. That dreadful counsellor would be sure to point out Dorothy's need to rescue a hopeless young man as uncoincidental.

When she waved him off the following morning with a bottle of Peter's aftershave, she felt a new resolve to rescue her own relatives.

'I have three staff off sick including my deputy,' Penny had explained on the phone. Dorothy had heard Derrick mumbling away in the background. She can't bear mumbling. 'So sorry to let you down. I so wanted to help you get it right.'

Dorothy had reassured her friend, despite the worried faces of Ben, Daisy and Estelle storm-trooping her mind.

'I'm sure it will all be just fine. After all, the solution is obvious. We need to get Daisy tested and then move on from this whole mucky affair.'

'I'm sure it will all come right. The important person is Daisy. Keep that in mind and you'll do right. Just make sure Daisy is heard,' Penny reminded her before hanging up.

'One of those days, Dorothy?' Gabby, her observant neighbour comments. Sheets of paper escape the coloured file as she juggles the milk and biscuits from the front seat of her car. She could have popped to the supermarket last night, but Penny had promised to bring extra supplies on her way. The leaflets threaten to flutter away in the breeze but fortunately Gabby stops it with a foot. She helps Dorothy pick them up, grabbing them one sheet at a time. Dorothy flushes as her neighbour pauses to check the headlines.

'Research for my creative writing,' Dorothy snaps as she snatches them out of a gloved hand. Why on earth didn't she bring them inside when the consultant gave it to her? Why leave it in the glove box as if the disease could be kept there too?

Inside, Dorothy rests against the back of the door. She feels ashamed. Why does it matter if the neighbours know there's dementia in her family? It's not catching or sinful. She blows out some air to steady herself and reads the top sheet of the pile. 'Genetic testing: a guide for young people.'

Her heart is pounding. She feels sick. How can this meeting turn out well?

Estelle is the first to arrive, looking how Dorothy feels. Her eyes are permanently sore and have lost their old sparkle. She's aged twenty years in the last five. What must it be like to find out the love of your life has an incurable disease, then that your beautiful daughter has a fifty-fifty chance of getting it too?

Dorothy attempts a hug but both women are unconvinced by the brief gesture. 'Come in, dear girl. Where's that granddaughter of mine?'

Ben follows before the door is closed. Dorothy longs to sweep that fringe from his face and plant a firm kiss like she used to when he was five. How he loved his mummy back then.

'Callie says she's sorry, but she's had to work, and, you know, can't miss the opportunity.'

'Indeed, onto the next thing, no doubt. We know the score.' As soon as Dorothy closes her big mouth, she regrets being snarky. Callie works hard and these aren't her problems.

She smiles with warmth, but the moment is lost and Ben has pushed past without even a cursory peck on the cheek.

'You said you'd collect Daisy,' Estelle challenges Ben without saying hello.

'I assumed she'd be here. I waited for her in the car park as we agreed but there was no sign.'

'She was probably inside given the weather,' Estelle snaps.

‘I went inside The Orchards. The woman on reception checked her rota and said Daisy had her psychologist appointment. When I phoned there, they said they aren’t seeing her for another week.’

Dorothy feels like giving up already. Penny would’ve diffused the heaviness of it all, made it harder for these two to fall out. She notices the Christmas tree in the window opposite and realizes she hasn’t given a thought to the twenty-fifth. Once upon a time the feast and surrounding days would’ve been organised with military precision. Since Owen went nobody seems to care about birthdays or Christmas. Nobody seems to care about anything. Well, that stops here. They need to regroup and move forward. She remembers what Penny said: think Daisy, only Daisy.

‘Let’s sit up at the table. The kettle is boiled, and the scones are still warm. We can catch up and peruse the leaflets, make a plan even if Daisy is late.’

Ben and Estelle do as they’re told. They sit. Estelle unbuttons her thick coat but doesn’t remove it. Ben perches on the edge of his chair, picking at the tablecloth like a toddler.

‘I haven’t seen Daisy for over a week.’ Dorothy is ashamed to admit that she’s completely lost track of her granddaughter. Ryan claims he doesn’t know where she is either.

‘She rarely sleeps at home.’ Estelle seems equally embarrassed. ‘Does she sleep at those flats, Ben?’

‘I have no idea, I’m sorry,’ Ben says. ‘Cheeky mare used our place last week when we were out but haven’t seen her since. She doesn’t talk about Kiera much these days. I get the impression she’s lost her initial shine.’

Estelle raises her eyebrows as if her daughter’s absence is Ben’s fault.

Dorothy blushes like a guilty teen when Ben mentions Ryan.

Estelle is tap tapping her nails on the dark wood. Dorothy wants to slap her hand and tell her to sit still. She watched Peter sand and repainted that table. He could fix anything. Would things be better if he hadn't gone too? Would Daisy listen to him? Do what he said?

'Maybe it's for the best to have a starting chat without her,' Dorothy says, pouring strong tea from a pot into delicate china cups. Ben takes a cream-laden scone. His mother slides him a plate.

'So,' Estelle says, notepad and pen poised. 'Shall we set an agenda?'

Ben speaks tentatively. 'Maybe we just need to chat through the issues and think about how to be a constructive team for Daisy over the coming months.'

'She'll have to arrange the genetic counselling soon to get it all done for the test in the summer.' Estelle bites on her thumbnail, a new habit that also irritates Dorothy.

'With all due respect, Estelle, it's not that straightforward. Daisy is saying she won't have the test, and it's her decision,' Ben says, his voice deeper.

'Ben, she might think she's grown up, smoking and drinking and shouting, but she's a child. She's got no sense of responsibility. She is unaware how bad Owen got. What he did. What this disease can do.'

'Well, surely that's the point,' Ben says.

Estelle had looked after Owen at home for years after his diagnosis, thinks Dorothy. They tried to help but it was her who carried the bulk of the burden. His slurred speech, chocolate binges and clumsy falls made life awkward but not unbearable. It was the rages that finished them all.

That's when Dorothy had to step in and follow Owen's wishes to end it all. Did she do right? Could they have managed for longer?

Dorothy is stunned back to the room by Ben's stern voice. 'She thinks more than you give her credit for. She's still the same bright girl. She's seventeen, she's lost her life, her dad, her education. Losing school was her final straw. Who can blame her for lashing out?'

Dorothy flattens her skirt as she speaks, not able to meet Ben's eyes. She hates it when he talks of last straws.

'She can't see a future, she's given up,' Dorothy repeats what Ryan said.

Estelle fires back without pausing for breath. 'It's not just about her. We all need to know, don't we?'

Ben looks away. Dorothy can tell he doesn't agree. She doesn't want to hurt her son or push him over the edge. Before Dorothy can say her piece to support her daughter-in-law, Ben inhales and launches his opinion in no uncertain terms.

'We might want to know for our peace of mind, but in a few months, she'll be an adult. If she gets the test, it's her decision, because she wants to know. If she's manipulated, and the test is positive, she'll hate us even more.'

'Manipulated! Thanks for that, Ben. If it was Callie or your child you might be less passive,' Estelle snaps.

Ben's head dips. 'Let's take a breather,' Dorothy suggests. 'I'll fetch some more tea.'

Before she can action a top up, Estelle bites back.

'If she doesn't have the test, she can't get a job, have children or enter a relationship. She has to know,' Estelle races on, checking her notes to make sure all her points are voiced.

Dorothy can feel her breathing quickening. This isn't right; it's not up to them but she wants to keep the peace. They need to come together. This isn't helping.

'It's none of your business, Estelle, whether she has the test.' Ben's voice is louder than is appropriate. He is shouting.

'I'm sorry. Who do you think you are, Ben?' Estelle slams her pen down.

'Hang on, everyone.' Dorothy puts her hand on Ben's forearm. 'We need to take a breather. Ben. Get more hot water, please.'

While he clatters around in the kitchen, the two women stay silent. Estelle doodles on her notepad and Dorothy flicks though the information pack, rearranging the sheets so they are in the correct order.

Ben returns carrying a tray with more scones. 'Sorry,' he says to Estelle. 'I shouldn't lose my temper but . . .'

Dorothy jumps in before the room heats up again.

'Can I please add my ten pence worth?'

Estelle says, 'Of course.'

Dorothy wonders if her tight mouth suggests otherwise. Is Estelle tempted to say, 'Don't you think you've done enough damage by sleeping with a cursed man?'

'Ben, I think what Estelle means is that it will be hard for Daisy not knowing what her future holds.'

'But it's *her* future and not ours, and if she'd prefer not to know, she's like the ninety per cent of people with a genetic risk who choose not to be tested,' Ben suggests.

'Don't patronise me, Ben. It's my daughter's life you're talking about. Life will be impossible if we don't know.'

Dorothy slouches back in her chair and fixes her gaze on the flashing reindeer in the neighbour's garden. Oh, to go back, when they looked forward to simple pleasures like how to decorate at Christmas. This is hopeless. When Penny cancelled and Daisy failed to join, she should've cancelled. Estelle has never enjoyed Ben's company. She has always considered him spoilt and immature. As Dorothy watches her son raging like this, she wonders if she has to agree. What have they come to? A family of screeching banshees. How shameful. She's glad Gabby next door has gone to see her daughter.

'Impossible for whom, Estelle? You or her?'

'How dare you! You have no idea what I went through with your brother.'

'Have some more tea.' Dorothy fills Estelle's cup hoping it's oil to calm troubled waters. Estelle pushes her cup to one side.

'It's alright for you and Callie playing the clever social workers, nicey nicey to her druggie friends. It's not you she screams at. She's just like him, shouting and yelling, throwing her weight around. I'm living in terror. I have no life at all.' Estelle is crying and Dorothy rushes forward to push a box of tissues at her.

'We were all hurt by what Owen became,' Ben lashes back.

'Yes, but it wasn't your partner who got thrown out in a cloud of shame for sexually harassing a child. Was it?'

All three of them startle at a movement in the kitchen. Dorothy is certain the back door is locked. Please don't let it be Ryan, that would take some explaining. As Dorothy turns to get up, she comes face to face with Daisy standing in the hall. How long has she been listening? She's obviously come in through the back gate. Her face is a mask of make-up with thick blackened eyebrows under her fringe. She's wearing a tiny skirt and a skimpy top that shows off a new piercing. It looks inflamed. She must be freezing.

'Well, well, well. It's the three wise monkeys,' Daisy says slowly. She makes Dorothy want to weep. She is trying so hard to be brave. Hands on tiny hips. Jaw jutted towards her audience but with eyeliner tears streaming down her perfect skin. 'Sorry. The new beast has pitched up. Just when you thought you'd got rid, the sequel started. I heard you. We all know I have the curse, so why bother? You want an excuse to lock me up. Kill me. Sweep the dirt under the carpet and live happily ever after.'

Estelle is still crying, dabbing her eyes with a flowery tissue. Dorothy opens her mouth, but no words come.

'Thanks very much for coming. I declare this committee over. I will never be tested.' She bends forward to stick her finger into her mum's face.

'Daisy, sweetheart, why don't you sit down and have a scone. Bens printed off some information for you,' Dorothy soothes.

'Gran, I know you mean well but it's none of anyone's business but mine. And I don't want to read about FTD 'cos I don't care.'

Daisy turns around to leave and it's only then that Dorothy sees what Daisy has been hiding. In between her granddaughter and the wall is another child. A much smaller child with chubby arms and clothes too flimsy for the season. His wide eyes show fear and when Daisy remembers what he's witnessed she scoops him into her arms.

'It's okay, maggot,' Daisy says, brushing his hair from his face with such kindness that Dorothy can't bear to watch. Daisy carries him into the room. The child buries his face into her chest like he's been there for years. Daisy pushes past her mother and with her free arm, she grabs a scone. She breaks it in two and taps his shoulder. He takes the scone but cuddles it like a teddy. With cream still around her mouth, Daisy pecks Dorothy on the cheek and marches out. Before Dorothy can gather herself, she looks across at Ben who looks as if he's seen a ghost.

25

Ben

Ben woke up early with an idea. A crazy idea, not at all consistent with his character but once you cross to the wrong side of the integrity line, it's much easier to keep going. He had to do something. Being his natural, passive, see-what-happens self hasn't worked. He can't sit about waiting for this woman – Sachini – to reveal their secret to Daisy. His niece has been through too much and he has to finish what he started. When he was lying in bed oppressed by the early hours, coming here seemed like his only option. Now, he's less sure but the sinister black case with the combination lock is tucked ready under the passenger seat. When she gets to the driver's door, he'll push the button and a few minutes later, it'll be sorted. This time the problem won't come back another day.

When he saw her in the playground, it frightened the life out of him but once he got back to his life with galleries and grown-ups, he convinced himself they wouldn't meet again. Storrington is not Brighton but it's big enough for two people to stay apart.

How has he been so naive? Of course, they were going to see each other. But how on earth has his wayward niece ended up childminding her kid? Does the girl know? Has she deliberately stalked Daisy? Does she want to ruin Owen's family like he ruined hers? Daisy displayed the pride of

Mufasa when she held that child up high. Does she know she's holding her half-brother?

That thought hit him like a sinister thunder bolt.

Ben can't believe that in trying to save Daisy, he's ruined everything for everyone. So many questions have kept him awake.

The family powwow at his mother's was appalling. He had known it wasn't a good idea but had been bullied again. When he saw Daisy, he knew she had heard what Estelle had said and he had thought his heart would break. That poor kid. He caught that fleeting look before she wrestled on her angry armour. He saw the tears teetering on her lower lashes. He saw the raw hurt at what her family were saying, but mostly he saw the disbelief that her own clan had turned against her and her father. He had never liked Estelle, but they had always shared a love for Daisy. Even in the most terrible of times, they had protected Daisy. But not now. They haven't protected her; they've done her harm. Today, it ends. Today he'll sort it out.

Sitting in his high van seat, he can see the Christmas decorations in the house windows. Somehow everything feels worse at this time of year. Daisy is a child. She should be creating a wish list, scoffing her advent chocolates and counting down the days not escaping to the streets feeling unsafe and unloved.

Before Owen got ill, Ben hadn't known a time when Christmas wasn't fabulous. Each year they would watch *A Wonderful Life* on Christmas Eve with a Chinese take-out. He remembers hanging his stocking outside his door. He didn't want the big man marching into his room. That had felt terrifying. His father had warmed a mince pie for Santa knowing he was coming from the cold and a carrot was left for the reindeer. Even though Owen was a teenager, he went along with it all. He would hang his stocking too and pour the whiskey to leave for Santa. Christmas day started with morning presents followed by a church service. His father insisted on that. His mother usually stayed home excusing herself with lunch prep. The rest of the day they would binge on enormous amounts of food, with a brief pause for the Queen to speak. Another of his father's rituals.

When Owen got married, there was an unwritten expectation he would continue to come home. So, he and Estelle went to her parents on Boxing Day even though that meant lots of travelling. Daisy has always loved Christmas. In the last few years, she has hand made them something. She's so talented. The year before last, she had painted an abstract picture of her father, full of colour. In the depiction, he was dancing with a small girl and musical notes were cascading from the clouds. She gave one to them all.

The last few Christmases have been unbearable. They could no longer make everything right for Daisy. Everything was wrong.

Ben parked early. The road outside the pre-school gets packed. He's parked close to the kerb so he can wind down his window when the time is right, act quickly and drive away. Job done, this time properly. When he collected this hire van, he pulled up outside the rental depot to test it. He got out, to assess what was visible with the tinted windows shut. Sitting here like a vile predator, he can monitor her but stay hidden until she's parallel to the window. He doesn't want to draw attention to a dodgy-looking vehicle outside the school.

He watches as the yummy mummies arrive first, far too early but plenty of time to gossip about those less fortunate. Before he has time to wonder what kind of mum Callie will make, he sees his target. The briefcase lies on the front seat. If Callie could see him now, she'd be horrified. Hanging outside a school, presenting as Mr Nice but with dark motives that horrify even him. He thought he was a nice guy. He was.

She isn't much older than Daisy and it shows. Her head is down, her arms folded. Her coat is too big and disproportionate for the twig legs hanging underneath. Her trainers are not the trendy ones worn by girls her age. They are functional shoes for walking and working.

Ben watches her, each step taking an impossibly long time. Is he up to this? He wipes his brow with the back of his hand. He looks at the case. She's getting closer.

She's passed the back wheels of the van. Her mind is on the playground. The fear of walking past those women, the ones in their four by fours with the classy clothes and freshly cut hair.

Ben moves his finger to the window button; the tinted glass slides silently down at the exact moment.

'Hello,' he says, trying not to sound like the monster he feels.

She jerks her head to the left. Eyes are wide with shock, fear.

She's racking her brains. Do I know him? I do. From where? Not a school dad?

'Hi, can I have a moment. I won't take long.' He tries to keep his tone even.

'Hello,' the young woman says with hesitancy, turning to face him, to take a better look, work out what is going on.

She's prettier than he remembers. Ben glances in his mirror. Has he been seen?

'You don't recognise me, do you?' he says.

Ben notices the way she keeps touching her neck, the eyes almost black. He remembers both.

‘I knew you didn’t recognise me,’ he says with a hesitant smile. ‘Four years ago, you . . .’

‘Hello Ben,’ she says before he can explain.

‘Look, this has to be quick. You said that to me once. You were desperate. You begged me to help. I did. I was stupid and hurt and confused but I did as you asked.’

Ben pauses for breath.

‘Now you have to do what I ask.’

The young woman turns to face him, moves closer to the window. He reaches for the case. He wants to show her what’s on offer if she does right. He opens the lid like he’s seen on the movies. His cash is all messy and spread about, not in neat rolls or even piles. By the way her child was dressed, she needs it. That’s the way he thinks about that child, *her child.* Labelling that quiet little person – the one Daisy referred to as ‘little maggot’ – as Owen’s child would take him too far.

She backs away, puts both hands up as if he’s holding a gun.

‘I do not want your money. Chez took it last time. I didn’t get a penny. I don’t want your dirty money. You can’t take my boy. Get away from me or I’ll call the police.’

Ben closes the case before it’s seen. He opens the van door and jumps down to go after her, but she’s gone. She’s running towards her son, taking the same path at the same speed as when he ran from here, fuelled by the same terror. Terror that someone is about to steal your life, all that’s yours, all that you love.

He watches as she runs to rescue her child when he wasn’t even in danger. At least he knows he’s right. The boy is who he thought he was.

26

Daisy

Daisy's well pleased. When she gets to the entrance, Penny and the pig are having a scrap at reception. They're too distracted to realise she came from the wrong direction, inside the building rather than outside. Nobody can find out she's staying in blue corridor. She can't believe her luck.

She's not been home for ages and since overhearing the family committee, she's not planning to go back. How could they say those things? How could they tell such lies? Even Ben has turned into a total dick.

Derrick is ranting. He is leaning across the desk with his fists on the desk like a gorilla.

'You need to say no, for goodness sake. We have enough to do. She's such a selfish madam, that daughter of yours.'

'Nothing to do with you then,' Penny snaps back.

'We told her not to marry that layabout. She made her bed . . .' he retorts, marching away. Penny has her head in her hands when Daisy says, 'Hi.'

'My my, who'd have thought it'd be you who'd brighten my day?' Penny says when she sees Daisy.

'What?'

'You're early and smiling. Have I missed something? Your resignation? You won the lottery?'

'Nope, just walked fast,' Daisy lies.

Before she can speak, Penny hauls herself over the desk and cups Daisy's cheeks in her hands.

'My angel,' she says and slumps back into her chair.

'Bit weird,' Daisy mutters, exchanging raised eyebrows with Greg, the chef.

Leaving Penny and going to lock her phone into the safe box, Daisy's ears pick up a high-pitched screech, a pause, and then another animal noise. Where's it coming from? It's horrible. This is a voice she can't identify. She can't even work out if it's a man or a woman.

In the corridor, it's all quiet apart from the squealing. It stops and then starts again. No staff around. Moving faster than her usual work pace, she races down yellow corridor to the noise coming from room seven.

She pushes the door. The room is empty and quiet. Maybe the noise was coming from the open window.

A different, quieter noise, like a washing machine after the spin, is coming from the floor. When she gets to the other side of the bed, bare legs are sticking out. She crawls under the bed. Selvi is stuck.

'Charles, Charles, Charles,' she's calling as if he might be under the bed.

Written on the whiteboard it says: 'Charles has gone to the shop, back at 9.30.'

What's Daisy supposed to do? Selvi is wailing. Should she pull her out by her legs? She's so skinny, she could break. Maybe she should start cleaning, pretend she's not heard. Daisy goes around the other side and crouches so the old lady can see her face.

'What's up, Selv mate? Charlie's gone to the shop, come out or you'll get cold.' The noise stops but Selvi keeps up with the sleeping lions. This is not fun. 'Come on, mate, are you stuck?' Daisy pleads.

Selvi stops whimpering and rolls onto her side. Her pin head collides with the bottom of the bed, ouch. She doesn't seem to notice.

'Hang on,' Daisy says. 'Stay still.'

On her belly, she wiggles under a bit, and pushes Selvi's head to the floor. The body goes limp.

Has she killed her?

She manages to cradle Selvi's head to pull her backwards and free. She slides out like Dad used to after fixing the car. Selvi has terrified rabbit eyes and looks like she's been in a wind machine. Daisy drags her into a sitting position with her legs sticking out in front like a Barbie doll. Then she helps her stand. Selvi sways back and Daisy jumps behind just in time.

They sit side by side on the edge of the bed. Daisy holds the bony hand.

'Selv, look.' She copies the way Charlie says it, and points at his blue words on the board.

Up Selvi gets and shuffles towards the board. Daisy follows in case she falls. Selvi puts her finger on the white surface to see if it moves. She looks like she's drawing snakes on a misted-up window. She's on a mission of some kind, then she drops her hand and walks off, bored of playing.

The clock has a loud tick. Daisy's life oozing away minute by minute. The numbers on the clock are large, like the one at the clinic.

'It's five past eight now.' Daisy points to the five and then to the eight. Selvi's eyes are hypnotised by the movements. Daisy's breathing is going very fast, but her new pet is calming; her eyes are fixed and open.

Selvi's eyes are like Dad's before he went. Empty, hollow, pointless eyes. Daisy refuses to wait for that. No one can force her.

On the sideboard, Daisy spots a flat tin with a dent in the middle of the lid, it's decorated with clouds. Its hinges are brown, it's stiff to open. Inside is a row of pencils ordered by colour.

Selvi's purring is getting louder, is she going to lose it again? Will she freak if her stuff is touched? Daisy moves dead slow, not speaking. Selvi moves towards her tin. For a moment she stares at the pencils, all in a row. Then, in slow motion, she reaches with an E.T. finger across the crayons so they roll. When one rolls, they all roll making a clicking sound. Selvi jerks away her finger as if the pencils are hot, then looks at Daisy like she's expecting something. Daisy has no clue what she's after. Impulsively, she runs her finger over the pencils just like the old lady had done. The chunky ring she nicked from the corner shop makes the clicking louder. Selvi watches the teenage hand.

'There are ten in the bed and the little one said, roll over, roll over, so they all rolled over and one fell out,' Daisy whispers the song and pushes a pencil over the edge.

Selvi laughs, she actually laughs.

Daisy does it again. 'There are nine in the bed and the little one said, roll over, roll over, so they all rolled over and one fell out.' She pushes another one, and it happens again. Selvi laughs. She actually laughs. Like Bill laughs, as if it's hilarious when it so isn't. Selvi's laugh makes Daisy laugh. Usually, she's like a corpse from the living dead. And now she's laughing. This is actually quite cool. Daisy elbows the old girl so they can have a giggle together, but Selvi doesn't move.

By the time they get to five, Daisy has had enough. She needs to get on with her jobs or Patsy will cop a strop. When she tries to walk off, the mental moaning restarts. So, Daisy carries on, singing a bit louder. Each time the pencil falls, giggles burst out of this strange little alien.

How long does she carry on? Daisy's not sure how long she sits there singing with Selvi, but eventually the door opens and Charlie's back. Usually, he bursts in with lots of chat about where he's been and who he's seen. But he's statue still and not chatting. His coat is zipped up to his chin, his flat cap is shielding his eyes and he's crying. There are tears dripping onto his cheeks. Daisy has no idea what to do. She's never seen an old boy cry.

'I heard her laugh,' Charles says, 'outside the door, I heard her laugh.'

What must he think? Daisy's face feels hot. Charles must've been listening. He's heard her playing a silly game and singing like a baby.

'It was my singing,' she whispers, blushing like an idiot.

'I thought my hearing aid was playing up. From outside the door, I heard her laugh but she doesn't laugh anymore, just frets and cries or sleeps.'

His tears keep going but he doesn't seem to care. 'How glorious it was to hear my girl laugh again. Thank you, thank you so, so much.'

Daisy panics. She doesn't need him squeezing her face. What's up with this place? Why is everyone so wacko today?

'You're welcome, I better go, I'm supposed to be doing the teas, Penny will shoot me.'

Daisy's shift has finally ended. She needs warmth and a rest. A place to be herself surrounded by her stuff. She waits for Penny to leave reception and scribbles her name and the time she left. Then she darts outside, walks around the perimeter and uses her key card to get into blue corridor the back way. She snitched a key card from Patsy's desk. Now, she has open access. A massive win for team Daisy.

Blue staff check hardly at all. The home is short staffed, and the blue lot can't cry out, so they get left for hours. She's kept a diary, so she knows the system. The toilets, main staffroom, dining hall and entrance are all in yellow corridor.

She stands outside the white door. The peeps in blue corridor never escape. There's a photo on the door. A hot bloke with his fake lady and ugly kid. The sea is behind them. Averting her eyes from the image on the door, she pushes the handle.

Her heart thuds hard. 'If you're found in areas outside your work, you'll be dismissed,' Penny had warned. Oh well, that won't be so bad especially now she has Sach and the maggot.

The radio is on; makes the staff feel less guilty. Daisy looks at coma boy. From her surveillance he gets left the most. She's never seen him move; he makes the occasional groan like a zombie waking from the dead. Once his leg made a couple of jerks under the cover. She nearly had a heart attack.

When she broke into blue corridor for the first time, she could not believe her luck. She now spends at least two or three hours here every day. There's a window that opens enough to smoke from and it looks out to a wall no one passes. The room is wide, the bed is enormous, and he sleeps all the time, literally all the time.

Today, he's curled up in his usual tight comma. At first, she found it a bit creepy being in a room with his body. Once she got over the ick, the dribble and smell, it was all good.

He never wakes, just mumbles. Daisy and her silent companion. And an unused en suite in the hotel package. Livin' the dream, Daisy girl.

There's nothing wrong with her hearing and all the nurses wear squeaky plastic clogs, so as long as she doesn't wear headphones, she can hear them a mile off.

Each time she arrives, there are rituals to complete. First, open top drawer and check through his wallet. Behind a crumpled plastic window is a smiling family: mum, dad and that ugly kid with the head too big for its skinny bod. Slipping her fingers inside to check there is cash, she's reassured. He can't use it. She's glad it's there just in case.

She closes the drawer with her knee, it needs fixing. She doubts anyone checks but if they do, they'll find it just as it was.

The mirrored wardrobe holds a box of cards. She loves reading his stuff, a proper nosey parker, Gran would say. She reads a few bits and bobs, an old Father's Day card, folded in two, too big for the shoe box. She unfolds it. A big pink heart on the front, held by a cartoon teddy bear. The writing says, 'To the best Daddy'.

The door slides shut with a click. She can see her reflection and the bed with its humped shape. Her body shivers. Is she a freak, wanting to be here? Alone with him.

Where are all the people who knew him before he was a bundle under a blanket? What would people say if they knew she came in here? What would he say? Who knows? He is still. No noise. Might as well be dead.

Daisy slips into the high-back chair she now considers hers. Much to her fury, she remembers yesterday. How dare they, especially Ben? They can't force her to be tested. When she's eighteen she'll do a bunk and be alone where no one knows her. She'll get sterilised just in case but when her words go weird and her mouth goes droopy and drunk, she'll be brave and end it herself. That lot will be the last to know. She had forgotten they were meeting to yack about her, forgotten she was meant to be there too. Sach had got a last-minute call to work so she'd rushed from work and got H from pre-school. She had wanted to scrounge some toast from Gran. When she saw the extra cars, Daisy had crept around the back to listen. She had to put her finger over the maggot's mouth to keep him quiet.

Her mother was on her throne, all haughty, legs crossed like she's still posh with a big car and a fancy house. Her high-pitched screech spewing over Ben.

Daisy grabs the soft blanket from underneath the plastic-covered chair. She tucks in both sides like she does for Haizeh. It's hours before the next catheter check. She sets an alarm on her phone and tugs the blanket up to her chin.

Closing her eyes, she imagines cuddling close to Dad, smelling his aftershave and feeling his chest move up and down. Soon, she's having their Saturday lie-in, waiting for mum to bring breakfast in bed. She sticks in her thumb and sucks hard. Then she's asleep. Easy as that.

Dear Daisy,

I can't control the future, nor would I wish to control yours. (Well, maybe just a tad!) You are you. So, what I am about to say comes from my spleen.

Don't believe what people tell you. Thriving in life is a choice, having good friends, a meaningful purpose and a supportive partner is not down to luck. Trust me, it's possible to up your chances of finding the life you deserve.

First, my baby girl, get to know yourself. Discover what's inside you that makes you think what you think, feel what you feel, do what you do.

I should have done that earlier, definitely before I got married or had you. I did lots of hurting because I hadn't figured that stuff out. My love for you is thicker than water (less thick than Greek yogurt) so you'll be surprised by this, but you'll have scars from your childhood, everyone does. If you leave those wounds unknown or unattended, they'll get in the way of future you. The future you I dream of.

To be able to love well, you need the ability to love yourself. To forgive others, you will need the ability to forgive yourself. To show compassion and care for others, you have to first learn self-compassion and self-care.

Journaling like I do is excellent but if you feel stuck, therapy can give you the essential tools to live a happier life. It helped me gain confidence, listen better, and talk honestly.

One more piece of fatherly advice, get to know your body. Women are more complicated than men. You're savvy so you'll do your research but be careful about taking medications with high dose hormones, they mess up your body. Chart your cycles and know your body. It's the best way to care for your biological health and spot any serious illness before it's too late.

If you only knew how proud I am of you. You have already given me joys beyond my deserving. To see you growing, learning, thinking and making friends fills me with all the confidence I need to sign out with dignity.

Daddy xx

27

Dorothy

Dorothy shivers. It's gone eleven p.m. Owen forced her to promise she wouldn't come here, to his resting place. Of late, family promises have become cheap.

Owen chose this place. He planned his exit with meticulous detail. This place was spacious and overlooked trees and a vast wild meadow. They were reassured it was never overrun by visitors, especially this section at the back.

Like her, Owen could hold an audience, be the life and soul. But he felt most restored after time alone, quiet time with his books and his music. He would have hated to be abandoned in a noisy place to be studied by random passers-by. The night security man at the gate offers a solemn nod. She plonks herself on the uninviting seat.

She's glad she can come when she pleases, when others have long gone. This is her second time. For years she did as she was told and stayed away. He wanted his life celebrated. He didn't want to be mourned amidst misery. She understood. This year she came on his birthday. After all that's happened, she needed a connection with who he was.

She flicks through her pile of dog-eared photos. Owen at his thirtieth, him in a ridiculous shirt for the Abba fancy dress. Her favourite was taken on a rare day out at Littlehampton. Owen and Ben sitting close on a low wall overlooking the waves. Peter took the photo and she's standing behind her boys, an arm on each. The sky is cloudless, and Ben is covered in ice cream. Owen is too big for the wall and his legs are sticking out at an odd angle. They all look so happy.

She shoves them back in her pocket, overcome with unwanted emotion. Why did she come?

The week he brought the letter was after his first set of tests. Dr Susie Venn had told him they needed to wait for the final results before she would confirm a diagnosis of FTD. Owen had noticed the deterioration. He didn't need others to point out that the content of his sentences was diminishing. The diagnosis confirmed what they had suspected for months.

When Owen turned up that summer evening, the neighbours were having a BBQ. Owen had stood on the door, smiled and inhaled.

'I love that smell,' he'd laughed. 'Whatever the veggies say, the smell of a burger is simply divine.'

Oh, how she loved her boy.

She had welcomed him over the threshold with a hug and resisted the temptation to help when he struggled to remove his coat.

'I won't wait until I can't smell, taste or see,' was his introduction to the evening's agenda.

She had insisted they ordered a take-out. He had agreed to stay quiet and humour her whilst they shared a lamb bhuna with pilau. His favourite. They had sat outside in the evening sun and laughed about Ben's latest plan to buy a narrow boat. Then Owen indulged her whilst she talked of his childhood as if they'd visited Littlehampton every weekend. He didn't mention she was rarely home when he was little.

The moment she finished her last mouthful Owen said, 'Let's go inside,' in the tone reserved for disciplining Daisy.

He began to gather up the plates. The top bowl slipped and smashed.

'I'm done. I don't want to wait. You have to promise . . .'

The evening was memorable for all the wrong reasons. It was as ghastly as many things have been since. He had leaflets for a clinic in Switzerland. She had cried and argued.

'It's my right to end my life when I want,' he had shouted. This version of Owen was new. Owen never raised his voice at her, not even as a teenager. His tempers were becoming increasingly frequent.

'When I look in the mirror. When I see Daisy and Estelle, I wish I'd never been born,' he'd raged with his hands above his head, like he wanted to rip out his hair in desperation.

She went over to him, tried to get close, to hold him but he had shaken her off, pushed her away and screamed in her face.

'You should've done what your heart desired. You should have killed me when you had the chance.'

When she fell back into the chair, her hand over her mouth, he knew he had gone too far, even in his diminished neurological state.

'How could you say such a thing? I always wanted you,' she whispered.

For a moment he stayed quiet. Regret on his beautiful face.

When he spoke, he had returned to himself. He spoke quietly of a time she didn't want to remember. A time when she was stupid, indiscreet, but mostly plain selfish.

'I heard you. When I was in secondary, I heard you talking to Carole Curtis, from the hospital. You did that all the time. Once I was upstairs, you and she would drink too much and talk too much. I used to sit on the stairs and listen. Mostly you ranted about men, the NHS or the doctors but . . .' He tailed off.

'What? What do you think you heard?'

'Mum, I don't blame you. But I know what I heard, and I know it's the truth.'

'Tell me?'

'You said you wanted rid of the baby. You wanted rid of me. You said that having grown up in a tiny town controlled by tiny-minded parents, that you wanted an escape, and a baby wasn't part of the plan.'

'That's all true. I didn't plan on a pregnancy as a twenty-year-old. I had finally escaped that dreadful fishing village; I had qualified as a midwife and I wanted to do well. I didn't want to end up like your nan, beholden to a man, waiting each week for my housekeeping while he went to the pub.'

'But you told Carole you had booked an abortion, that you had been sedated on the operating table with your legs in the air.'

'That was true. And then your father came, or should I say your sperm donor. Peter was your dad.'

'How come?'

'I was on the table. But my heart wasn't in it. However much I wanted my life back, I couldn't kill a baby. I'd worked on the wards long enough to see miscarriages and I knew the truth. But didn't have the courage to stop it.'

'How did my father help?'

'He had always wanted you. He didn't know what I was planning but he went to the flat and found the appointment card. He made a massive fuss at the clinic. He thumped a security guard and burst in. He literally dragged me off the bed and out. When I arrived home, I was bare footed with a split gown. We cracked open a bottle of gin.'

‘How wise,’ Owen snapped.

‘Fair. I wasn’t wise and I never got my clothes back.’

Owen hadn’t been able to resist a smile.

‘But from that day on I made plans. We found a flat. I told work and they were fine about me taking maternity and then returning. I promise, from the moment I left that table, you were wanted. I wanted you.’

‘Well. My father was soon off.’

‘He did love you, though. We both did. If what you have is genetic then I think he probably had it. He had a terrible temper and was so stupid.’

‘Thanks for the heads-up.’

‘I’m so sorry. That was clumsy.’

They had finished the evening on good terms, but she wasn’t surprised when he turned up the following evening, a fat envelope in his hand.

Dorothy had promised she would take the burden of following his wishes; not Estelle or Ben, but her. She had promised to help him finish well. She had promised she would follow the instructions and see it through. She had promised that they wouldn’t return to weep and wail.

She pulls herself off the seat and retraces her steps. Her ancient body trembles as she stands. She’s sure she’s aged ten years in the last three.

There’s Christmas carols playing in the high street. Impressive lights hang from a pole outside each shop. A Christmas tree, an angel and a star. Music that would’ve once lifted her spirits has no impact whatsoever. You’re a miserable so and so. She would love to wrench each tasteful display from their anchor and haul them under the approaching cars. She can’t wait for Christmas to be over. At least in January, she'll have permission to feel this sorrow and despair.

She spots the late-night shop. Maybe sourdough toast with Callie's homemade marmalade might give her a welcome boost. Callie's homemaking is a new thing. She hasn't had time to ask Ben about that. She hopes they're nesting. She'd love another grandchild. Head down, she crosses the road.

'Dorothy,' she hears.

Please don't let that be a neighbour. She wants to be alone, needs to be.

'Gran.'

She whips around. Only one voice would shout that. She can't see anyone. When she's about to give up, doubting her sanity, it comes again.

'Gran, wait. It's us.'

Daisy and Ryan rush out from the Twitten opposite Tesco. That's why she couldn't see them. They must've seen her when she passed the entrance.

'Gran, what are you doing out? It's far too late,' Daisy says like she's the community warden appointed to watch over the wandering elderly.

'I would ask you the same question. And it's most definitely too late for that little one.'

The little boy who came to the house is hiding behind Ryan. Ryan looks sheepish and drops his cigarette as if she was born yesterday. She wonders if Daisy knows he's been around hers.

'We're taking him home. His mum is doing heaps of extra shifts at the hospital, and we mind him.'

Dorothy crouches to speak to Haizeh.

'I bet you're tired little man, aren't you?'

He nods, looks at her from under thick lashes.

'Here you go,' Dorothy hands him a packet of sweets from her pocket and stands up. 'What are you two thinking? He's only little. He shouldn't be dragged around in the middle of the night, inhaling smoke. He should be tucked up, snug as a bug,' she says with her hand resting on the little one's head.

Daisy looks at her feet and it's Ryan who speaks.

'We tried to, but Chez is at theirs and Daisy isn't a fan.'

''Cos he's a total dick.'

'Daisy! Watch your mouth.'

Ryan can't resist a smirk.

'Right,' Dorothy announces. 'You're all coming back to mine.'

Daisy looks at Ryan, and Ryan looks at Daisy. They both shrug. Dorothy inhales and begins a quick march up the high street holding the little boy's hand. He doesn't protest.

'I'll follow on when I've got some snacks. I know where she lives,' Ryan says, running back to the shop.

'You do?' Daisy asks before running to catch Gran.

28

Ben

Thanks to his mother, Ben's most unwanted Christmas present was a ticket to see dead bodies.

'It's art, I thought you were an artist,' she had said when she saw his face. Then he saw Daisy wink at her grandmother.

As he opened the envelope, he knew he'd been set up. The previous summer, Dorothy, Ben, Callie and Daisy had gone on a rare day trip to the Science Museum in London. It was the sort of thing Owen would've done with Daisy. Ben knew that Daisy would decline if he proposed such a trip for her upcoming birthday, so he bought tickets and told his mother to give them. Daisy continues to show respect for her grandmother even when she is narked.

His plan had worked. Daisy was in a good mood, and they had enjoyed the day and ended in McDonald's. Daisy spotted the poster for an exhibition of plasticised bodies. Callie has an insatiable curiosity for the macabre in science, it's why she and Daisy get on. She jolted out of her seat and rushed to the advert as if supernaturally powered. She returned and sidled up to Callie.

'Hey, do you fancy a romantic break in the new year, you and Ben?'

'What a good idea,' Callie laughed, knowing Ben would hate such a thing. He's stupidly squeamish.

The memory of that conversation came flooding back at gift-opening time. Dorothy handed Callie and Ben identical rectangles covered in Santa wrap. Daisy sat with her arms folded and a smug look.

Apart from a few moments like that, when their old family with its banter and ease peeked out, Christmas was dire.

Estelle invited them just for lunch, not the usual Christmas Eve then Christmas Day breakfast and lunch. Ben suspects Estelle hoped Daisy might come back for Christmas week. She hasn't been sleeping at home. Estelle thinks she's sleeping in the flats on the estate with her friends. He's looked around the park a few times, but she hasn't been there. He saw that girl with the matted hair and piercings, but she has a new set of disciples. Neither Daisy nor that boy she likes were there.

Ben misses Daisy. He knows that's pretty sad for a grown man, but they were mates.

On Christmas Day, Daisy arrived home a few minutes before lunch looking like she hadn't slept. No one had much to say. His mother worked hard with gentle questions about Daisy's work and music. Daisy was civil, responding with one or two words.

He nearly choked on a stuffing ball, when out of the blue his mother had said, 'I bet Haizeh's excited about Santa,' as if Daisy has a family and lives in a modern semi with her professional husband.

Ben resisted the temptation to jerk his head away from his end of the table and fire a hundred questions at Daisy.

Is it that boy from the other day?

Why is he with you? How do you know his mum?

Is Ryan the dad? Of course, Ryan isn't the dad. Ben knows exactly who the dad is. But does the kid think Ryan is his dad?

You can't do that.

You must stop.

You have no idea.

Instead, he pretended to have little interest. He listened to the back and forth between his mother and Daisy.

'Don't forget to take my little something. I've left it under the tree with some new clothes for Ryan.'

'That's kind.'

'Well, he clearly needed some, didn't he?' His mother had laughed.

'Yes, he did. His dad doesn't give him any money.'

'And what are Sachini and Haizeh doing today? Do they even celebrate Christmas?'

'Gran.' Daisy rolled her eyes. 'Sach is Sri Lankan, but Haizeh is British. Of course, they celebrate. He's learnt all the Santa stuff at pre-school. He was well excited this morning.'

Ben repeated that name in his head. Sachini. Sachini. That person he's feared. That person he terrified. Sachini. Hearing her name spoken here is discombobulating. This is the shadow who filled him with terror and guilt. But she's a person with a name. She's not a monster, she's a mummy who has clearly done right by her child. By Owen's child. Mostly, Daisy is a pale reflection of the bright-eyed genius that was his niece, but when she spoke of Haizeh and how she'd been helping Sachini whilst she worked to escape the room she was in, Daisy lit up. Her face was animated, there was light in her eyes, and it made Ben cry.

For a horrid moment, the room fell silent. Daisy's voice, Callie and Estelle's chatter faded to nothing. The table laden with Christmas indulgence blurred. He could see nothing but an abandoned, fatherless child and a young woman who thought he might steal her boy. What kind of monster did that make him?

Ben made a silent promise. He promised he would make things right by everyone.

He promised he would tell Callie. Tell her there is a child. Owen's child. Haizeh. This family need to do right by Haizeh.

He reckoned using those dreaded tickets would give him time with Callie. For once he wasted no time. By the close of Boxing Day, he had made a date with his wife and booked online train tickets. If he has to suffer a load of dead bodies to get quality time and have a big conversation, so be it. Annoyingly she couldn't get out of a pre-booked meeting, so she is meeting him at Victoria. The teenage shop assistant at Paperchase is pulling the last of the tinsel from the window display. Already there are Valentines cards on display.

'Ben.' Callie envelopes him from behind before he has the chance to catch his breath or smell the obligatory Lush store at the station.

Ben laughs turning around to hug her properly.

'Come on, old girl, let's get this over with.'

'Shut up.' Callie gives him a playful shove reminiscent of their dating days. 'I can't wait. And you might surprise yourself.'

He does. The exhibition is absolutely fascinating. Bodies on bikes, playing sport and even mid sexual act, revealing the internal anatomy in all its glory.

He's jolted away from planning a cycling holiday for the spring by an intense feeling of sadness. It's like something is gripping his chest. It catches him before his brain has had chance to catch up.

Inside neat glass cabinets, a sequence of tiny foetuses have been placed in his eye line. The first one is the size of a fingertip, just five weeks from conception, undeniably a human form. An obvious spine is curled over with stumpy little arms and an eye already placed in the tiny head. For a few seconds, he's overwhelmed at the miracle of human life. Before he can take a second breath, a quick succession of dark thoughts smack him repeatedly in the face. Thoughts about life and death. Dad. Owen's father. Genetic curses. Foetuses and babies.

As his gaze is dragged to the final exhibit, he sees a life-sized model of a pregnant woman with a perfect baby in her womb. Callie is distracted by some wall art and is not looking where he is looking.

He studies the model. Her hands holding her unborn baby as if it's on the outside. He's glad he didn't see Sachini when she was heavily pregnant, it would've been too painful. When she stood in Owen's front porch, barely older than Daisy, Ben knew this couldn't have been an equal relationship. He was deeply troubled and knew he couldn't allow her to suffer more than she already had. His brother was three times her age and her supervisor. In that moment he lost all respect for his darling brother and that cut too deep. He had hoped he could stay deluded despite the evidence. Like his mother. Like Daisy. But he couldn't. There is right and there is wrong and what Owen did to Sachini was very wrong.

The guilt confuses him. But looking at this artistic representation he gains clarity. It's his misplaced loyalty to his brother that is wrong, not his behaviour towards the girl. He showed compassion. He gave her extra money that was his. He offered a hanky to wipe her tears and reassured her somehow it would all come right. *Sachini and Haizeh*, he whispers to himself. He can't wait any longer. Walking over to his wife, he taps her gently on the shoulder, glad no one else is around. She turns to face him; he holds both her hands.

'I let her keep the baby,' Ben says. 'There was no abortion.'

29

Daisy

Daisy sits cross-legged on the floor of what she now considers *her* room. Her room at The Orchards. Her room in blue corridor. She can't believe she's survived this dump for nearly six months. She perches on the end of the bed to prise open the creaky wardrobe. 'Don't worry, it's only me,' she reassures her sleeping partner. She's glad she can't see his face; it would mess with her head. She nods to the bed bundle, You okay? No response. She'll take that as a positive.

Her stuff is hidden so far back in the wardrobe that she has to get on the floor to retrieve it. She wonders if her body ached when she sat here last week or if these are the early symptoms. Her FTD file is with her letters in the tin. She nicked it from Primark. It's just the right size, shame the hinges are a bit wonky where she dropped it in her rush to escape the store detective. She knows she is becoming clumsier and stiffer.

The subjects are separated by colourful dividers. She should have an A level Biology file, not this. The sections should be photosynthesis, anatomy and biochemistry not the nature of the disease, testing dilemmas and genetic counselling. She has a new section for updated research and useful telephone numbers. Google has saved her most frequent searches. The FTD association is first up. It tells her she last went on this site at six thirty a.m. Every day she hopes the information will change. She longs to open the home page and see an announcement in capital letters: 'CURE FOUND'.

But the home page has not changed. A cheerful speech bubble asks if she's a new visitor to the association for Frontal Temporal Degeneration. Daisy hates that word. Degeneration. It's so aggressive. Degenerated Daisy. There's a drop-down menu and one of the options is 'Find Help – Share Hope'. Liars! Nothing helps and there's no hope. The site is brightly coloured with search options in compatible shades of lemon. A graphics geek worked hard to make a monster look less terrifying. Sorry, mate, epic fail!

At eighteen she can find out. She scribbles some facts she hasn't noticed before. Ninety per cent of people choose not to have the test . . . A new person has been appointed as the Sussex advisor . . . A pop-in café has started online (announcement in sugary pink). The section for young people has been updated. Get peer support. As if being around other degens might help. No thanks.

She's had enough. She forces the file back in the tin and shoves it back in the wardrobe. It's filthy in there. She uses the arm of the chair to get off the floor. Yep. She's definitely getting stiffer.

The negative thing about this comfy chair is she can see her reflection. The pattern of the light shows up the scar across her eyebrow. She rearranges her jagged fringe to vanish it.

After that, Dad went away.

Mum told the social worker she could no longer cope. Dad was smashing everything. They had locks on the bedrooms as he got confused at night. He didn't know what he'd done until after, then he'd cry, be ashamed. He hated what was happening. For some reason, he picked on Daisy more than anyone. He'd shove her if she got close. Call her stupid for losing the remote when he'd put it in the fridge.

Daisy's thoughts spin until her knotted stomach makes it impossible to keep still. Whatever position she shifts to, her mind won't stop racing, her breathing won't slow. She digs deep into her pocket. She's tried to give up but sometimes nothing else works. She's shivering. Her hand knows what to do. The coldness of the metal provides the sign. Her whole body relaxes, relief is close. The bad feelings ooze out of the tiny holes in her thigh as she makes the rhythmic stabs.

When she's cleaned up, she flushes away the evidence. She paces the room with only an hour to kill before her shift starts.

Daisy opens her room door a crack, she leans and listens. The morning staff won't be for another half-hour but occasionally Patsy does a random check. Daisy leaves blue corridor by the fire exit; another broken thing Derrick hasn't fixed. One day she'll call the police and get him done. She circles the building and goes out the gate, over to the pub and then retraces her steps to the main entrance. She almost got caught last week coming the wrong way. Before she can disentangle her bag from the sliding doors, Penny is pushing a hideous green apron in her face.

'Take a chill pill,' Daisy snaps, snatching the offending item.

Penny makes that face but doesn't say anything. She nods towards yellow corridor.

'Charlie's asking for you. He's had a bad night. He wants half an hour for breakfast in peace and says you're the only person who settles Selvi. Can you go?'

Daisy gives Penny a hard stare but is secretly pleased Charles has asked for her.

'S'pose.'

Charles has changed the photo on the door; Daisy doesn't get why he does that. A smart lady in a navy suit is smiling. She is holding hands with a little boy the same age as Haizeh. He's dressed like a sailor, looks a bit stupid. It's Selvi and her son Chester. The door photos were Derrick's idea. When she's bored, she kills time matching photos with the zombies plodding about in the corridors.

'Look. It's who you like,' Charles says to Selvi's back, she ignores him. 'I am sorry, love, I can't remember your name, my head's not so sharp these days.'

'No worries, it's Daisy.'

Selvi is in a long white nightie. Daisy can see she's naked underneath, which gives her the total ick. She looks like a cartoon ghost, moaning like a lunatic, saying the same word over and over. Sounds like 'where' but she's not looking for anything.

Charlie holds out some pants in front of her. 'These?'

She ignores him. Her hands are covering her ears, like a hear no evil monkey, but she's the one making the noise. She totters to look out of the patio doors into the gardens. Her eyes are fixed on something, but there's nothing there.

Charles walks up behind his wife and puts a hand on her shoulder. 'Selvi, love, Daisy is here, have a look.'

He uses his other arm to steer her but she's not moving, he gives up and talks to her back. His voice is soothing, makes Daisy wanna lie down. The new night nurse didn't clear off until two a.m. so she's had hardly any sleep.

'I'm going for breakfast, be back soon,' Charles says, like Selvi gets him. Then he says to Daisy, like there's loads of choice, 'I'm going to the daffodil restaurant. Can you keep an eye for half an hour?'

Selvi turns around, keeping her ears covered; her eyes are not seeing eyes, just blank staring ones.

'Sure, it's easier sitting in here than cleaning toilets,' Daisy says.

As he leaves, he turns back and waits.

'She'll be fine.' Daisy smiles.

Gently she pushes Charles out the door.

Selvi hasn't noticed it's just Daisy now. Daisy can't figure how she can stare for so long. Penny said in the Bible someone's wife turned into a pillar of salt for looking backwards. Selvi's as pale as salt.

'Alright, Selv?' Daisy's taller. She bends to look into her eyes. Selvi doesn't respond. Should she stare her down or get on with something else?

The empty bed looks very inviting, she could easily take a half-hour kip. Selvi can't tell. She slings her legs over the armchair and rests her feet on the bed. All the rooms are set up the same. She keeps forgetting room thirteen isn't hers. She was sure she heard breathing outside her door last night. It was pretty terrifying, but she worked out she can fit in the bottom of the wardrobe if she curls tight. No one came. Maybe it's the ghosts. All the peeps who've died prowl about haunting the lazy night staff who don't bother to check people. Coma boy should be glad Daisy's his sleeping partner, that she's keeping an eye. Who knows what would happen if he needed something?

Selvi seems happy enough staring at the wall, so Daisy closes her eyes. She feels herself falling asleep until her head jerks back and hits the wall with a thud.

'Ouch,' says the old lady and rubs the back of her head.

'Thanks, mate,' Daisy replies.

The sudden movement has agitated her. Selvi starts to pace. She won't stop. She rocks from side to side, like she's winding herself up.

The tin of pencils is on the side. She hums the bed song that made Selvi laugh and unhooks the catch. A slipper smacks it clean out of her hands. The pencils go flying.

Daisy swears. Good job Selv can't snitch. Crawling on the floor Daisy puts the pencils back in a colour spectrum and stands slowly. Charles is always slow and quiet. She returns the rusty container with one eye on the other slipper.

'Okay, so you're not in a singing mood today, I get that. Just give me the heads-up, next time. No need for the GBH.'

Selvi looks puzzled but stays calm.

'What do you fancy then?'

On the bedside cabinet there are three books on Charles's side.

The top book is called *Contented Dementia*. Selvi is walking up to the window and back to the bed, over and over. She doesn't look very content. The second book is a Bible, not the brown one Penny puts in all the rooms – that's on the shelf – this is black leather, the pages have gold edges, a big chunk of gold in a black box. Selvi snatches the heavy book with remarkable vigour. Daisy puts a hand across her face and ducks, waiting.

Nothing happens, Selvi looks as if she's reading, but it's upside down. After a few lines, the book slips onto the floor, it lands with pages crumpled underneath, like Daisy's new bike when Dad smashed it in the road.

'Am guessing you're done with reading for today, then. I hope that hubby of yours won't be cross when he sees his holy book with creased pages.' Selvi goes back to her pacing. Daisy does her best to press the pages flat.

This is more exhausting than babysitting Haizeh.

Daisy, read to me.

Daisy, dress my doll.

Daisy, chase me.

Daisy, lift me upside down.

She's glad Ryan's been helping. Sachini has been in a right state since Christmas. She says she's got to move Haizeh's school, that she needs to double her wages to get away. She said there's a man after her, but she won't say who. Daisy bets it's Chez or one of his mates.

Selvi's still pacing.

The last book on Charles's bedside cabinet is a children's book she recognises. They had the whole series, she loved them.

It was Dad's job to do bedtime unless he worked late. He would get home, change out of his suit and race down the last few steps, burst into the sitting room and grab her in his arms. Together they would fall back onto the large brown sofa, so it nearly tipped up.

'Owen!' Mum would shout. 'Be careful.'

They must've read other books, but she only remembers the old-fashioned book and these feisty girl ones.

Both her parents approved of these books; she remembers Dad bringing home the first one. 'Look at this, a book where the girl isn't waiting to be kissed by a handsome prince.'

When her grandparents gave her books Dad considered 'soppy trash' they went on the fire.

'This one is *Blaze and the Terrible Night*,' Daisy says to Selvi.

On the front cover, a girl dressed in red trousers hangs off a rope swing. Her face shows determination, and her hair is short and spiky. On her feet, she's wearing heavy black boots with laces all the way up. They're similar to the ones Daisy has on.

Selvi seems content on the same path through the carpet flowerbed. Wiggling to get comfy on the bed, Daisy opens the book for a sneaky peek, but she hears Charles. She shuffles his reading material back and jumps in the chair as if she's never moved.

'No smiles today, then?' Charles looks sad.

'Not really, just that, over and over,' she says, nodding to Selvi, still pacing.

'Come here,' Charles says to Daisy. He points to the exact route Selvi is tracking, they move to let her pass by. 'Look, the carpet is almost threadbare. You'd think she'd run out of steam, wouldn't you? She's been doing that since three a.m.' He breathes a long sigh.

Daisy wants to go. She's missed her break.

'She went normal for a few minutes, though,' Daisy says, trying to cheer him up.

'What do you mean?'

'She started reading from your Bible.'

Charlie smiles. 'She does that, she knows her Bible. If you find the right trigger, sometimes she'll sing. She can do rhymes, numbers, days and months if she's in the mood. Occasionally a line from one of the books she illustrated will burst out. I love it when she briefly "goes normal".' He smiles. 'Each time, I imagine there's going to be a miracle, but she rarely stays like that for more than a few minutes. She's lost in there and I can't rescue her.'

The voice in Daisy's head is pleading, *please don't cry, old man.* She searches for a question. 'What did she illustrate?'

'She was a fabulous artist. She did lots, but we made decent money out of books that were forward-thinking for their time. It wasn't like now when girls can do whatever they want.'

Charles goes over to his side of the bed; Daisy knows what he's looking for.

'*Blaze and the Terrible Night*?' Daisy reads, trying hard to look curious.

'I wrote the words, and she did the pictures. We were a good team, me and my girl.'

For the first time, Daisy reads the names at the bottom of the book.

Charles and Selvi Bandara.

'No way. *You* did these?'

'We did.'

'Wow, that's so cool, they are awesome stories, we had the entire series, I was Blaze, and my friend was Spark. We told her younger sister that the only girl left was Burn, that made her cry.'

Charles is laughing. 'We wrote them for our daughters. Selvi hated all the Disney princess stuff. She said it made girls appear useless. She wanted girls to feel strong and brave.'

'That's why Dad liked them. That's what he wanted for me. I can't believe you wrote those books, that's so cool, I know a proper famous person, I can't wait to tell . . . my gran.'

A knock at the door stops Selvi in her tracks.

Patsy comes in uninvited. She completely ignores Charles.

Daisy opens her mouth to quote Penny – ‘People’s rooms are their homes and should be respected as such’ – but Patsy jumps in without making eye contact.

‘Can you start the tea trolley please? It’s ten minutes late already.’

‘My fault, I’ve been rambling. The lass has been trying to return to her duties. I’ve had a peaceful breakfast thanks to her. I think she reminds my wife of our eldest daughter.’

Daisy flashes him a grateful smile, that’s three smiles, a whole week’s worth. She’ll have to be extra grumpy for the rest of the day. Patsy leaves, muttering something about the schedule. Charles winks at Daisy.

‘Bye, Selv mate.’ Daisy offers a wave.

Selvi mumbles. Maybe she wants to say, Goodbye Daisy, I won’t tell you’ve been looking at his stuff and swearing if you don’t mention the slipper.

30

Dorothy

Dorothy is full of the joys of spring, literally and metaphorically. Outside in her garden, the tip of a daffodil is poking through the mud. Yesterday, her and Pen treated themselves to a potter around Leonardslee Gardens. It has been years since she has been. It was the first place Peter took her when they started walking out. She's not wanted to go since he died but there's been a lessening of the pain just lately.

He loved it there, with its glorious statues. They're a bit abstract for her taste but there's a lovely restaurant and they serve a divine cream tea.

'Your granddaughter is doing rather well,' Penny announced yesterday, wiping the cream from her lips.

'Really?'

'Indeed, she has quite a knack with our old folks. Astonishing. She's even dropped the false lashes!'

When Penny said that Dorothy had realised she has been feeling better because Daisy is better. Still blooming obnoxious at times but recently she's been lighter, brighter.

When she first came around with little Haizeh, Dorothy's heart sank. She didn't want Daisy thinking pregnancy was an escape and a flat. The look on Ben's face showed he feared the same.

But Dorothy has changed her mind.

'She's different, Pen,' she told her friend.

'Different how?'

'I'm not sure. I think caring for her new friend and the little boy has given her purpose.'

When Dorothy was home lying in bed last night, she realised Daisy's new purpose had rubbed off on her. She can see that Ryan has taken a shine to Daisy and watching the two of them with the lad is lovely. For the first time in months Daisy is laughing. Not the spiteful titter she's been fond of lately, but a childlike belly laugh. The other day, Ryan and Haizeh were play fighting on her carpet. Dorothy was watching Ryan make silly faces which Haizeh found hilarious. Then she saw Daisy. Daisy wasn't sneering, or sulking. She wasn't on her phone or distracted. She was leaning forward, doubled over, laughing. A proper side-splitting uninhibited laugh. Dorothy had stopped in her tracks. She couldn't resist it. She squeezed into the chair next to Daisy, slid her arm around her shoulders and hugged her. Just at that moment Ryan got silly again and the two of them had laughed and laughed as the boys rolled around the floor. It was like their old family. Laughter and silliness not tears and fear.

She realised she felt better. Since Christmas the pain has felt less raw, and she knows that's because Daisy is changing. Dorothy is lapping up her maternal role with the three of them. Yesterday was 8 April, Peter's birthday, and for the first time in years she felt relaxed. She let it pass with a nod of acknowledgement but no heart-wrenching sobs.

Things are looking up with Ben as well. Callie text yesterday to thank her for the body exhibition tickets and to say they both found it fascinating. Ben's been in Milan for the last fortnight on a work trip, but she popped into the gallery. Kasia, who she's warming to, allowed her a sneaky peek at Ben's work. It's good, genuinely positive like it used to be, before Owen, before everything went so wrong. Finally, things are looking up.

Today, she's treating Daisy and Haizeh to a trip to Lewes to that awful soft play shed that Daisy used to love. She's finally going to meet Haizeh's mama. Dorothy and the little chap have become great chums, but she's not yet met his mum. Usually, he's with Ryan or Daisy as they help out whilst mum is working. Sounds like the father wasn't dissimilar to Jonny. Did a bunk when the going got tough. At least Jonny pretended for a year. Daisy says Haizeh's father ran before the baby was born.

Dorothy can't wait. Daisy used to love it there. They are going by train as Haizeh has never travelled on one. Ryan got him some Thomas the Tank Engine books from Oxfam so now he's obsessed with the Fat Controller and James the Red Engine. Dorothy hopes he's not disappointed with British Rail. With the delays and mucky seats, she's usually disappointed.

Just as she's packed the last item, there's a long press on the doorbell. That can only be Daisy. She's still a little blighter at times.

'Perfect timing,' Dorothy says as she opens the door.

She crouches to embrace Haizeh before greeting Daisy and . . .

'This is Sachini, Grandma.'

Dorothy smiles at the slip of a girl who looks younger than Daisy. She doesn't know what she expected but it wasn't a mere child who looks exhausted and malnourished. There's no doubt that she's Haizeh's mother. They are two peas in a pod. Dorothy wants to tell her to loosen her ponytail. It's scraped back in the most unflattering way. If she let down her locks, all the boys would be running.

'Hello,' Sachini says with eyes to the floor.

'Do come in, dear. I'm nearly ready.'

Penny honks her horn to let them know their taxi to the station is ready and waiting. One by one they pile into her friend's battered Ford. Dorothy hopes the grubby passenger seat doesn't mark her new slacks. In the back, Daisy sits between the little boy and his mother, her legs pulled up to her chin. With anyone else she would complain she was squashed and insist she sat in the front or at least by the window. This friendship is changing her, thank heavens for that. Dorothy can't help the odd glance in her mirror. She's grown very fond of the little one. She hopes the girl will be easy company. So far she's said very little.

Much to everyone's amazement the train is punctual. Soon, they are speeding from the station accompanied by Haizeh's clapping and joyful chattering. He's perched on Daisy's lap, close to the window but can't keep still. He bounces up and down, down and up. He squeals with joy as he spots cows, chimneys and two kids messing about near the river.

When Haizeh calms enough to lean back into Daisy, Dorothy digs about in her bag for refreshment. She empties the treats onto the table.

'Enjoy,' she says, grateful everyone is smiling.

'Thank you, auntie,' Sachini says every time she takes anything.

'Thank you, auntie.'

'Thank you, auntie.'

'Give it a rest Sach. Chill. Say, cheers old biddy or something.'

'Daisy!' Dorothy chastises. 'It's rather nice to be around someone with manners.'

Over the din, Dorothy shouts, 'I'm not sure I'm going to cope with this place.'

Releasing an impatient sigh, Daisy says, 'Oh Gran.'

Sachini looks rather out of place. She's in a long navy skirt that would make Dorothy feel old-fashioned and a brown long-sleeved jumper with a polo neck. Dorothy's concerned she'll be boiling. Haizeh wears smart trousers and a shirt that would suit an elderly man. Usually, he has clothes that are far too small. These fit but she worries he'll roast in the play area.

'What you doing with wet bog roll?' Daisy asks Dorothy as if it's not obvious.

'Cleaning the chairs. I don't want chocolate stains on my clothes, and it'll be a shame if Haizeh spoils his.'

'Whatevs,' Daisy mutters.

Before Dorothy can respond, Haizeh comes running back.

'Auntie, Auntie, come see,' he says pulling Dorothy by the hand towards the inflated dinosaur in the middle of the huge ball pool.

She does her best to match the little one's enthusiasm as he jerks her from one activity to the next. He has a go on each thing but is often put off by the boisterous children who are free of inhibition. Dorothy is too old to be getting in amongst it all.

'Let's go and find Daisy,' she offers eventually. 'She'll be able to dive in with you. Keep you safe.'

Dorothy remembers the first time she came with Daisy. She wasn't a child who needed an adult for security. She was brave from birth, like her father. She was always a socialite and within minutes of arriving at a new place, Daisy would present a new chum as if she had known her all her life.

Much to her surprise, she returns to see Sachini spreading leaflets on the table.

'I've been looking up FTD and found this pack for younger people. I wondered if it might help you consider those big questions, help you decide about the test?' she is saying. Dorothy hangs back, keen to eavesdrop on Daisy's reaction.

'I have three of them. We have a family one, Ben got me one and then Gran gave me one three weeks ago. Didn't you?' she says, turning to Gran angrily.

Sachini looks embarrassed. She hurriedly gathers up the pamphlets and shoves them into their brightly coloured folder.

'Sorry, I'll go and get us a drink instead. What would you like?' she says, standing so Dorothy can sit down.

'Hot chocolate,' Daisy demands.

'What do you say?' Dorothy can't suppress it. Manners cost nothing. She wasn't raised to be like this. She sighs as she sits down next to Daisy, watching Sachini walk towards the counter. 'It's because we all care. You are lucky to have people who do.' Haizeh climbs on Daisy's lap and snuggles close, stretching his arms around her back. Daisy nuzzles into his neck. At least someone can reach her.

'I've got my own file, thanks,' Daisy snaps.

'Well done. What does your file say?'

'That the evil that smashed up my family will slowly smash up me. I've got it, it's obvs. My fingers shake and I mess up sentences. Just like him.'

Dorothy reaches for Daisy's hand. 'I know it's hard, pet, but even if you are FTD positive, you have plenty of time to explore life, pursue a career, have . . .'

Dorothy is relieved when Sachini arrives with a tray of drinks and cake. Daisy takes an oversized mouthful of carrot cake which appears to lighten her mood.

'Daisy, I'm sorry. I should mind my own business. When I was you age, I was pregnant. It was very lonely.'

'Yeah, but there was an answer to your problem. Kill it, have it, give it away. If my body had the same choices, I'd be good with that.'

Dorothy takes a sharp intake of breath. She wants to say, 'Daisy, how could you?' She thinks of the conversation she had with Owen. Life is so much more complex than these youngsters realise. Life isn't black and white.

'Harsh but true,' Sachini replies. Dorothy finds herself admiring this young lady; she's not defensive. Daisy stays quiet but pulls Haizeh closer and unconsciously kisses the top of his head, saying, 'You alright, me little maggot.'

It makes Dorothy smile. Owen and she were obsessed with the film *Matilda*. He used to call Daisy 'his wee maggot'.

'I just want to help,' continues Sachini. 'You've been a saviour for me. I'd like to help you. What are you thinking about the test? It must be confusing. I wouldn't know what to choose.'

'Yeah, not the best eighteenth present. Free gift from the NHS that I can't pass on to Oxfam. *They* want me to have it, so they can delete me like my dad.'

Dorothy is not going to let that one go.

'That is simply not true, and you know it. We . . . I guess we just feel a test will give you clarity.'

‘I have clarity, I’m not stupid unlike my family who haven’t even realised there’s a twelve-month wait so I can’t have it this year anyway.’

‘I can pay. We can find an independent neurologist in London, make a day of it,’ Dorothy offers.

‘Yeah! Wouldn’t that be a fun day? London Eye, a theatre and pick up my death sentence, maybe stop by the Tower on the way home. You can’t buy a solution to everything, you know.’

With that, Daisy throws back her chair, and stands. Holding Haizeh under his bottom, she walks away with him attached like a mummy kangaroo.

‘I’m so sorry,’ Dorothy says to her guest, who seems so kind and desperate to help.

‘No worries. She’s not angry with me. It’s fine, I get it. She’ll be alrighty in ten. She reminds me of my father. He was like that.’

‘What happened to him?’

‘He was killed in the war back home. That’s why I’m here.’

‘Now I understand why you and Daisy have become best buddies so quickly. You have lost a father and the life you knew, like she has.’

‘Yes. And she’s funny and kind.’

Dorothy wants to ask, ‘Is she?’ She knows that’s not fair as Daisy is often kind. Lately, she’s seen that again. She is grateful for this young woman who is being a sweet friend. She had previously thought the relationship was a one-way street. Daisy helping a single mum who didn’t care. She can see that she was wrong.

‘There you go,’ Dorothy says five minutes later, passing Sachini a decent coffee and a chocolate brownie. Sachini smiles. It is lovely to see the previously tense young person starting to unfold.

‘What have you got there?’ Dorothy asks, hoping she won’t be seen as a nosey parker.

Sachini has emptied her purse on the table. There are a few coins dotted about.

‘I like to pay my way,’ she says, pushing a crowd of ten and twenty pence pieces towards Dorothy.

‘Oh no. Please. It’s my pleasure.’

Sachini reticently puts the money away and in doing so exposes a few dog-eared photos inside her purse. It’s a scruffy black wallet that looks like it should belong to a man. Dorothy wonders if it was her father’s.

‘Can I see?’ Dorothy asks.

Sachini seems hesitant but tugs out the pictures from behind the wallet’s windows.

There are five photos. One is black and white. A family photo. Mum. Dad. Two young children. The mother is very serious and has a headscarf covering her hair.

‘Kind faces,’ Dorothy offers. ‘Aaah I can see who this is,’ she adds, putting the other three photos in a row. Haizeh as a newborn, then sitting on a wooden rocking horse and finally in his school jumper.

‘He’s a good boy. I love him so much.’ Sachini beams as they both look at her precious boy.

‘He’s very beautiful. And that sweet smile. I have to admit I’m already rather fond of the little chap.’

Dorothy spots one more photo still behind the wallet’s see-through pocket. It’s less close up. A photo of two adults walking down some stairs outside of what looks like an office block.

'What's that one?' Dorothy asks.

'Oh, that's the only one I have of Haizeh's father.'

'Daisy said he ran for the hills when you were pregnant. Why do you keep the photo?'

'He's still Haizeh's dad and maybe one day he'll want to know. Sometimes other people want to know. I like to show them. He was a respectable man.'

Sachini takes out the photo and puts in between them on top of the newborn one.

Dorothy turns it around to face her. That building is familiar.

It can't be.

Her neck is feeling damp. Her hands are trembling. The noise is overwhelming, but she can't hear or see.

She has been shown this photo before. She could never forget that. That day when she was happily mopping the floor. Humming along to the radio. Then he was there. That dirty, pitiful boy thrusting this photograph in her face.

'What do you say about this then?' the boy had spat in her face.

He had shown her a baby scan with her own surname typed underneath, but she'd torn it in two and thrown the bits in his face. She knew her son and he wouldn't have done that. He loved Estelle. He adored Daisy. He was a loyal and faithful son like his stepfather, not a philanderer like his biology intended. But then that vile-smelling kid had reached into his back pocket and pulled out a photograph. A photograph of her son leaving his office with a very young lady clinging to his arm. She hadn't looked too closely. She hadn't wanted to see.

He had demanded money. Two thousand pounds to pay for an abortion in a private clinic. So, they don't kill her in the process, he had spat out.

'And if I don't pay?' Dorothy was stupid enough to ask.

'Then this photo will be in the *County Times* on Friday.'

What could she do? The next day, she had gone very early to the bank, as if people watching her would know. She gave the cash to Ben and abandoned him to do the handover. She couldn't face the idea.

Dorothy's sight blurs. She is going to faint. Her words are jumbled as they tumble out.

'Sachini,' Dorothy gabbles, knocking over the bright red drink Haizeh has discarded. She doesn't care.

'Sachini,' she repeats, as the young woman scrabbles to gather her photos and mop the spreading liquid.

'Who is that man?' Dorothy finally manages to say. She is standing, her palms on the table to steady herself. 'What is the name of that man you are clinging onto?'

'Owen,' Sachini answers in a whisper and then adds, 'Owen Bowen-Jones.'

31

Ben

Yesterday, Daisy had called to ask for Ben's help; he's embarrassed to admit it thrilled him. When he saw her number, he would never have guessed what she was after.

Daisy lets herself in the front door while he's having breakfast. She's early and smiling.

'Come in whilst I finish my toast, then we'll head out,' Ben says offering Daisy a kiss on the cheek. She even accepts a quick hug.

'Have you seen Gran?' Daisy asks popping some bread in the toaster.

'Not since I got back from Italy. Is something up?'

Ben's mind goes straight to worst-case scenarios.

'Dunno. She took me and Haizeh to soft play on Friday and had some sort of funny turn.'

'That sounds stressful?'

'It was. She called a taxi and left me with my gob hanging open. I had to pay for the train home as we missed the connection.'

'I hope she's alright.'

'Yeah, she is. Penny called to say it was just that vertigo thing she gets. Gran's been texting every day, she doesn't want visitors, says she feels chucky all the time and is staying in bed.'

Daisy looks at her watch and panics.

'We need to go. I promised I would be there at ten.'

Ben lugs the large box of musical instruments that they've rounded up. When he's shunting it into the van, the yellow tambourine falls and crashes to the pavement.

Daisy used to love that tambourine when she was little, banging away at the most inappropriate moments.

He retrieves the yellow metal and brushes off the dirt. When he settles into the driver seat, Daisy is waiting patiently, smelling of perfume. His asthma never quite packed its bags, and the scent sets off a coughing fit.

'Make your mind up, smoke or perfume?' she laughs with a childish giggle rather than the mocking sneer he's become accustomed to. This giggle has resurfaced recently. She's now the one joking him out of a moody place.

They drive in companionable silence. Daisy jiggles to the music in her ears leaving Ben with his thoughts. They turn to that day in London with Callie. She was typically chill about his big reveal; looking back, he doesn't know why he was so worried about telling her. In the middle of the museum he had got teary, so she had looped her arm through his, led him downstairs to the café, and sat him at the table like a child. She had returned with a huge slab of chocolate cake and a can of coke.

'You did the only thing you could. Sounds like she was planning on keeping the baby, her choice was nothing to do with what you said. What's beyond me is why you've kept it to yourself. It's not your baby. Your affair.'

Ben had tried to explain the chaos of his psyche, his sense of responsibility towards her, his mother, Daisy, Owen and Estelle . . .

'They all need to know. I need to let Mum off her guilt and tell Daisy the kid she's minding is part of our family.'

'No, you don't, not straightaway at least,' Callie had said. 'Haizeh is four. All that's changed is you know who he is. A few more weeks won't make a difference. There's nothing to connect him to you and Daisy, and this town is small but not that small. We can tell them all when everyone's calmed down about the test.'

Sitting in the car with Daisy next to him, Ben isn't sure. There's so much that could go wrong with that plan. But, for now, he's going to follow his wife's wisdom. So far, she's shown more than him; he couldn't bring himself to tell her about the van and his bungled attempt to return the blackmailing favour.

When they arrive at The Orchards, Daisy leans against the automatic doors so Ben can follow with the box. No part of him wants to be here, in this place, with all its shadows. He's here for Daisy and he plans to get the job done and scarper ASAP.

'Come in,' Derrick says with a bark that wouldn't be out of place in an army camp. Then he gestures a bow to Daisy. Odd man. Penny comes rushing out. Unlike her husband, she never plods. He's met them several times at his mother's. A mismatched couple, Penny warm and cheery and her husband a pessimistic grump.

Wiping her hands on a tea towel, Penny announces, 'We're almost ready.'

They go into the day room. Armchairs are filled with ageing bodies, some more slumped than others. At least half are asleep, their heads bent low into their chests.

Daisy used to love the film *Toy Story*. She loved it when the humans left, and the toys came alive. Watching Daisy, he has a similar experience. She's a different person in this place, she's coming alive.

She's crouching in front of an elderly lady who looks too old to be alive, her body smaller than a child's. A few tufts of white hair don't stop the pink head shining through. Daisy is clasping the lady's hands, but neither is speaking. The old girl lifts her head just a fraction and Daisy bends lower to meet her eyes. Ben presumes this is Selvi, her favourite resident. The man next to them stands up and greets her with an Estelle-style peck on her cheek. Ben waits to see his niece flinch but instead she turns her face so he can kiss the other side.

Daisy backs into the middle of the circle still looking at her friendly couple before standing stiff and clapping her hands like a primary teacher.

'Good morning, everyone.' She extends the syllables to make her speech clear and slow. 'Welcome to the first singing group. This is my uncle Ben.' She points at him. 'He's here to play the guitar.' A few of them nod and smile in his direction. Daisy holds his guitar high in the air.

'Uncle Benny Hill,' one lady shouts.

'I'm sure you're right, Clara,' Daisy laughs. No hint of irritation at being interrupted.

Derrick points to a chair. Ben guesses that's for him. Penny has dragged an upright chair from the dining room and is perching on the edge as if not staying.

'Penny, can you give out the instruments, please?' Daisy says with new authority.

Penny is quick to her feet, taking instruments to the people with open eyes. Charles takes a wooden stick with bells on it. He tries to put it in his wife's hand, but she doesn't respond so keeps it for himself. Derrick joins in. He takes another bundle of musical toys and gives them out.

Daisy claps again even though no one is speaking.

'We're going to start with the alphabet song.' She looks over to him. They've practised a few tunes she downloaded from a website about singing for dementia. He hopes she won't be disappointed. She saw on a daytime television programme that one lady who hadn't uttered a word for six months started talking again after singing.

Looking round this room, he's not overwhelmed with optimism.

Daisy raises her arms to conduct, and Ben plays the first few chords to accompany her singing. He can't sing and play.

A . . . you're adorable . . .

B . . . you're so beautiful . . .

C . . . you're a cutie, full of charms . . .

D . . . you're a darling . . .

Charles sings along. Daisy said the two of them have been practising, so she now knows the words of a few ancient songs. He has a surprisingly good voice. There's a big smile on his face as he bashes the small bells onto his palm.

Penny's disappeared and Derrick is leaning back with his arms folded. Ben can't tell if he's waiting to hurry back to reception. A few more bodies have woken up. There is a cluster of five, four ladies and a man, who look the most alert. This little group join in, bodies gently moving as Daisy ploughs on.

E . . . you're exciting . . .

F . . . you're a feather in my arms . . .

It's so strange to see a young woman dressed in the shortest skirt, hair freshly dyed, clapping and singing to a song so far removed from her world.

Charles nudges Selvi as he sings the next three lines.

J . . . we're like Jack and Jill . . .

K . . . you're so kissable . . .

L . . . is the love light in your eyes?

Ben glances at Selvi; she hasn't dramatically changed. It would be great if she leapt up singing a solo. But she's moving her fingers. Is it just a timely coincidence?

Penny bursts back in doubling the volume as she claps and sings, her body swaying to the music like she's at a wedding reception waiting to join the floor.

M . . . N . . . O . . . P . . . you could go on all day . . .

Q . . . R . . . S . . . T . . . alphabetically speaking, you're okay . . .

She then dances over to her husband and drags him to his feet as she sings:

U make my life complete . . .

V means you're very sweet . . .

Just when Ben thinks there were no miracles, Derrick, yes Derrick, smiles. It's not a megawatt grin but it's a definite small smile of pleasure. If Ben was a betting man he'd have put his money on Selvi's resurrection before a rhythmic sway from Derrick.

Everyone pauses ready for the last verse. Derrick takes the opportunity to sit but his arms stay unfolded, and his leg keeps tapping to the beat. Some of the residents are humming or just making noises. But most of them are now joining in, one way or another.

Daisy sings the last lines louder than everyone, grinning at Penny.

A few people stand up and clap. One elderly man looks like he shouldn't and Penny rushes over to support his elbow. One lady who hasn't so far moved a muscle joins in the clapping.

Ben can't believe it; Daisy has on the biggest smile. 'Right, for this one we all have to stand up.' The strict teacher lifts up her hands to illustrate. Penny mumbles something to her husband. Maybe he's mentally updating his risk assessment for this activity.

More residents than Ben expects stand up.

Charles puts a hand under his wife's armpit. Nothing happens.

'Okay, Selv mate, you do you!' Daisy says.

Daisy begins marching around in a room full of people, knees higher with each stride, arms pumping at her sides. She'd make a great Zumba instructor. Penny beckons Derrick to stand next to her.

Oh, the grand old duke of York, he had ten thousand men,

He marched them up to the top of the hill . . .

Ben speeds the tempo as everyone sings. His anxiety has eased. Maybe singing does have a unique power over the brain. Daisy adds new verses, demonstrating further actions that aren't familiar to him. They go a little faster each time and the small group of ladies are nudging and laughing like schoolchildren. It's beautiful to see.

They end with 'My Bonny Lies Over The Ocean', a song Ben has never heard, but Daisy said it's on the list for old people. She's right. Selvi is moving her arms in time with the music. The song finishes to more clapping. This room has come alive in the most astonishing way. Daisy bounds over to Ben and reaches for a hug. It's the first spontaneous offer of affection for months.

A young man dressed in chef's whites interrupts, poking Daisy with a tray of Penny's homemade cookies. More staff arrive to help the frailer ones drink their tea. Derrick goes back to his door guarding position, but his cheeks are flushed.

Daisy is bright red. The glow that vanished when she left her old school is visible. He hadn't noticed until now that the false eyelashes are missing.

'Wasn't that marvellous, Ben?' Penny cups Daisy's flushed cheeks with her hands. 'This girl is a wonder. Next week we'll advertise in the community magazine so other people can come. Who'd have thought The Orchards would have its own singing group?'

As the residents are helped out of the room, Daisy's posture deflates.

'What's up, chicken?' Ben says. 'That was wonderful.'

'Nothing.'

'Come on, I know you better than that.'

'I thought it might wake up Selv.' She starts to pack up the magic instruments.

Ben pulls her into a hug which she readily accepts.

He whispers in her ear. 'You never know. Maybe next time.' As she pulls away, he notices a black mark behind her ear. It's a little guitar-shaped tattoo. Underneath are five tiny letters. *Daddy*.

32

Dorothy

'Grandma, are you in there?'

'Grandma – open the door.'

Bang bang. The pounding of a fist hammering on the window is not helping Dorothy's sense of fragility. No one has ever called her Grandma. For a few years, toddler Daisy called her Tutu. Nobody knows why but she did that for years. Dorothy has pictures signed to Tutu from Da which is what she called herself before going to school.

When Daisy matured, it because Granny and then more recently Gran.

Dorothy is home alone. Fortunately, she's always had bouts of vertigo and that's the party line. She's unwashed. The fridge is empty and there's dust on the mantelpiece but for once she doesn't care.

Thankfully, Sachini rescued her on Friday. Dorothy was as pale as a ghost when she had finished her tirade. It was all she could do to stay standing. She had wanted to reach across, over the cups and the leftover cake, and smack that girl across the face. She wanted to call her all the dirty names under the sun. The labels Dorothy's mother threw at her when she got pregnant. The insults the midwives whisper behind hands when a teenager disappears, leaving her baby behind.

Wisely, Sachini ran away. She ran to get Daisy and told her that 'Auntie' had had a funny turn.

Dorothy insisted she didn't need their help, that she just needed Daisy to call her a taxi. She told her she must take Haizeh back into soft play so they could get their money's worth. Sachini dutifully followed.

Daisy had obviously called Penny, as by the time she arrived home, Penny was on the doorstep. She felt such a fool. Penny fussed, taking her blood pressure and checking her blood sugar. She had wanted to call Dorothy's GP, but in the end, Penny left after tucking Dorothy in bed like one of her grandchildren. She couldn't tell anyone the truth as to why she was in such a state. She felt too ashamed.

The next morning, she closed the heavy curtains. This is her fifth day of ignoring them all. She keeps her phone off and has ignored the door. Each day she switches on her phone and sends reassurance to Penny and Daisy. Then she switches it off again. Ben has been away and no one else is asking.

But still the doorbell rings and rings. Then the letterbox flaps open. There's a pause. No doubt those 'don't miss a trick eyes' are searching for clues. Is she dead? Is there evidence of new movement? Has she been burgled or simply gone away? He'll have seen her car. This is the third day in a row he's been. He rings. He bangs. He shouts and eventually he gives up.

Today he's persisting for longer than is helpful for her state of health. It's shame that's keeping her stuck. She doesn't even know what she's ashamed of. Treating that young woman as if it was her. Being a stupid fool and falling for a child who is her grandchild by a sordid affair. Or refusing to believe her son would do that.

She's known all along. No one gets sacked for being unwell.

She heard the hushed tones when Estelle rushed off to take a call. What other offence would make Owen's colleagues cross the road when they saw his mother? Sometimes things are best left unknown. Unsaid.

She had thought of finding a Catholic priest to say it aloud to, just once. All those things she hadn't told anyone. The almost termination. Her poor parenting, at times neglectful. What she bullied Ben into. And what she knew Owen must've done. But she kept hoping they were wrong. She just couldn't go there. He was her son.

As the months went on, she did what she does best. She looked away. If she covers her eyes, puts her fingers in her ears, then it'll disappear, and the calm will return. It always does. But not this time. Oh Owen, sweetheart. What on earth were you thinking? That fragile girl, the same age as your daughter. How could you?

At last, the banging has stopped. Thank goodness. Dorothy shuts her eyes and reclines in Peter's chair. She grips the arm rests as if she's a nervous passenger.

'Hey, Grandma. I've been knocking. You ghostin' me or summint?'

Dorothy's eyes fly open ready to fight. She thrusts her feet onto the footrest. The chairs pings to upright and she's ready to run.

'Oh my. Oh my. It's you.'

'Who did you think it was. I've been shouting for an hour.'

'How did you get in?'

'Easy. Wrenched open the kitchen window. You're asking to get done over.'

'Well. Thank you for the warning but I'm too unwell for visitors, especially ones that break into my home.'

'What else was I gonna do? Daisy said you'd had a funny turn. I thought you were dead.'

'I've texted her. She knew I wasn't.'

'Not seen her.'

Dorothy can't help feeling sorry for poor Ryan. A cold unwelcoming bedsit. Dumped by Kiera for an older crowd and now Daisy has found a new bestie with whom he can't compete.

'Go on then. Make us a cuppa.'

Dorothy listens as Ryan does the washing-up. Then the Hoover starts. Finally, she hears the kettle boiling.

'You don't look ill. Are you faking, Grandma?'

If she didn't feel so terrible, she'd chuckle. He cuts right through the niceties but is spot on.

'I'm feeling rather low,' she admits.

'What's up?'

'Oh Ryan, I can't burden you with my troubles. Nothing that won't come out in the wash, I'm sure. Family troubles. Nothing for you to worry about.'

'I'm good with women's troubles. When my ol' lady still lived at ours, she and her mates were always yacking to me. I'm good with bloke troubles or is it your menopause?'

With that, Dorothy starts laughing. She laughs and laughs, a manic high-pitched crazy kind of laugh until that gives way to tears. Lots of tears and before she knows it, she a lady of many decades is being comforted by a boy who should still be in school.

'There, there,' Ryan is saying whilst patting her liver-spotted arm. 'Don't you worry, there, there.'

Ryan goes to the downstairs cloakroom. Dorothy tries to gather herself but fails. Still with his filthy cap resting to one side, he thrusts a handful of toilet tissue in her lap.

'Wipe ya tears, I'll make more tea and then you can tell me all about ya worries.'

And she does. Pouring out her tales of woe to the boy with grubby hands and a kind face makes her feel lighter.

She tells him about her boys. Owen so serious and Ben rather sloppy. She tells him about Jonny and his genetic curse. Then, she takes a deep breath, and she tells him about the day Owen was diagnosed. The relief he wasn't a druggy. The guilt about the relief and inviting a blood curse into their family. But mostly the terror of seeing Daisy disintegrate like her father.

Finally, she tells about that day. The day when a kid like him shattered her life with photos and a baby scan.

'It's Sachini, Ryan,' Dorothy confesses.

'What's Sachini, Grandma?'

'Sachini is the girl.'

'*The girl*? With Owen? Nah, that can't be right. If she's the girl. Then – the maggot would be your grandkid?'

'Exactly,' she says, relieved she's voiced it.

'But you said the bloke who blackmailed you wanted dosh to get rid of a kid.'

'Well, Sachini must've changed her mind and kept her baby.'

'Nah, that ain't right. I'm telling ya, it ain't right.'

'Of course, it's not right. It's so terribly not right, Ryan. I'm ashamed of my own son.'

'Nah, I mean, you've got this wrong. Chez did Borstal with our Gary. He told me he had a kid. He def said that.'

'He's Sachini's cousin not her boyfriend. It must be another child.'

‘I’ve never seen another kid. He’s always hanging at Sachini’s place.’

Ryan grabs his jacket and bends to peck Dorothy’s cheek. ‘I’ll sort it,’ he says.

With his hand on the door handle, he turns back. ‘Have a shower, Grandma. You stink like an old person.’

The front door slams.

Dorothy has no idea what to think.

33

Daisy

'Well, well, early every day for a week,' Derrick chuckles as if he's made a joke. Daisy ignores him as she signs in.

'Where's Charlie?' Daisy demands without looking up.

'He will be delighted to see you. I popped in when I arrived, and he looks shattered. I think she's been pacing all night,' Penny says.

'I need my work dress.'

'Tell you what, I'll let you off for good behaviour, just this once. Pop it on at tea break.'

Daisy can feel a smile creeping out, but she turns away before Penny or Derrick see. She realises she's happy here.

She goes to switch off her phone but sees she has a voicemail from Sachini.

Since they went out with Gran last week, Sach has left about twenty messages that Daisy has been too busy with work to listen to yet. It's doing her nut in. Daisy loves the maggot and Sachini but it's hard work helping look after a toddler and Sach is taking more and more hours. She wants to move to Steyning which Daisy thinks is super pointless. She's only been here five minutes but now she wants to move five miles up the road. One minute she said she was here to look out for her nan and then she's trying to move further away.

She pops in the staff bog to listen.

'Daisy. Where are you? Stop ignoring me. I need to talk to you about your gran. About your dad. It's important. Call me. Like now. Call me.'

Daisy presses 3 for delete and turns it off. She has no idea why Sach mentioned Dad. She didn't even know him.

Daisy pops in to see Clara. The bedroom door is green. Her photo shows a beautiful lady leaning on the front of a black car that looks a bit like a taxi.

'Good morning,' Clara says with a big gummy smile. She's always cheery but doesn't wear her teeth. 'Do you know what?'

'What?' Daisy knows exactly what but tries to look interested.

'My parents have just dropped me off. Isn't it great here?'

'Not bad at all, Clara mate.'

Clara tells Daisy this every morning. She's nearly a hundred but at least she's happy mad, not like poor old Selvi or Dad.

For a change, Charles is pacing and Selvi is sitting on the bed looking out of the window.

'It's Daisy, who you like,' Charles says with more enthusiasm than she feels.

Selvi doesn't move.

'You go, Charles, we'll be fine here, won't we, matey?'

Charles slips out without making a sound.

'So, what shall we do today then Mrs?' Daisy's sure Selvi moves her head towards her voice. 'Shall we play some music, have a dance or do some colouring?'

Selvi continues to stare out the window.

'Wait here. Don't move. I'll be back in two seconds,' Daisy says as she speeds out the door, nearly knocking Bill over.

'Give me your answer do.' He grins.

In the laundry room, Daisy grabs a massive pile of clean pillowcases and runs back to room seven.

Selvi is where she left her. Daisy scatters the bundle all over the floor.

'Right, matey, you've got to stop space staring, we have work to do.' Daisy prods Selvi's arm.

'Like this.' Daisy puts a pillowcase on Selvi's lap. Immediately the housewife appears, and two mechanical sticks bring the far corners back to her lap.

'Hoorah.' Daisy claps. 'You're folding.'

Once Selvi connects with something, she's like the maggot, she wants to do it over and over.

Daisy plonks pillowcases and tea towels from the floor onto the bed between them.

Selvi folds each piece.

Daisy turns her phone back on, relieved there's no more messages.

'You'll like this,' she tells Selvi and clicks play.

A head appears through the door.

'My, my, what have you done?' Penny shouts over the music.

'I'm sorry, I know it's against the rules, but I was trying something with her, honest I was.'

'Daisy, I'm delighted. It's beautiful to see Selvi working to music. I'm going to get Charles.'

‘As Time Goes By’ is playing, one of Gran’s fave tunes. When Charles comes back, Selvi is sort of singing. It’s a bit muffled and odd but she is folding tea towels and making noises.

Penny grabs his hands, and they start dancing to the music. They’re laughing, he pulls up Penny’s arm and she twists round.

Meanwhile, Selvi continues to fold, stare and make a noise that isn’t sad. Daisy lies on the bed watching her manager dance with an old man. No one seems to care that she’s not working.

After three more songs, Charles lets Penny go. Pulling his jumper over his bright red face he collapses into his armchair. Selvi has stopped folding but isn’t sad or cross.

He nods at Daisy with the biggest grin. ‘She’s a keeper,’ he says to Penny. Daisy doesn’t know why Penny’s crying.

Daisy loves a Thursday as it’s her half day and blue corridor run on a skeleton staff. So, she can get to her room by two p.m. and she won’t be disturbed until gone five.

She empties her pockets onto the bed. Greg the chef gave her some homemade chunky cookies he made for coffee time.

‘You don’t mind, coma boy?’ she says, taking one of his bedside tissues to wipe her face.

He doesn’t respond. His bed lump looks a bit smaller; Daisy hopes Penny is not tricking her with pillows, she’ll snitch a peek before she goes, not now though.

Daisy studies the sideboard, loads of smiling faces. Happy couple time on a boat. At the top of the Eiffel Tower. In a separate frame there’s a little girl with a wide mouth, screaming about something. That kid wasn’t going to be ignored by her parents. Daisy looks at the wife straight in the eye. What happened to 'til death do us part'?

Daisy has a mini fridge in the back corner of the wardrobe. Risky, but, a girl needs a beer. Coma boy doesn't need the clothes hanging in colour order so it's a perfect hiding place.

She retrieves two books, she's part way through both. Charles Dickens is on the top, Dad desperately wanted her to read *A Tale of Two Cities*. He'd read it as a teenager and loved it. He wanted to reread it before he got too old. That thought that he didn't get the chance, hurts her heart. She puts Dickens back in the hideaway.

Her comfy position happens without thought, she snuggles into the soft chair, legs on bed. She has a beer, a cookie, her tin and Jane Eyre. She can manage a few chapters. This life is not so bad.

The story sounds so much better when it's read aloud. Drama was her best GCSE result. She knows coma boy appreciates hearing decent literature.

'There are few people whom I really love . . .' She mimics the posh estate agent who sold their home . . . 'And still fewer of whom I think well. The more I see of the world, the more am I dissatisfied with it.' Yeah, too right. She scribbles that quote in her notebook.

Coma boy creates a movement she ignores. She mustn't allow her mind to process him as a human, a man who lived and loved. And lost.

What do you make of that? Guess your world is not that satisfying right now. When did you realise the fate that dragged you here? Was it the first time you forgot your glasses or when they walked you in and pulled the door shut?

She shakes those thoughts from her head.

Last week he had a chest infection and people were popping in and out all over the place. She lost her haven. Nightmare!

Daisy creeps out the back door. It's easier now. This is home.

Distracted by her phone she misses the footsteps gaining on her as she crosses the pub car park. A stream of messages from Ryan are arriving. So, when someone grabs her from behind, she's startled out of her tiny mind.

'What the . . .'

'Calm down, it's only me.' Sachini pulls her friend close for a hug. 'You've been ignoring my messages,' Sach says, linking arms with Daisy to walk.

'I've been at work.'

'For five days?'

'I'm babysitting Robbie later, I can't have the maggot overnight. I'm knackered.'

'I know. It's fine, it's not that. Can we go for coffee at Costa?'

'Sach, I can't. I'm due at Ben's for supper in five. I've not seen 'em for weeks. I'm sorry, really.'

'I need to talk, Daisy. Something has happened. It's bad.'

Daisy stops. 'Not my gran?' She couldn't cope with that. She's lost too many already.

'No. Nothing like that.'

'What then?'

'I can't speak here,' Sachini insists.

'I'll see you in a couple of days. I'll call, I promise. Talk then,' Daisy says, speeding off. She can't be late. She wants to be better.

Sachini doesn't move.

'Daisy. Your gran saw something when we were out.'

Daisy keeps walking, disinterested today in Sachini's dramatics.

'Daisy,' she raises her voice, but Daisy keeps walking.

Daisy is jerked backwards by her hood. She struggles to break free. She's tired. She's in a rush. What's got into her friend?

'Daisy, your gran saw a photo of Haizeh's father.'

'Cool, so what?' Daisy's miffed she's never seen it. She's begged loads but Sach denied she had any pictures. She wouldn't even tell her his name.

'Daisy. I'm sorry. I didn't mean it this way.'

Tears are streaming down her friend's face. Daisy doesn't understand but she knows it's bad. She knows something is about to change. She knows it's one of those seminal moments like when her granddad went upstairs. And died. Like when Dad saw her shoe and slapped her face. And never came back. She can see from Sachini's face, it's going to be one of those moments.

'Daisy, it's your dad. Haizeh's dad is Owen. Haizeh's father is your father.'

Dear Crazy Daisy,

From the first time you gazed at me with your big eyes and that goofy grin, I feared a time when I would die a small death. I've been preparing for this since you wobbled to a stand without holding on.

It's the time when one miserable day, another man will become your number one. At least now I'll avoid my demotion to Crazy Daisy's number two. You've inherited Ben's immature toilet humour, so the thought of me as your number two will make you chuckle.

People don't tell you this but loving another person for more than two years is hard and it's tempting to throw in the towel when the adrenalin rush slows to a dribble. If there was a perfect man I'd search the world with a fine-tooth comb and find that flawless prince. Sadly, there isn't one. If you choose to marry, it'll be a man who does stupid things, works too much and forgets to love you as you deserve. But if he's kind, intelligent and appreciates how lucky he is to have you, that's all good. After the honeymoon memories fade, the lust will diminish. One day, you'll open your eyes and see less prince and more paunch. The whites of his eyes will be cloudy and the hairs in his ears more evident. Greener grass might feel tempting – listen to your dad. It's not.

Tell him how you're feeling and if you've chosen well, it'll pick up. A year down the line you'll catch his gaze in a crowded room and share a private smile. You'll realise it's back, and that the intimacy is deeper and more rewarding than ever before.

Every day I dream of your wedding day and how proud I'd feel walking you down the aisle. I'm less of a fan of the giving you away bit.

Maybe you will stay single, you certainly don't require another human to complete you. You're more complete than any person I know. You have inherited the best of our family tendencies, none of the flaws. Well, maybe you have a tad too much of Uncle Ben's humour and a sprinkle of Gran's OCD, but you're ever so almost perfect.

Whatever you do, however you choose to do life – you'll be better than I can possibly imagine despite my planet-sized imagination.

Daddy xx

34

Ben

'Ben, Ben, wake up.'

Am I dreaming?

Callie is shouting.

What on earth is happening?

'Ben.'

Ben sits up, startled and sleepy.

'It's the doorbell,' Callie says flicking on her bedside light. 'It's been ringing for ages.'

Ben squints at the clock. 'It's five a.m., must be kids.'

'But it's been going on and on.'

Ben stumbles downstairs and snatches back the door. Before any words come out, he's pushed aside by the full force of his niece. She's tiny but never gentle.

'Out of the way,' she says. 'Where is Callie, because this ends now.'

Daisy's foot is on the first step, her body poised to race upstairs. She changes her mind and swivels around. Daisy looks down from the third stair, pointing her finger in Ben's face.

'I know the games you've been playing. My dad was ill, but you' – her finger is almost touching his nose – 'you're a monster, playing with people's lives. You're sick in the head.' She taps at her own head.

Ben pulls her down towards him. She loses her balance, grabs the handrail and has to step back down to balance.

'How dare you come marching into my house to speak to me like that?' Ben has never shouted at her. He's always tried to stay calm, not be rattled, but he's done with this kid. Sorry, Owen. 'Get out of my house.' He pushes her towards the door, clutching her hood, frightened of what he might do next. She spins round, wriggling free, and puts her face so close he can feel her breath, and shouts, literally spitting out words.

'You can't do this. I'm not staying quiet anymore.'

'Since when have you stayed quiet?' He refuses to step aside.

'Ben!' Callie says quietly standing between them. As his heart rate slows, Ben is flooded with shame and a terrible fear.

'I hate you!' Daisy is shouting, tears streaming down her face, rolling unchecked down her neck and onto her jumper.

'What on earth is going on?' Callie looks at Ben and then at Daisy.

'Ask him,' Daisy screams.

'I have no idea what she's on. But I can't do this anymore. I thought you had finally grown up,' Ben says, looking pointedly at Daisy before walking into the kitchen.

He falls into a chair, runs his hands through his hair and rests his head in his hands, defeated.

Still in the hall with Daisy, Callie take charge. 'Right. Well, I don't want the neighbours woken. Sid next door will call the police without hesitation. Ben, put the kettle on. Daisy, sit in there and calm down.'

In the kitchen, Ben presses his palms onto the work surface. *Breathe, Ben, breathe* . . . He knows what's coming.

At first, he'd wanted to believe she was drunk, or stoned, been out all night. But the look in her eyes was of shock and distress. It is raw fear, and he knows: she's found out about Owen, about the baby.

He returns to the lounge 'Okay,' he says. 'I can't stop this, but I can make it less terrible.'

Carrying two mugs, he consciously slows his breathing and evens his tone.

'Daisy, I'm sorry you are hurting, but you can't turn up in the middle of the night shooting your mouth off and screeching like a wild cat.'

'Don't patronise me. I'm no longer some silly kid who you control. Callie deserves the truth. She needs to know who you really are. What your family are really like.'

'I agree,' he says, sitting down. 'Tell me what you've found out and how.'

He listens as Daisy tells what Sachini had said about the day at the soft play with Dorothy. Apparently Sachini had a photo of Owen in her purse and the two women stumbled upon a different but equally ugly truth. Dorothy found out she had another grandchild and Sachini realised they were Owen's family. Sachini got to Daisy before her grandmother could spill the beans.

Eventually, her breathing slows, and she relaxes a little. But just as Ben reaches out to hold and comfort her, she ramps it up again.

'And then she told me you and Gran tried to kill him. You wanted rid of Haizeh. You wanted to kill my brother. I hate you. I hate you. I hate you all.'

At that she collapses into Callie's arms like a much younger child. Callie strokes her head and whispers soothing sounds. She meets Ben's gaze and raises her eyebrows. Where do they go from here? How did he ever think this could all be cleaned up, swept away? No harm done.

Watching Daisy cry, his thoughts are scrambled. Their surname is so distinct. Did Sachini know all along who Daisy was? Did she deliberately target her, them? Is this some kind of revenge? Is this what she's been planning from the moment she posted that sweet-smelling letter through his letterbox? What's she after? What does she want from his family who are already on their knees? And just when he saw a glimmer of hope.

Ben tries to explain but every time he starts a sentence Daisy revs up for another fight. In the end he gives up. Now is not the time. In the end he slopes off to the kitchen. He can hear Callie soothing their niece, trying to make his nonsensical behaviour sound right.

'It all happened so quickly Daisy.'

'We don't yet have all the facts.'

'Your father was unwell.'

'Everyone did what they thought best.'

'No one intended to hurt you.'

Ben stays out of the way. When the voices stop, he checks the girls are asleep, covers them both with a duvet and then creeps out the front door.

He knows there's no point, but he has to go anyway.

Ben sits himself down. It's eerily quiet. This is where he comes for his one-way conversations. She doesn't know he knows, but his mother comes here too. He's seen her name in the book.

'Don't worry. I'm used to being ignored.'

He doesn't expect a response. If he got one that would be miraculous but visiting him is strangely therapeutic. He talks anyway.

'I'm keeping everything ticking over, mate. I hope you'd be proud. Daisy's doing alright.' Ben never mentions that his brother's prodigy has dropped out of education. Whilst he was in Italy, Estelle had texted Ben thirty-plus times about Daisy's recent carry-ons.

Ben, she's not been here for three days . . . Can you tell her not to smoke at home? . . . She's stolen my new trousers.

Meanwhile Penny is telling his mother the complete opposite.

You should see her with the residents . . . She's been early every day for a month . . . She's transformed the life of one couple . . .

Ben knows he's being stupid. He knows Owen won't come back to life, tap him on the shoulder and ask a question but he still watches what he says.

Ben looks over his shoulder to check he's still alone. What would people think if they saw him in the dark, chatting away to his brother as if that was normal?

'Oh mate, why you? Who'd have thought you of all people would get a degenerative disease. You were the definition of alive, vibrant, awesome. I was so jealous of your model looks. If that wasn't enough you had to get a brain the size of a planet.'

Today, Ben can't kid himself. His brother has gone. Ben pulls up his sweatshirt hood. It's freezing. He thrusts his hands in his trouser pockets and sets off for home.

Oh Owen, what were you thinking? And what a mess I've created trying to save your reputation, keep you intact. Daisy says you first lost your smile but, Owen, you first lost your nature. The kind and faithful father was dead long before we knew there was a problem to be solved.

35

Daisy

Daisy hates this feeling. It's not even lunchtime and the bus is full. There's no escape on public transport when it's crowded, her breathing is a struggle, and she wants to chuck. But she can't walk two miles, she's tuckered out. If Ben and Callie thought she was going to leave it, they're more stupid than she thought. When she woke up, Callie was still asleep even though it was light. So, she closed their lounge curtains to make it dark and crept out. Ben's car was gone. She reckons he's at the studio.

She's hot with panic but she doesn't want to take off her jumper. After Sachini said that stuff, she needed release. Now the cuts and burns are red raw. She thought Sachini liked her. But she'd just pretended to be mates, wheedled her way in and then screwed her over. Now Daisy hates her more than she ever liked her. She hates her and Ben and even Dad. That's what messes with her head the most. Who even was he?

Sach has been ringing constantly. Daisy's deleted every message without listening. Thankfully, Sach doesn't know her address or about her room. She'd have turned up, barged in, blown her cover, selfish witch that she is.

She said if she talked, it would help but now Daisy knows that she was just getting intel on them all. On Ben, on Dad. Daisy had told her how she missed him, how he'd changed. She'd told her about the shouting and thumping. She'd told it all to her, not to Gran or Ben, but her. They had even discussed the test. She had told Sach things she's not told anyone. Daisy even gave up fags for her.

'He's Haizeh's dad,' Sach had yelled like it was nothing.

Why would she do that? Purposely ruin Dad, her beloved Dad. How could she? Had she planned it all along, is she jealous? Had she known all along that he was her dad?

Daisy stole some photo albums from Ben's office. Ethan let her in. She's checked each picture for dates to work out the timeline. She's studied them over and over, looking for clues. Studying Dad in photos taken at parties, photos at home. Photos when she was little, of day trips, holidays, birthdays. Was it all a lie?

Nodding goodbye to the driver as the bus pulls away, Daisy runs, head down, a hefty bag clutched to her chest as if she's escaping a war zone, desperate for safety. She's two minutes away.

Dropping her stuff on the step, Daisy pounds both fists on the door.

'Let me in, Gran. Dorothy. Gran. Open the door.'

Gran slowly opens the door, a crack. She has her hair in plastic tubes under a net, a hideous dressing gown over a long pink nightie. She looks miniature and old.

'A please would be nice.'

'Sorry,' Daisy says, retrieving her stuff to push against the just-open door.

'Do you know what time it is?' Daisy says whilst Gran undoes the chain. 'Why aren't you dressed? Are you sick?'

Daisy looks around. She can't believe Gran's place is so messy. Without a word, she heads for the sitting room and dumps four albums stuffed with envelopes of loose pictures onto the tartan two-seater. Gran's furniture is from her parents' old bedroom. She has the tartan chair.

'You know that thing you're on all day?' Gran says, pouring a sherry. 'It's called a telephone for a reason.'

'I need to know stuff.' Daisy announces plonking herself on the floor.

'What's so urgent it can't wait?'

'Dad.'

'I need the toilet and my warmer dressing gown. Make us some cocoa while I sort myself out,' Gran says before stomping upstairs.

The recipe books with their dusty covers lean against the microwave. Daisy spent hours baking from those pages. The aqua kitchen tiles here are more modern than in Gran's big house but the kitchen layout is the same. Microwave balanced on top of the fridge. Windowsill with boring vase holding daffodils from the garden. Everything the same. She craves her childhood routine. Dad working all week but home early on Friday for swimming and Toblerone. That was the routine for as long as she can remember until it wasn't. When they thought he was working away, was he?

Gran's fridge is always spotless. Today, the glass bottle sticks when she takes out the milk. Stirring the steaming liquid is soothing. The wooden spoon going around and around in the battered saucepan that's older than Dad.

'Well done, that smells marvellous, put it in our mugs and take it through. I'll find some chocolate biscuits.' Gran has on what she calls her cleaning rags. Trackie bottoms and woolly cardigan, dressing gown under her arm.

Daisy cups her mug, enjoying the warmth, and waits whilst Gran settles herself in the chair.

She clutches the shortbread tin with both hands and pulls it towards her, pretending she might not share. She's done that all Daisy's life.

'Gran, I'm not five.'

Gran ignores that snipe and slides the tin across to Daisy with her foot.

'Spit it out then. What's this honour visit from my elusive granddaughter?'

'I want the truth,' Daisy says.

'What about?'

'Was Dad a good man or not?'

'Before he was ill, you mean?' Gran clarifies. There are two Owens known to them all. The old one and the ill one.

'Yeah.'

'He was a very good man, even as a child – like you were, eager to please, kind.'

'But when he was older, with Mum.'

'I think your mum would agree he did his best, as a husband and dad.'

'What's that supposed to mean?' Daisy snaps.

'Well, no man is perfect.'

'Right, so you're saying because he did the odd bit of dusting, he could sleep around, abuse a few trainees . . .'

'Hang on.' Gran plonks her mug on the side table and cocoa sloshes on the mat. Your dad was a faithful and loyal husband. By not perfect I meant he worked too much, occasionally had a few too many, and was sometimes grumpy. There's no way he would have cheated on your mum. He loved her. Where is this coming from? She didn't say he was unfaithful, did she?'

‘He got a teenager pregnant.’

Daisy watches as Gran’s face droops and her skin loses colour. She knows the truth.

‘Who told you such a thing?’

Daisy sorts through the photos she knows so well to retrieve two. One is Dad sitting on Gran’s lap as a little boy. The other is Haizeh, his last school picture.

‘They look alike. Same mouth. Same hair,’ Daisy says, getting up and dropping them on Gran’s lap.

Gran pulls her hand to her mouth. She says nothing. Daisy hopes she doesn’t have a stroke.

‘No. They don’t. No more than any two boys look alike.’

Daisy ignores the defensive tone.

‘I’ve been looking at loads of stuff. I found his old work diaries. And Ben said he went away with work. He was probably sleeping around all my life. Anyway, she told me.’

‘Who told you what?’

‘Sach told me Haizeh is Dad’s and that you agree.’

Gran is moving her hand over her mouth, taking it away and putting her other hand there. It’s her ears she should be blocking.

‘Oh . . . oh . . . Daisy. I honestly don’t know what has gone on. If he did that, he wasn’t himself.’

‘Well, when he wasn’t being himself, he was a predator. I can’t believe he would do that.’

‘But it wasn’t him! He was already ill. Your real dad wouldn’t have done that, I promise you.’ Gran is using her firm voice and Daisy isn’t a fan. She’s not a child. She won’t be patronised and deluded anymore. She opens the albums and rips out the secured photos. One by one she tears them in two, then four, then tiny pieces. She throws the confetti memories in the air. That's her life. Gone.

'Oh Daisy, stop. Come here. Don't do that, sweetheart. Please don't cry.' Gran stands to pull Daisy into her arms. Eventually, they collapse as one into the armchair, Daisy on Gran's lap as if she's small.

They cry for a very long time.

Before Daisy can ask Gran what she knows and what they should do, there's a crash and loud voices out the front. It's a man and for a minute Daisy thinks it's Ben but then she hears a long string of swearwords and knows it's Ryan. If they stay quiet he won't know they're in. She puts her finger to her lips, but Gran disentangles herself and goes to open the door.

Ryan stumbles in with one hand behind his back. It's only when he's properly in the room that Daisy spots something off. Ryan is hiding something behind him and it's whimpering like a sick dog. She sees a leg, then one arm and slowly it dawns that behind Ryan is not a pet but a skinny girl. Cowering behind him is a girl. The girl she hoped would stay her best friend forever. It's the girl she trusted. The girl she despises.

With her eyes to the floor, her face blotchy from crying and hair wild, is Sachini. Sachini is cowering behind Ryan.

'I told ya I'd sort it,' he says to Gran.

Gran says nothing but then she sees what Daisy sees. Sachini is handcuffed to Ryan.

'Oh, my giddy aunt, Ryan. What have you done?'

'My ole man says if you can't trust em, cuff em. I can't trust her.'

He points at Sachini with his free hand.

Dorothy steps forward and sweeps Sachini's hair out of her face.

‘Sweetheart, I’m so sorry. What has he done to you?’

‘Hang on a minute. I ain’t done nothing. It’s what she’s done to you. And Daisy.’

Daisy cowers in the chair, sucking her thumb. She’s had enough and can’t make sense of any of this. Why is Ryan here? Who is he sorting, and for whom? Surely Gran hasn’t asked for this.

Gran wags her finger at Ryan.

‘Get those cuffs off now. This minute. Whatever is going on, restraining someone half your size is not the answer.’

Daisy watches as Ryan does as he’s told. He gets a tiny key out his front pocket and unlocks the links. Sachini stays where she is. Head down, hands together.

‘Right, you sit there, Ryan,’ Gran says, pointing him towards the foot stool. Gran takes Sachini’s hand and leads her to the two-seater and together they sit, like it’s a dance that’s been choreographed. For a moment Daisy is distracted by happy memories of a school hall. Girls too young to know, in brightly coloured leotards, waiting to be shown how to move by their ballet teacher.

Ryan doesn’t sit. He gets his phone and starts to play an audio. It’s Sachini’s voice. She bows her head and stares at her entangled her hands.

‘I asked her for the truth, and she told me. I recorded it for you.’

Everyone is listening.

‘I lied,’ the timid voice whispers.

Silent tears drop from Sachini’s face onto her hands.

‘I didn’t mean it. It wasn’t supposed to end like this. I wasn’t supposed to meet Daisy and Dorothy. They weren’t supposed to know Haizeh. I didn’t even know they were related to Owen until last week.’

Ryan stops the recording. 'Listen to this bit, Grandma.' He nods to Dorothy. 'You won't wanna hold her hand. You'll want her cuffed and lobbed in the road.'

He's trying to sound like his older brother, who Daisy hates.

Ryan restarts the audio.

'I felt so ashamed. My mother would have disowned me. My brother would've killed me. It would've killed my grandparents to know.'

At that point the recording becomes incomprehensible. Ryan swears and bangs his phone on the wall as if that'll help. Then he gives up.

'You.' He points at Sachini. 'You tell 'em the rest.'

Gran turns to look at Sachini, reaches for her hand. 'Tell the truth and we can sort it out.'

Sachini doesn't look up. She whispers, 'I met Owen at work. He was nice. He knew I was unhappy. I hadn't been in the country very long and he gave me a map book and helped me workplaces out. He drew red circles around places to avoid. The White Horse pub and the warren. He circled places I would enjoy like the park near the Hormare estate and the walks near the pond.'

Daisy can feel tears pricking at her eyes. Dad did the same for her.

'Go on,' Dorothy encourages, patting Sachini's hand.

'Things were terrible at home. Chez and his older brother were around a lot. They pushed me about, called me names, took my money and . . .'

'Take your time,' Dorothy soothes.

Daisy is glaring at her, her face hot with anger.

‘I don’t wanna hear this junk. How you and my Dad got cosy and then . . .’

‘Daisy,’ Gran says, putting up her hand like she’s a traffic cop, ‘this is hard, but we all need to know the truth. I’ve avoided that for too long.’

‘Chill,’ Ryan interrupts. ‘It’s not what you think.’

‘I’m so sorry,’ Sachini continues. ‘It wasn’t on purpose. Owen saw my black eye. He took me to the first aider and they both listened whilst I told them what Chez was making me do, how he . . . came to my bedroom at night . . . how he touched me and . . .’

Nobody speaks. Sachini struggles to form her words through her tears. Daisy doesn’t know what to think or feel or do.

‘Owen was kind. He wasn’t very well, and his words were muddled but he told me to go to a refuge where they’d look out for me. I wanted my child to have a father like that, a father like I’d had. Not a violent animal like Chez.’

Daisy can’t hold her tongue any longer. She jumps up, pointing her finger right in Sachini’s miserable face and shouts, ‘So you put your body on offer when Dad couldn’t control himself and made him inseminate you with his kid. Now, there’s another kid with this curse and it’s your fault. You did that.’

Ryan pulls her back.

Sachini shouts back. ‘Daisy, you’ve got it all wrong. Owen never touched me. I was already pregnant. Haizeh belongs to Chez. I hate him. I don’t want him to be the dad. But he is. I needed to get away from him. That’s why Owen took me to a refuge.’

Daisy is confused. ‘So, Haizeh isn’t my brother?’

‘No.’

36

Dorothy

This morning, Dorothy had woken with a start.

At first, she had thought it was her alarm and that puzzled her.

Then she had realised it was the home phone. Rushing to answer she had bashed her ankle on the door frame.

The last voice she had expected to hear at six a.m. was Daisy.

'I'm gonna do it,' she'd said. 'And you have to take me.'

Daisy hadn't given her chance to say about her plans for a walk with Penny.

'Get me at work in an hour. Oh, I've asked Sachini to come. Can you get her on the way?'

Too sleepy to reprimand Daisy for bad manners, Dorothy wondered what on earth had changed her mind.

Dorothy had been mortified when Ryan dragged Sachini to her home on Thursday. But it has been such a relief for everyone to understand the truth. Thankfully the dramatic atmosphere had quickly dissolved, and Daisy had made a huge saucepan of hot chocolate. Dorothy had sent Ryan home. This mess wasn't his.

Wrapped in Dorothy's heated blanket, Sachini had told her story without interruption. She explained it was never her intention to deceive. She was terrified to discover she was pregnant by her cousin and desperate to protect her family. But another cousin worked it out and told Chez where she was. On the way back from the refuge, Chez was rooting around in her bag for money, and had stumbled on the photo of her and Owen. At that point, Sachini had looked up for the first time and smiled reassuringly at Daisy.

'The photo was taken at a work do. Owen's walking was less steady, and he had stumbled on a step and I grabbed him just in time. Then, someone snapped a photo.'

Sachini's head dropped back down as she confessed that hearing Chez's plan to pretend it was Owen's to get money would mean her family wouldn't find out and . . .

'I could pretend Haizeh had a kind father not an evil one.'

Sobbing, Sachini had continued.

'I wanted to believe he was conceived in love. Once the radiographer typed Owen's name in black and white, I started to believe the lie. I couldn't face that Chez was his dad.'

Dorothy knows how easy it is to create stories in your head that, if repeated enough times, become the truth.

'But I promise I didn't know. Daisy told me her surname was Stultus. She's still in my phone as that.'

Dorothy knew Daisy was using a new name. Most of the time she has no idea what her granddaughter was thinking. She still hasn't remembered to ask where she got the idea for such a stupid name.

If Dorothy hadn't been so quick to believe Owen was capable of such a thing, she would've studied that photo and perhaps seen there was nothing going on.

Much to Dorothy's surprise, Daisy's anger had quickly dissipated.

In the end, when there was nothing more to say, Dorothy had taken control. She had insisted Daisy and Sachini slept in her bed and gone to find the little boy. In his hurry, Ryan had left Haizeh with Chez.

How dare that man stomp about, treading on people's feelings and terrifying women?

This time it was her hammering on a door. Hoping to take him off guard. Make him cower. Chez had opened the door in his boxers. Undressed, she could see he was just a kid.

She had stood too close to him, but it hadn't given her the sense of redress she had hoped for. It made her feel like a bully. So, in the end she had demanded he bring Haizeh to her car. When he was strapped safely in the back. She had followed Chez back towards the flat and whispered a last sentiment.

'From now on, you'll only see your son when I'm present. And if you don't cooperate I'll be reporting you for blackmail.' Sachini had told her he was on licence for GBH and scared of going back to prison. He hadn't argued or said goodbye to his son. She hopes he'll disappear and not come back. Imagine having a father like that.

The following morning, Daisy had called Ben and, whilst Callie took Haizeh to the park, Sachini had filled in the remaining gaps for them. Sachini told Ben she had kept her promise.

'I went to live with another cousin up North, but I couldn't leave my grandmother alone when she got ill, especially with Chez around. Until I came back he thought I'd terminated the pregnancy. When he met Haizeh, he promised he'd change but not tell anyone he was the father'.

Looking at Dorothy and back to Daisy and Ben as she finished her story, Sachini had said, 'Every time I told someone Owen was the father, I had felt comforted as he was a gentle and kind man. I'm sorry I said he hurt me. He didn't.'

Dorothy is still trying to understand why Sachini allowed Chez to come back into their lives, but she can't judge. Dorothy had fallen for a rotter, Owen would have never been born, or got ill if she hadn't given in to Jonny, over and over. With hindsight Dorothy was desperately glad Ben had encouraged Sachini to follow her heart and keep her child. Both her boys are good men.

Just time to call Penny.

'So sorry Pen. I've promised to help Daisy this morning.'

'Don't you worry. We'll do it next week.'

'I'm collecting Daisy from the home. I think she's worked a night shift.'

'Under eighteens don't do nights but I'm sure she has her reasons.'

Having cancelled Penny, Dorothy had jumped in the shower with renewed vigour and a lightness of spirit. She was even looking forward to seeing Sach again.

Dorothy pulls slowly into The Orchards car park, and watches as Daisy runs out from the back door, a rucksack hauled over her shoulder. Dorothy hopes that's allowed. She needs to keep this job at least until she finds an alternative.

'I didn't know you worked night shifts. You must be tired,' Dorothy says, thinking Daisy looks surprisingly bright eyed. Doing some honest talking has helped everyone.

'Just occasionally. If they're short staffed.'

Dorothy gives her granddaughter a tight hug, she can smell shampoo and her mother's Chanel No 5.

Daisy climbs in the back next to Sachini. Dorothy feels hurt but she's learning to keep her mouth shut. There's a lot of bridges to build. Dorothy starts the engine but can't help noticing the two girls in the back. They're both unusually tiny for their age, in height and weight. They could easily be twelve. Dorothy watches as Daisy clips her seatbelt but then reaches for her friend's hand. The two girls greet each other with a knowing smile. Dorothy knows they were talking late into the night when they stayed with her.

She was too shattered to actively listen like she might've done six months ago but when she had got up to use the bathroom, she caught a few sentences from downstairs.

She had heard Sachini beg Daisy for forgiveness about the lies she had told about Owen. She had felt proud of the way Daisy had responded.

'I get it,' she had told Sachini, 'you lost your dad. My therapist said it's terrible for girls to lose a dad. We're both messed up,' she had told her friend.

That had made Dorothy smile after a long dark night. 'We're all messed up,' she had thought to herself.

'I'm sorry I'm a few minutes late. Your mum called on the way out and then I stopped to reply to Ben who has been texting.'

'I hope you didn't tell them.'

'Daisy, I'm sorry but I did. They deserve the truth. There's been enough lies.'

In the mirror, Dorothy catches Sachini do her besetting head bow.

'Sachi,' Dorothy says. Her voice gently stern. 'Look at me.'

Fortunately, they've stopped at a traffic light so Dorothy can wait for Sachini to give eye contact.

'You need to forgive yourself. You were very young, and Chez took advantage of you. You haven't done anything wrong. From now on, look people in the eyes.'

Sachini nods and Daisy goes to speak but changes her mind.

For a few hours, the three women travel in silence. Each lost in their own reflections. Sachini breaks the quiet.

'Daisy, are you sure about this?'

'I'm sure she is,' Dorothy interrupts, hoping Daisy will go through with it.

'I dunno. I've avoided it long enough. I can't stay at The Orchards forever and this one is only a preliminary interview. I can change my mind at any point, can't I?'

Before Dorothy can speak, Sachini takes the lead. She squeezes Daisy's hand and speaks to her as if she's her small child.

'You can, Daisy, you can change your mind at any time. But I promise it'll be okay. I promise.'

'Gran,' Daisy says, 'are my CDs still in here?'

'Indeed.'

At that, Daisy unclips her seatbelt and climbs in the front. She unfastens the glove box and sorts through her old CDs.

Click. Click. Click. That noise of plastic cases being flicked at speed takes her back. So many car journeys. Driving Owen to and from school. Later, the long runs to Cambridge and back. Then Ben and his terrible noisy music, and finally school runs with Daisy. The two of them would choose a CD and sing like no one was listening to Bruce Springstein and later *The Greatest Showman*.

'This one.' Daisy shoves a disc in the gap. Dorothy hasn't had music in the car for ages. Songs are too painful. Each one triggering a memory she'd rather not face. A missing lover. Lost sons. A wayward grandchild.

Lost in her thoughts, worrying she might cry, the first track begins.

Daisy returns to the rear seats, knocking over Dorothy's travel mug.

'Soz,' she says.

'No worries.'

With only a few miles to go, Dorothy catches Daisy's gaze in her mirror. She jigs about in her seat in time with the music just like they used to when Daisy was twelve. For the first time in ages, Daisy grins and does the same. The song builds to a climax and all three women sing the chorus.

The sat nav directs Dorothy into a side road and then a car park with blue and white signs. The car jerks as she slows to a stop. She pulls hard on the handbrake.

'Daisy, how did you get on with the physio?' Dorothy asks before they get out.

'Fine.'

'What did she say about your legs?'

'There's no weakness.'

Dorothy sighs with relief and gets out the car to open the door for the girls. Her rear doors still have child locks.

Dorothy smiles as Daisy links one arm through hers and the other through Sachini's as the three of them march towards the intimidating doors. They're much the same as at The Orchards. They choose who comes in.

A man near Owen's age pushes past them to get in front.

'You're welcome, mate,' Daisy mutters. 'I'm not going to fight you for first place.'

Dorothy notices his weaving walk. Most people wouldn't, or if they did, they'd think, one too many, bit early for that, be ashamed.

'So sorry,' a young woman about Daisy's age says, rushing after him.

His head nods, most people would think he was saying hello to the nurse coming the other way. He stumbles onto the inside mat.

'We can do this together,' Dorothy says, putting her arm around Daisy's shoulders and giving her a hard squeeze.

The ugly blue letters above the door have no character. No imagination has been applied to the interior design in this place. Patronising boxy letters, making no effort to be kind. The G has fallen just below the E. No one cares enough to sort it out, maybe it's deliberate, a clever sign. Faulty letters to welcome faulty genes. Genes that she welcomed. Genes she fell for. Genes that left her son for dead and could do the same for this beautiful bright girl.

Dorothy supresses an inappropriate urge to jump and tear down those letters, one by one, cascading them onto the floor until they're all broken. Then she could break off the large arrow from the wall and smash it over the head of the receptionist. How dare she be distracted? How dare she giggle with her colleague?

Sachini takes the first step. She holds her head up high and demands the receptionist's full attention. Dorothy and Daisy hang back, clinging to each other like old times.

'We're here for a preliminary screening interview,' Sachini says. 'Are we in the right place for the genetics clinic?'

37

Ben

Ben is loitering at the edge of the green space, sheltering from the wind. Observing. The weather isn't ideal and it's too noisy even with his beanie pulled down to his eyes. May is supposed to be warm. There are kids everywhere, screaming and pushing. Laughing and running wild. He's anxious, an inane grin plastered across his face. Callie, Sach, Daisy and Haizeh are competing on four swings, in a neat row.

Daisy is in perfect sync with her new friend, a fresh openness in her face. As she swings forward, her long legs point to the sky. She's regained her healthy skin in the last few months, but with all that's happened, Ben has missed her becoming a young woman.

Haizeh is making a huge fuss.

'I need a push. It's not fair. Everyone is bigger than me.'

What a turnaround from the first time their eyes met. When Ben first spotted this little boy in the school playground, he was clearly terrified of everything. He could barely make eye contact, much the same as his mum. Two quivering souls on the edge of a community. A normal kid is emerging from what was a little shadow.

Daisy slows her swing, and with a dainty jump leaves her seat and goes behind Haizeh. No demand is too much. Ben remembers when Daisy's every wish was his command. Heels have been replaced by bright plimsolls and her fresh face is back on display. The thick foundation has gone and he daren't comment on how pretty her natural hair looks. Daisy places her hands over Haizeh's grubby ones and pulls back the swing with exaggerated enthusiasm.

'Hold on, maggot,' she shouts as she lets go.

Who'd have thought the catalyst for his distress, the spark underlying the catastrophic fire, would turn out to be the solution, the saviour.

'Push your feet out,' Sachini shouts to her son. She's also found her voice.

Today his mother is treating them to a family day at Legoland before Sachini returns home. Tomorrow, she's flying home to Sri Lanka. This last year has changed his mother. In many ways she's a calmer, more accepting version of herself. But also, she's somewhat diminished.

'Come on, dull boy,' his wife shouts from the top of the slide. At the moment he would rather watch, take it in, process his thoughts and feelings. It has been a lot.

At work, Kasia has been going on and on, accusing him of being weak and foolish.

'You cannot let her get away with it.'

'She deserves to be punished.'

'She must write a statement for the press.'

'The people of Storrington need to know the truth.'

'Owen deserves justice.'

She rants on and off all day. Hands on hips like a stroppy teen, her accent more pronounced in anger.

Initially, Ben felt the same. When his mother demanded he came to the house, he had refused. After all the hurt Sachini had caused. He wanted her punished. He wanted to avenge his brother.

Ben had deliberately dragged his feet that Saturday. He had sat in his car and made excuses to not go in.

But when he did. Sachini was hunched in the window corner, shaking with tears. Rocking back and forth, apologising over and over. Nothing anyone could say had effect. She was clearly as broken as them. He had crumbled. In the end, it was him who had taken her into his arms and soothed her.

Ben is convinced Sachini is the smallest human he's ever met. What was the point in being unkind? Listening to this tiny creature whisper in fear, he had seen what his mother had already discovered. Sach was as much a victim as them. She had been hurt and abused, displaced by war and coerced by someone who claimed to love her. Owen wouldn't have wanted her hauled over the coals.

It has been nice to briefly scapegoat another, but he knew the truth.

Owen was a shadow by the time Sachini pitched up with her accusations. Owen would've undoubtedly been sacked for his lateness, mistakes and increasing aggression. It was some months before a diagnosis explained the way he was.

After his mother threatened Haizeh's father, she insisted Sachini pack her bags and leave that damp flat behind her. Sachini and Haizeh have been staying in Dorothy's double bedroom whilst she's in the spare.

Penny has sourced heaps of DVDs about life in Sri Lanka, so Haizeh knows where he's going. They've been cooking Sri Lankan food. Daisy got an app so Haizeh can learn his native language. He's practising please and thank you, hello and goodbye so he can chat to his new grandparents. After the initial shock, his grandmother had welcomed them with open arms.

Sachini is desperate for them all to visit next Christmas. He's sure his mother will pay for a return visit, Haizeh has become like a second grandchild. He saved everyone. He's an easy chap to enjoy.

In the last few days, Daisy's constant fight has dissolved.

On Sunday, she came around with Ryan and the four of them played board games. They haven't done that for such a long time.

'It's not fair,' screams Haizeh because Daisy has gotten higher than him on the swing. He pushes Callie away as she tries to comfort him and runs towards Ben. It feels positive that he's gaining some spirit and energy.

Sachini jumps off her swing and runs after her son, calling his name. Eventually she catches him.

'Look,' she says, holding her phone and pointing to the screen.

Everyone crowds around Sach and her screen. The one with a large crack across the top.

Leaning over the screen from Sachini's side, Ben can see an elderly man towering over a much younger woman who is a rounder version of Haizeh. There's no doubt about his heritage.

'Press play,' Sachini instructs, deliberately distracting her stroppy boy.

The video starts, unfocused at first.

As the video plays, they watch a lady. She's frantically waving, her hair blowing about in the wind. She gabbles away in her own language.

'Ammamma,' Haizeh mutters pointing at the screen, mesmerised. His tears and tantrums forgotten.

His grandmother buzzes about pointing at a variety of market stalls, explaining each, her voice animated. Colourful displays of food and material. Blue skies above, a contrast to the noise and dust of the surrounding streets. Car horns hooting. Sirens. Shouting. Ben feels dizzy as she appears and disappears to finish a rapid-paced guided tour. Finally, the relatives wave and all of them wave back even though it's not live.

'Cool, eh?' Sachi says slipping her phone into her bag.

'I'll tell you what, let's get lunch, my treat,' Callie pipes up.

Ben gives her a sideways glance. She's never been one to bother about regular meals. She scoffed breakfast less than three hours ago.

After lunch, Ben and Callie make their excuses. The press loved the exhibition and several local business groups have got behind the studio. This afternoon was the only day everyone could meet. Ben has finished a series of self-portraits. Callie says they're his best yet.

'I'm going to miss that little man,' Ben says, placing a hand on his wife's leg as they drive.

'Yeah, I've loved watching you with him. I used to love watching you with Daisy. You're a natural with kids.'

'Really?' Ben checks her expression to see if she's joking. He has always thought of himself as a big kid.

'For sure,' Callie laughs, 'and that's a good thing as I think us two might become a three.'

Fortunately, they're on a straight road as Ben swerves to miss the kerb.

'Are you saying what I think you're saying, Mrs BJ?

At that Callie looks down and cups her stomach in that way pregnant mothers do. Ben accelerates into the approaching hard shoulder and handbrake slides to a stop.

He thumps his seatbelt clip to escape and swallows his wife into the biggest hug.

38

Daisy

'It's so lovely here, isn't it?' Clara says with a lopsided grin. Daisy tries hard not to be revolted by the blob of dribble on her wrinkled chin. Daisy can't agree it's lovely but since she's been staying here, at The Orchards, life is easier. Penny claims she knows all that goes on, but she hasn't noticed the wardrobe stowaway in blue corridor. A runaway tear escapes as Daisy thinks about everything coming to an end.

'It is lovely, isn't it?' Daisy smooths down Clara's fringe, pulling out a piece of egg yolk with her fingers. She wipes the egg under the cushion of her seat.

'My parents are around somewhere, working on the estate. Don't forget to say goodbye to them when you go.' Clara points out of her bedroom window.

'I'll remember,' Daisy reassures. 'What classes do you have after you've finished your food?' Daisy strokes her hand to prompt the next mouthful.

'German and then Literature,' the shrivelled old lady replies with genuine happiness.

Bless her, if I'm at school at ninety, I won't be happy.

'I love books,' Daisy answers, hoping she'll get a chance to read some more Dickens to coma boy before she leaves.

Today couldn't be worse. At handover, Penny said the hospice are taking over coma boy. He's going downhill fast, and they don't know how long he's got left, could be only a week. For the last few days, his room's been spilling with strangers at unpredictable times. Daisy's hearing has become her superpower. She can tell who's coming by footsteps. If it's Penny or Patsy she climbs in the wardrobe. If it's the night staff or a visitor she crawls into the small space under the bed and listens to everything. No one thinks to check there.

Someone knocks on Clara's door. Daisy recognises Penny's ring tap.

'Come in,' Clara and Daisy shout at the same time.

'I'll sort Clara,' Penny says, touching the top of Daisy's arm.

'Hello,' Clara says, as if Penny is new. 'Have you seen my mummy? She's in the garden, I think.'

'I'll find her after breakfast, Clara. Eat your egg.'

'This school is lovely, isn't it?'

'Yes,' Penny says, impatience in her voice.

Daisy knows she's Clara's fave. 'It's okay. I'll have my break later,' she says, full of pride. She gently swipes Clara's mouth with a wet wipe. The perfumed smell combined with egg brings up the ick.

'There's someone at reception for you.' Penny takes the spoon. 'Clara will be fine with me for once, won't you Clara?'

Daisy is short of time today, she can't afford any hold ups as the virtual dementia bus is arriving at two p.m. She arranged it after she saw it on the news. Staff get to wear dodgy glasses and painful socks, so they get to see what it's like to have dementia and be angry and confused and scared. Penny said she could book it and has agreed all the staff must have a try.

Clara puts her hand over her mouth and pushes away the spoon. Daisy loves that. She's the only one who gets Clara and Selvi to do what they're told.

'You need to do the spoon slower and move it from the front so she can see it, or it shocks her,' Daisy explains. Penny does as she's told.

Daisy shuffles along with as much speed as Bill. She knows it'll be her mother at reception for her and she doesn't want to chat. She'd rather be feeding Clara or even cleaning the bogs. If Daisy wanted to chat, she'd go home. Most nights Daisy sleeps here, but she has loved Sach and Haizeh being at Gran's. She refuses to think about them gone.

Derrick gives a nod as she swaggers past reception.

'No need to sign out,' he says.

Well, that's a first, usually she has to sign out to water the plants.

Searching in her bag for a cigarette, she vows to give up. The genetics nurse said all neuro conditions are made worse by smoking. But she's going to get this week out the way first. She hates goodbyes.

Daisy lights her cigarette and takes that first calming drag. She doesn't spot the grimy yellow taxi outside the entrance until she looks up and sees her. Daisy's cigarette falls to the floor. Why is *she* here? She's not welcome here. Daisy told her that, over and over. And she's brought him. Daisy won't cope. It's not fair. She can't do it. The car park is spinning, her throat tightens. Her legs are proper shaking, she has to lean on the wall for stability. *She told her*. She told her she can't do goodbyes.

She's on her phone, her back towards Daisy, waving her hands about as she does. In a long flowery dress with a black jacket and scarf she looks like she did that first time.

Just as Daisy is ready to turn and run. Run away. Hide in the wardrobe with her hands over her ears. Haizeh sees her and runs. He catches her legs with his arms and squeezes. He has on the outfit Gran ordered. Smart black jeans and a striped rugby shirt.

Daisy's crying so hard, she staggers back but manages to stay upright whilst he clings on.

For a moment, time stops as Sachini and Daisy search each other's face. Sachini has tears streaming down her face as she runs towards them.

'Go, just go,' Daisy shouts.

Putting both hands up to protest, she bends to untangle Haizeh from her legs. But as Daisy pulls free, Sachini grabs her.

'I couldn't go without saying goodbye,' she says. 'Please Daisy, please Daisy.'

Daisy is frozen. If she lets these feelings in, if she acknowledges this loss, she'll unravel. She knows it. Whatever her psychologist says, she knows if she has to do another goodbye, she'll break and never mend. Cry and never stop.

With Haizeh close to her feet, she can't escape. Her body is stiff as Sachini pulls her close. She keeps her head high. Her eyes to the sky. If she doesn't look, she doesn't feel. She needs to be back inside. Clara will be alone. Selvi will be frightened. Coma boy will have nobody.

But she can't move. Her body responds without her permission. She collapses to the floor. Her bag overflows. Her purse, her book and her teddy spill out. She covers her face with her hands and rocks. No one speaks. Then, a small warm body appears next to hers. She feels it squidging closer and closer. He rests a hand on her knee and a head in her side.

'Don't cry, Daisy,' Haizeh whispers.

Sachini crouches down on her other side. The three of them stay like that, a crumpled bundle of brokenness for too long.

'Here.' Sachini pushes a tissue at Daisy. It's neatly folded, and kind of pointless for the job. Daisy uses her sleeve instead.

Haizeh jumps up and holds both hands out to Daisy to pull her up. His mum helps. Together they wrench her off the floor and repack the bag.

Standing in front of Daisy, Sachini holds both her hands. Daisy supresses an urge to break free and run. She's can't watch them go. She absolutely can't.

'Right, you get your bum back in there and do more fabulous deeds. You are transforming lives. I'm going to tell everyone in my country about you. My best friend. The best friend we've ever had, Daisy BJ. You're gonna to do amazing things – well, more amazing things. Your dad would be so proud.'

'Go on.'

Daisy gets a shove towards the automatic doors. 'Don't look back.'

She doesn't look back but can't stop the tears even when faced with Derrick.

'Alright?' he says as if saying hello.

I'm obvs not alright.

The mirror in the staff room is steamed from the kettle. It's hard to do her eyeliner.

'You want tea?' Silviya says.

'No. I'm in the middle of breakfasts,' Daisy snaps.

She rushes her jobs. She takes each breakfast to the able clients. She feeds Selvi hers whilst Charlie pops to the restaurant and pulls Clara's blanket over her so she doesn't freeze. Penny and Derrick don't ask her to do anything extra.

Back in her safe space, with feet over the chair, she gets peace. Coma boy is more curled than usual. A bed body now.

His flaky friends have come now it's too late. Popping to say their meaningless goodbyes. She reads the visitors book.

'Where were they when you were all alone? Nowhere to be seen then, were they matey?' she whispers in his direction.

His breathing has changed, it's noisier, gets in her head, harder to ignore. 'You and me, we've muddled along alright, haven't we? I hope you've felt protected.' He doesn't respond.

All week, she's been smuggling stuff out. Her many journals are heavy. All that is left in this room is her Dickens collection. She'll leave those till last. Here, in her sanctuary, she's okay. Where will she go now? He's fading fast.

'Hang on in there, coma boy,' she says aloud, dropping Jane Eyre on her foot.

She reckons he hears. Whenever she has read, he's very still. She knows he loved the dramatic effects, crazy accents and actions.

Outside, no one is around. The large garden container has been a good place to hide stuff, but summer is coming, Greg says they'll need it.

Sitting outside in the memory garden, Daisy leans back. The sun is hot. Goodbyes are the worst thing; the waves keep coming. She can't stand this pain. Someone is reaching deep inside her, ripping her to shreds. She promised Sach she wouldn't burn or cut but knowing the sharps are so close, it's hard. Flashes of warm holidays smash into her head, making her cry. She's no longer sure if they're real memories or planted from the photos. Dad runs from the sea, laughing as he flicks water at Mum's sunbed, flopping down on the towel next to her. They were such a good family. She misses him so much.

Please Dad, no more goodbyes.

39

Dorothy

When Dorothy answers the phone, there's silence followed by heavy breathing. She hopes it's not one of those filthy callers.

'Do . . . ro . . . thy,' a female voice gasps. Someone is crying.

'Hello. Hello?'

'It's . . . Estelle.'

'Are you alright, dear?'

'Matron has been on the phone,' she says, steadying her voice. 'The infection has taken hold. They've suggested we go in.'

For a moment Dorothy can't speak.

'What do you need me to do?' she asks her daughter-in-law. They've not spoken since they disbanded monthly breakfasts.

'Find Daisy. I don't know where she is. She won't pick up her phone.'

'She was on a dementia course over the weekend, but she should be back at work today.' Dorothy hopes Daisy was telling the truth. If not, she has no idea where she is.

'I'm going now. I'll call Ben. He's on my way if he wants to come,' Estelle offers.

'He may not want to . . . after all, we agreed, didn't we?'

'I know . . . but this is probably it. We need to say goodbye . . . I think.'

Estelle can't continue. All Dorothy can hear is her gut-wrenching sobs.

'It's okay, Estelle, dear. Whatever you decide is okay.'

Dorothy waits. There's no hurry. She can hear Estelle attempting to gather herself, regain her usual tight-lipped composure. She knows all about that.

'Estelle,' Dorothy prompts.

'What?'

'You did right by him, dear. You must know that.'

'Thanks. We all did our best.'

'Let me know if you catch up with Daisy – I'll keep trying her mobile.'

Dorothy replaces the phone and staggers to sit down. Could this be it? They've been told that before.

At the end of that summer night, she had promised if he didn't go to end his life in Switzerland, she would watch him like a hawk. She promised that if he got close to doing what he most feared, she would take immediate action.

So, after many tears, he had compromised. Out of love for her he had agreed to stay alive. She wasn't surprised when he turned up the following evening with the letter. Owen was unlike himself but still a lawyer.

'This is legally binding,' he had told her. His words were a little skew-whiff, but his sentiment was clear. She had withdrawn the cream letter from its crumpled envelope and unfolded it on her lap. Several times she had edged it sideways to avoid her tears ruining the perfection he wanted. The letter was beautifully written with only a few misspelt words and a slight coffee stain on the corner. He had watched her read. Her fingers had trembled as her mind struggled to contend with what he was asking, what she was signing her name against.

He didn't sit down. He stood with his hands in his pockets but couldn't remain still. His balance was shot to pieces, but he wouldn't sit. He was no longer employed but had dressed in a formal grey suit with a white shirt and a navy tie. The only tells were a missed button and a smudge of sauce on his white collar.

Her beautiful son had begged her to handwrite her signature.

So, she had signed it. He had taken a fountain pen from his inside pocket. The one Peter gave him when he graduated from Cambridge. She had signed it and he had signed it. He used a paperclip to attach the scribbled note from Mrs Forni, the expensive lawyer, to confirm Owen still had capacity to make his wishes known.

Struggling to process Estelle's call, she retrieves her comfort letter and unfolds to read. The three folds are less crisp. Did she do right? She kept her promise. The day he did what he most feared, the day he did that, she kept her promise.

Dear Mamma,

I'm writing this on Daisy's birthday. How did our girl get so grown up? Thank you so much for sacrificing so much to support us. I don't know how long I've got.

Already, I see the look on your face. When you furrow your brow to cue me in, it's the stare you gave when I was small. It stopped me in my tracks when I was tempted to back chat, kick a ball indoors. I was always scared of that look. It still stops me in my tracks. How long before that look gets ignored? How long before I'm what the consultant called behavioural? How long before I'm hurting you, or worse, harming Daisy? I am already a man I don't respect and often despise. So, I need you, the only person who truly knows me, to stand by what you promised yesterday. This letter formalises what we agreed, so you won't dither when the time comes. So, here is what you promised.

When the time comes. When I lay a finger on my girl, my beautiful Daisy, you step in and do what we agreed. Please don't invite discussion from Estelle or Ben and especially not Daisy. I'll tell them it was my decision . . .

The time had come three years after his diagnosis.

It was a Saturday evening. She was spending more time with Estelle, trying to keep the peace, trying to avoid the inevitable, knowing what she had agreed. They had enjoyed a meal out at Pizza Express and Owen had been fine. On their return, Owen had got himself more and more wound up over two apples Estelle was saving for a crumble. Then, Daisy ran in from the garden. In her hurry to tell them about a fox cub, she had left her trainers in the hall. Owen had tripped on one of them. He stumbled but caught himself. When he regained his balance, without hesitation he had swung around and slapped Daisy full in her face. Dorothy replays that moment over and over. The look on Daisy's face, the blood streaming from her eyelid. Then his face. The way the colour drained when he saw what he had done.

He had withdrawn to his room and when she went to calm him, he was packing a bag.

His copy of the letter was on his pillow. So much of his brain had gone, but he knew.

'It's time,' he had said thrusting the paper in her hands. 'And you promised.'

She had gone home to collect some things she wanted him to have. His graduation photographs. Daisy's scan picture. A wallet of Peter's she had wanted him to have. She also gave him Jonny's watch. He had always been fascinated by that.

Thankfully, Daisy was in bed when she returned. She went upstairs to the master bedroom and pushed open the door. Owen was dressed in a crumpled pair of work trousers, torn on one of the pockets. He was distraught. A screwed-up photo of Daisy was in his hand. He was mumbling, 'All about Daisy, all about Daisy.'

When she had taken him in her arms, he had allowed her to hold him for a few seconds before disentangling. His overnight bag was open on the king-sized bed. He retrieved the shaver she had got him for Christmas and the alarm clock that folded into a leather case and threw them on top. The shaver missed and bounced on the wooden floor. Dorothy didn't dare retrieve it. Owen tried hard to zip up the bag, but his arms wouldn't cooperate. When she had tried to help, he had swiped her away and ignored her tears. They had left with the bag gaping open.

Owen stood outside Daisy's bedroom long enough to break Dorothy's heart. He had kissed the wooden sign saying his daughter's name and turned away. He allowed her to take his arm as they descended the stairs.

Estelle had clung to him, crying and tugging at his jumper. The green one Dorothy had knitted before they were married. 'Not yet, please not yet' she had begged.

Owen had kissed her on the cheek, 'Goodbye. Say cheerio to Daisy.'

Her car was parked on the gravel drive. Dorothy had left open her passenger door and her son had stumbled inside. He had held his leather bag on his lap as if clinging on for dear life.

They had driven in silence. The journey wasn't long enough. Owen had visited several times to understand how the routines worked. They drove up to a barrier where a security guard sat in a box. She showed him the letter and the barrier lifted. When she tried to help him out of the car, he had pushed her hand away.

'On my own. You promised you'd let me do this alone. You promised you wouldn't look back.'

She couldn't understand his evil condition. She couldn't understand how someone could be so rational and focused and yet so chaotic and mad. He had held onto the long white railing to stay upright and insisted he wouldn't enter until her car was out of sight.

She kept her promise. She had driven away. She had driven as far as she could given the terrible state she was in. When, finally, she had parked and calmed herself, she took out the letter and read the final instructions.

When it's done, when you've dropped me at the institution, don't look back, just like when I cried at school. I mean that. Go eat breakfast at my favourite café. Swim in the sea and dance to my records. This is your last duty of love. To let me go.

She broke that promise six months ago. Night security opened the gate. She convinced herself, if like Nicodemus, she went at night, it wouldn't count. After she went the first time, she had to go back. Whilst there's nothing of him left, it gave her peace.

Watching him, it was obvious: like birth, death follows an exhausting labour.

When she left him last week in the early hours, it was impossible to unhear the sounds of impending death. She said her final goodbye. Today, her job is to support everyone else to say theirs.

40

Ben

Standing in the car park, Ben shivers. Will he regret being here? This day has been so long coming. He needs it to be over, they all do. He waits whilst Estelle stays in the car frantically calling Daisy's phone. No doubt it will go straight to voicemail. Owen wouldn't recognise his wife. She's gaunt and pale in her baggy t-shirt and loose trousers. All her curves have long gone and the grey in her hair is obvious.

The day his mother delivered Owen's final letter is forever etched on his mind. It was late morning. Callie and he had just finished eating their Sunday cooked brekkie. They were still in their dressing gowns. Callie had yelped with embarrassment when she had seen his mother coming up the path. It was too late to hide or get dressed.

As soon as he saw the look on his mother's face he knew something had happened.

'I'm sorry,' his mother had confessed handing him a cream letter with Owen's precise handwriting on the front. The letter was dated three years previously.

To my one and only Benji boy,

Please forgive me. After many hours of soul searching, Mum and I have agreed a plan. I wanted to go to Dignitas next week. She wanted me to stay longer for you, for Daisy, but mostly for her.

The compromise we've reached is sufficient, the best I can do to protect Daisy, given what I know will happen. So, if you're reading this, she's kept her promise. She's taken me to a place of my choice, my final resting place. There I'll end my days behind closed doors. We saw them, didn't we? When I went for the tests, when you were brave enough to hold my hand, we saw the ones who were lost. I do not want to be seen like that. Not by you or Estelle, not by Mum, but especially not by my beautiful Daisy.

So, I've gone. I forbid you to visit me. Consider me dead. Mum has another letter with my last wishes, but Benji, if I meant anything to you, please let me go.

I love you more than you'll ever know. You're her daddy now.

Owen

Apart from that one time when he couldn't stay away, he had done as Owen wanted. For the love of him, he pretended his brother was dead and insisted Daisy did the same.

Estelle switches off her phone. 'Who knows where Daisy is. Maybe it's meant to be, that she's not here to witness more horror,' she says as a single, unrestrained tear escapes.

Dorothy arrives as Estelle locks her car. She comes between them. The three clasp hands and move forwards, desperate to break the touch line but with no desire to finish.

Walking across the familiar car park, Ben feels Dorothy tighten her grip. Two figures stand at reception. The doors slide open before he presses the buzzer.

'Hi Ben. You okay, love?'

'Yep, all good,' he lies.

Penny gives each of them a hug. Derrick fiddles with his pen.

Penny takes both of Dorothy's hands in hers. They don't say anything.

'You know your way,' Penny says nodding to Ben.

Ben follows Estelle along the corridor, turning left past the dining hall and toilets. They stop at the entrance to blue corridor and Patsy appears from nowhere to let them in. Her key card changes a small red light to green and the wide door opens automatically. Patsy waits to let them pass. Ben allows Estelle and his mum to clamber ahead, hand in hand. United with purpose one last time.

He walks the corridor of doom at the slowest pace possible. He's been once. He has no desire to be here, but Estelle persuaded him he would regret it if he didn't come. Will he regret coming?

The door of room twelve is open. A visitor sits with her head in her hands. A plastic cup designed for a small child sits on the bedside cabinet. Here, silence wins.

Ben pauses outside the next room. The timetable of care is no longer there. He has faded behind the closed door, but the photo taken in Spain has retained its colour. He has to smile back. That grin is so infectious. Of all the people who didn't deserve this, it was him.

Slowly he pushes the silver handle.

The bed is the same. The man lies on his back instead of curved liked a comma. His blanket is pulled up to his chin.

It's immediately evident his soul has gone.

Estelle is in the armchair taken from Dorothy's old bedroom. She has her legs tucked under her and has sunglasses on. On a dining-room chair, dragged in for the occasion, Mum sits upright, back straight, no slouching today.

Ben hears before he sees.

'It is a far, far better thing that I do, than I have ever done . . .'

A bold voice reads aloud as if she's alone on a stage auditioning for the star role. Her accent is that of an articulate young woman who has enjoyed a private education.

Ben springs behind Dorothy who is struggling to breathe.

'Take some deep breaths,' he says, squeezing her shoulders.

As Ben stands tall, holding the back of the chair, the metal cold under his fingers, he can hardly believe what's before him. Someone is in bed with Owen. Sitting up, with her legs under the covers, she's sitting next to her father, reading. Ben recognises Charles Dickens, Owen's favourite. Dressed in violet pyjamas covered in teddies, Daisy's elbow rests gently beside her Daddy's awkwardly positioned head.

She inhales deeply.

'. . . it is a far, far better rest that I go to, than I have ever known.'

'The end,' a small but assertive voice declares. She closes the book with the authority of a head teacher and then looks up as if she's only just noticed the room is full.

'He wanted to reread *A Tale of Two Cities*. He said he loved it so much as a boy. But coma boy bailed before the end. Maybe he remembered that bit.'

As Daisy's eyes meet his, tears roll down her bare cheeks. No make-up today.

'I think you're right. Your dad never stayed at a party when he'd had enough. A bit like someone else I love,' Ben says.

Daisy manages a small smile as she climbs out of her father's bed.

Callie crashes through the door, her jacket half off her shoulders.

Behind her is Penny.

'He's gone.' Daisy collapses into her aunt's arms with body-racking sobs, years of supressed hurt haemorrhaging at last.

Perhaps they can now remember Owen for who he was.

Coma boy.

Ben can see his mother overtly cringe at the nickname Daisy has chosen. Owen would've laughed. Daisy's way of differentiating her dad from who he became.

As Estelle and Penny pack Owen's things into a small box, Ben notices Daisy clinging to a wrinkled old wallet.

'Won't be needing this now.' She nods towards the bed.

'You made sure he never went short, didn't you?' Penny smiles as she puts her arm around Daisy's shoulders. She turns to Dorothy and says, 'Every time she came in, she added a note to his wallet.'

Daisy gives Estelle a sideways look. 'He hated running out of cash. You insisted he used a credit card, but he always liked notes in his wallet. His beer money.'

Estelle embraces her estranged daughter and Daisy yields.

They huddle out of the room.

Ben walks next to Daisy. Penny still has her arm around Daisy's shoulders on the other side.

Ben leans closer to hear what Penny is whispering in her ear. 'Room thirteen is yours until we employ another staff member on site, so you can put your things back for the time being.'

Ben has no idea what that's all about.

Three years later

Daisy

I can’t move for boxes. All my books have come out of storage, and thirty of Dad’s records. Lifting them out, one at a time, I brush off the dust and read every title and track before ordering them on the wonky shelf. I finally made it. I tear out my course timetable from the front of the Sussex University book and attach it to the crumbling cork board.

On Monday, I start a medical degree. I want to specialise in older people and dementia. My education for the next six years will be funded by the Selvi Bandara Trust, a trust set up by Charlie from book royalties. Selvi died not long after Dad. Charles has moved to live with his daughter but he’s getting better with FaceTime. We chat on a Friday about politics, history and Selvi.

I shuffle my duvet into a new cover, poppies on a white background. The wardrobe here is half-size and, looking at the three cases of clothes, I have no idea which ones to hang up. The cheap furniture tilts as Dad’s heavy coat positions itself on the unstable coat hanger. Turns out Mum kept his fave grey coat.

I miss Dad every day even though it’s almost three years since he was carried out of room thirteen on a broken stretcher. When Ben told me Dad had left and didn’t want visitors, I was pleased, it was a good excuse; I was terrified of the person he’d become. Things were better with him gone. He’d got spiteful and I was afraid. I didn’t want to visit.

I missed him so much and felt guilty for abandoning him, but he couldn't face seeing me and I couldn't face seeing him. Then, I screwed up with friends, and Mum and with everything and things got very messy!

When Gran made me work at The Orchards, everyone stayed quiet about the elephant in room thirteen, including me. Initially, I planned to get sacked ASAP but being in that place, with its freshly washed laundry, strict rules and baking smells allowed me to find my younger self and then find him again. When Dad left, Ben gave me all his letters except the last one. They were each carefully numbered and in a separate yellow envelope. That was my favourite colour. At first, I hid them. I was tempted to chuck them away along with him. In the end I squirrelled them into my secret tin. Reading them aloud with Dad helped me remember who he used to be. By then, he was too far gone to realise, so he wasn't ashamed, and I wasn't scared. Gran said she was shocked I had been hiding in Dad's room, but I reckon she secretly hoped being in that place might help, that I might end up visiting him. I hate being so predictable.

It took me ages to decide what to do about the freaking test. I completed the genetic counselling. It was awful, but I went to all three sessions. Mum came with me after the first one and Sandra gave me some extra therapy to thrash it all out.

In the end, I did it.

Tom, the gorgeous vampire nurse who did the hospital counselling, stole the blood sample he needed. I saw a flicker of recognition in his face when he spotted my self-harm scars. Tom smiled and patted my hand but didn't comment. Mum likes me to wear long sleeves, but I won't. They're my battle wounds. I fought for Dad, I fought to stay alive. I'm strong and I survived.

I didn't collect the results. The result is waiting patiently in a filing cabinet. No one knows what it says. I've gifted it to Tom for now. Let him have it for safe keeping. Maybe if I'm stupid enough to lose my head over a bloke I'll want to know. Or maybe I'll have IVF and hope for the best. Right now, I can live despite the uncertainty. Who knows what the future holds for any of us?

Burying Dad helped everyone move forward. Gran went back to work. She does some agency midwifery at the hospital even though she's ancient. She needs someone to soak up her wisdom now I'm here. Mum is working in a legal team to support vulnerable kids. The two of us have come a long way and we're still working our stuff out but we're no longer hurting each other. I've agreed to go with her on a city break in the summer. She wants me to choose where in Rome to scatter Dad's ashes. Italy was his favourite place.

Mum and Gran have promised to come for a Brighton shopping trip. I've relapsed into some geeky habits so can't take too much time out. I never thought I'd choose a university this close to home, but being close means, I can do weekends at The Orchards. Beer money for when Ryan visits. Penny has moved singing group to once a month so I can run it when I'm back. Penny kept her promise, she'd known all along I was in room thirteen. She'd told all the senior staff to keep out when I was there. I'm glad we had his last months together. I'm convinced coma boy knew I was there. When I read or sang, he was definitely less grunty. Every day, I showed him the cash in his wallet and told him not to worry and that I loved him. We listened to heaps of music, and I acted out his favourite classics. My favourite is still *Jane Eyre*.

Gran paid for Sachini to come the summer before I left Storrington. We all went to Center Parks at Longleat. Gran, Ben and Callie and Owen Junior, my nephew. I love saying that. Haizeh adored his new friend. They spent every hour in the swimming pool. The maggot has grown so much. He has a cute accent that sounds more like his mum. I was chuffed he remembered me from FaceTime. Sach and I email every week, but it was awesome to hug her. I might go visit them at Easter. I got some money from Dad's company gave when they found out he hadn't hurt anyone, even with his illness. I haven't told the family yet, in case I don't make it.

Ben says, 'No more family secrets.' He reckons we're all gonna commit to a future of openness. In his dreams!

As I pin up my family photo on the crumbling cork noticeboard, Sir Owen catches my eye.

'You'd be proud of me, Dad.'

Giving him a quick kiss, I carefully put a dot of blu tack on each corner of the back of the photograph. I turn it over and push the corners with my thumbs to secure the photo above my bed.

'Thank you,' I tell him. He poured so much into little me and that will see me through.

Sitting against my pillow, I have to finish the final proofread of the manuscript and read Dad's last letter. I rip it open and put the envelope aside. I inhale his smell. For reasons unknown to me he sprayed all my birthday cards with his aftershave. He said it was what his father had done with his. Carefully I unfold the crisp folds and breathe him in. The letter inside is written with his fountain pen and on paper that matches the envelope.

Dear Daisy,

By the time you read this, I'll definitely be dead, and you may well be an adult. Sending you the biggest hug. I hope you're able to forgive me for leaving when I did and not saying goodbye.

Given what's happening, I've spent many hours pondering what I want my legacy to be. It's how I spent most of my teens. How could I make an impact? What sort of stamp did I want to leave on the world and how many rhetorical questions could I ask while walking alone in the woods? I spent so much time wandering aimlessly, never sure which way to go. Obviously, someone was eating the breadcrumbs.

I wanted to make a difference, but I didn't know how. I considered writing my autobiography, but my writing was already rather messy. I thought about moving to a commune, but the application form was too complicated.

And then it hit me, my purpose was you. From the day you, my little smudge, captured my heart from a monochrome screen, my job was to make you my footprint in this world.

Daisy girl, you are my legacy to the world and nothing I leave could improve on you.

Hold on to justice and courage. Stay fair-minded and kind. Above all, be humble. Then you'll come right, and you'll know you've done me proud.

Forever yours,

Daddy, Dad, Sir Owen.

Drinking in every word, I remember who he was, who he is. My unique beautiful father, to whom I owe everything. After some reasonable sobbing, I refold it and reunite it with the other ninety-nine in my battered tin.

A few months after Dad died I spoke on Sussex Radio about my story and what I'd learnt at The Orchards. Unbelievably, a literary agent was listening. He said he'd been looking for a new client and then he heard my voice and loved the way I spoke. My unedited thoughts and feelings from my journals will be published as a book next year to include Dad's letters. It's our last hoorah. Mine and his.

Owen and Daisy. I'm giving all the proceeds to the Frontal Temporal Dementia society to help more families like ours.

The draft book cover arrived this morning. It'll first be published as a hardback. It's been designed by Lauren Densham, she's my favourite cover designer. Her work is awesome. The front cover is a picture of me and Dad before he got sick. Under the photograph is my name and his. It's our story but titled 'All About Daisy'.

Printed in Great Britain
by Amazon

32555729R00182